Last Flight Home

J.B. Lawrence

ISBN: 978-0-9861822-0-4

Published and distributed
by Possibilities Publishing Company

www.possibilitiespublishingcompany.com

This is a work of fiction.

For Dicky and Leandro

1

My father sat on his throne with his shoulders hunched forward and a scowl on his face, looking a bit unseemly for his station and not at all, I felt, as a king should look. And where usually a bite of food lightened his mood, by the second course of the feast, we were all wondering if the fun-loving King Jorgen Buteo would ever show up.

My father was a great wit, and everybody loved laughing when he tore apart some remark by an unwitting guest or the behavior of a drunken baron. He left not even the slightest misspeak or curiosity unaddressed, and the voice that could be heard over the clash of battle could also freeze a boisterous partygoer in his or her seat.

The feast was the send-off for the annual eyas hunt that was to start the next morning, and this year's hunt was especially important because it was to be my first. But my father had been distracted and agitated for hours, and now he pulled at his beard and stared through the open doorway to the veranda. His seat at the head of the feast table offered a view past all four Sun Point mountain faces and, on a clear day, all the way to the dark silhouettes of both Sentinel mountains.

I tried to see what he was looking at so intently, but the only thing out there was the pink light of our sun Telios as it backlit the Shoulder Mountains. His eyes didn't move from the dimming glow, and I glanced across the hall at my mother, who was surrounded by her entourage of ladies and looking bored.

My attention was pulled back to the impromptu bout of Slip that was about to take place in the center of the hall. Lord Hengry, one of my father's closest friends, was busy handling all the bets being made on or against me. That sneering Captain Jasko and drunken Lord Rogell stood beside him. They boiled my blood when they taunted me by saying that my beard was like the down of a newborn falcon and I would never match up to a fighter like Cony Teilyr.

Cony was the finest Slip man of all the Austringers, and after too much barley wine, I had boasted that I would have no problem taking his title. It was a threat no champion could turn down if he didn't want people to believe he was afraid of a non-ranked opponent. Even without the barley wine, I was confident that I posed a real challenge to Cony because I was the best Slip man in the amateur ranks.

Slip was the favorite Austringer game among the rank and file, and since no Austringer could become a baron without serving first as a common warrior, the barons also had a well-established taste for the sport.

Jasko and Rogell continued to taunt me and warned Cony not to lose them any gold. Lord Hengry was also getting on my nerves. I wasn't sure who he was cheering for as he waved his fists full of gold rings, the currency of betting. Luckily, my best friend Markyn was also there—aggressive, incoherent, and drunk, but at least he was rooting for me.

Slip consisted of three sets in which contenders tried to remove one another from a pre-established ring by using the opponent's energies against him. No punches or kicks were allowed. A contender only had to win two sets, and matches often did not go past the second set.

Cony looked across the hall at my older brother, Aillil, who sat beside my father at the feast table. Aillil smiled back and nodded, letting Cony know that he had no problem with his best friend teaching me a lesson.

Cony and I started in the regulation stance, with the outer edges of our right feet touching and the backs of our right hands pressed against each other at shoulder height. This stance was intended to start both contenders at an awkward balance that a savvy Slip-man might exploit.

Everyone probably expected me to push my hand toward Cony in a typical but often clumsy opening move. Instead, I swept my hand away from him. The move left me off balance for a fraction of a second, but I countered by shifting my left foot and twisting in his direction. Cony knew this move but was not ready for my speed. His weight pitched him forward over my back, and a quick push of my hips sent him out of the ring.

The toss would have sent him into the feast table if the damned barons hadn't been so tightly packed around the ring. They all screamed as Cony landed in the laps of three barons, knocking them onto their backsides.

It was the first time in years that Cony had been thrown, and he got up off his cushion of barons with a new look in his eye—one that could kill giants. He didn't like surprises, especially when it concerned his clout in the Slip ring. Thank the Sirens I was too drunk to care.

He got back into the starting stance, and when I positioned myself, he growled, "Good show, Prince. But that will be your last win until the day I no longer climb these crumbling cliffs."

My heart was pounding all the way up into my throat. I was so excited I wasn't sure I could go another round. The crowd cursed and laughed, and more gold rings were passed from hand to hand as the more daring gamblers switched their bets to me.

Lord Hengry started the second set, and Cony moved more aggressively this time. In my drunken state, I couldn't think of any more tricks, and he exploited my split-second pause with a backhanded push that knocked me off balance. I stumbled backward, and all Cony had to do was get his foot behind my body then bump me out of the ring.

It was considered more skillful if a Slip man could rend his opponent so off-balance that all he had to do was give a light push of a single finger to tip him out of the ring. But Cony was still angry about his first-round loss, so he gave me a hard push to the back of the head as I stumbled clear of the ring—a push that some spectators considered too similar to a punch, while others argued that it was within the regulations of Slip play. Unfortunately, this time the crowd was ready and got out of the way, which meant there was no one to break my fall when I bounded out of the ring.

In the third set, Cony beat me handily and saved all the obvious bets from losing. The crowd let out a sigh of relief, and after much shifting of gold rings into various hands, Lord Hengry helped me to my feet.

"My boy," he said, "I appreciate your courage, but you should be more careful about who you threaten. Even Aillil stopped trying Cony." He slapped me on the shoulder. "Either that or learn more than one trick. I switched my bet after your first-round win, so you just cost me ten rings."

"Me, too," interjected Captain Jasko.

I was surprised. Jasko was a cranky old captain of the Austringer army who made no secret of the fact that he did not care much for Aillil and me. His breath stank of wine as he leaned toward me and said, "I put ten on your skinny ass after that first round. That's ten rings you owe me, boy."

He grabbed me by the shoulder, and I twisted out of his grasp and said, "I owe you nothing."

Jasko started to respond, but Lord Hengry pulled me toward the feast table, where full glasses of barley wine waited.

"Don't let those cranky old warriors get to you, Tyrcel," Hengry said as we walked away. "They're just angry that they can't move like they used to."

At the table, Lord Hengry and I sat down across from Aillil. Hengry handed me a glass of wine and began rambling in his usual fashion, this time about the hunt I would be attending the next day. He talked about the cliffs of Hunter's Bluff, the highest southern-facing cliffs of the Shoulder Range, and how in the mornings, our sun Telios made it the warmest place in the Midlyn Range.

"It's logical, Tyrcel, that the falcons would make their homes in those nooks," he said.

He was taking that patronizing tone that infuriated me. As my father's oldest friend, Hengry had helped raise me, but at eighteen, I had long ago outgrown his lessons.

He babbled on. "Even in these colder days, there's enough heat to warm those cliffs. Even these days, Tyrcel."

I looked restlessly around the table, and my gaze fell on Aillil, who sat on father's right with his elbow propped on the back of the empty seat beside him. He was pretending to watch the ladies dancing at the other end of the hall, but he kept looking back at father, whose lips were moving as though he was deep in conversation.

We had both heard the rumors circulating around the Overhang that my father was slipping into madness. But the mediums say it's not uncommon for great men to be able to communicate with natural objects and animals—which, if nothing else, I hoped my father was doing whenever he sat alone talking with himself. And Aillil held his roost master in high regard because he was directly descended from the ancient Austringer sages who had communicated with the first falcons of the Midlyn Range and he had a natural gift with our sacred birds.

But even so, Aillil was embarrassed and angry about my father's behavior and didn't like to talk about it with me.

To father's left sat Lord-general Landys Tuecyr. He, too, noticed my father's lips moving in silent conversation. His eyes met Aillil's, then they both quickly looked away.

Lord Hengry seemed to take my lack of response as an invitation to continue his lecture. "Up there, Tyrcel, you'll see farther north than you've ever seen. Almost all the way across the straits."

He took a drink of his wine then lowered his glass slowly, as if he was taking extra care not to break it. He sat back in his chair, his chest heaving under the weight of a huge feast, too many cups of wine, and too much excitement around the Slip ring. Everyone at the table waited for him to continue, but he lowered his chin to his chest and seemed to be falling asleep when he mumbled through his beard, "Keep your eyes open up there, Tyrcel."

I waved a hand impatiently as though to swat him away, and from across the table Lord-general Tuecyr said, "For what exactly, Hengry?"

Lord Hengry's cheeks glowed a warm pink much like the hue of the setting Telios, his sleepy face suddenly turned serious. "I've heard rumors floating around. Strange things from Port Tallion." He fixed his gaze on Tuecyr and added, "I believe it's perfectly reasonable to remind a young prince to keep his eyes open. These are difficult times for Austringers and our northern neighbors."

The lord-general smiled. "I didn't say it was unreasonable. I was just curious what Tyrcel ought to be on the lookout for."

To everyone's surprise, my father chimed in. "Doing a fine job as usual, hey, Hengry? It's good to know you're still keeping up on the latest gossip."

His quick laugh and good-natured teasing seemed to put everyone at ease. Father sat with his hands draped over the ends of the throne's ornately carved armrests while Hengry looked down at his beard.

Father winked at me and said, "Hengry is right, son. Those are the warmest cliffs to hunt. And it's always wise for young princes to keep their eyes open."

I got flustered whenever father focused his attention on me in public, and I hurried to defend myself. "I am well prepared for this hunt, and I can climb as well as any Austringer."

"Yes, but can you stand on a ledge no bigger than a pebble and hold onto a crack above you while rooting through a falcon's roost?" he asked.

My face flushed, and I had no response because I had never hunted an eyas before.

Lord Hengry decided to add to my embarrassment. "And can you do all that while gently placing a live and squirming eyas—so delicate and fragile— into a leather rucksack that is dangling over your shoulder?"

Again, I had no response.

Tuecyr, who never had a problem scolding Aillil or me, added his own question. "And have you ever been climbing while being attacked by a mother falcon whose only drive is to defend her nest?"

I held my tongue.

Tuecyr smiled. "I promise you, you may be able to climb as well as any Austringer, but you will never climb fast enough to escape a determined mother. She'll have your eyes out before you know what direction is up."

"For the love of the Sirens," cursed father. "Landys, why do you always have such heavy thoughts? Why in all the Midlyns am I cursed with such a sour lord-general?"

"My apologies, King Buteo."

Father waved his hand in the air to silence Tuecyr. His mood had changed again, and despite the fact that it was still early, he proclaimed, "Telios has gone down, and I wish to make the blessing for tomorrow's hunt."

He stood and raised his chalice and waited for the rest of the partygoers to do the same.

"At first light tomorrow, my youngest son, Tyrcel, will be making his way toward the sacred hunting grounds that have provided the falcons we Austringers have worshipped and used to keep our people alive. Tomorrow he will possess his first falcon."

He stood for an uncomfortably long moment with his chalice in the air as he smiled down at me. He wobbled a bit, and his toast became less formal. "He might be greaner than a kid goat's teeth—"

"And not much smarter," Cony called drunkenly from the far end of the table.

All the older warriors at the crowded table joined in with their own taunts. It was a verbal gauntlet that all eighteen-year-olds had to navigate, and as a prince, I got the worst of it. My mother, who was standing behind father's chair, gave me a look that I knew meant for me to keep calm.

Father finally interrupted my drunken tormentors to say, "At least he has his brother to watch over him."

The room erupted in cheers and laughter at that insult. I was livid but had to keep my mouth shut because no Austringer warrior gets near a falcon without suffering through some sort of hazing. An Austringer falcon was much more than a pet, and if a man couldn't handle some verbal abuse, then how could he possibly handle an unruly hunter falcon?

As the laughter died down, father finally lowered his chalice. He closed his eyes, and everyone watched him expectantly, the smiles still on their lips.

"I have spoken with our Telios," father said, and people glanced at one another nervously.

He was speaking of the one remaining sun around which our planet, Axis Solan, revolved. The disappearance of the other sun, Solan, was one of father's favorite wine-induced topics. When he was a young prince, the planet had been warmed by two suns. The smaller one, Telios, shone on the northern cliffs of the Midlyn Range, while Solan cast a searing heat down on its namesake planet.

It was because of Solan that centuries ago the first Austringers moved to the cooler peaks of the mountains that filled the Midlyn Range. But for decades, Austringer astronomers had noticed odd behavior coming from Solan, and mediums in the City Valley warned of threats that the sun was dying and the planet would be destroyed when it did. Most Austringers dismissed the mediums' rantings, but eventually Solan did begin to shrink. The days grew cooler, and when the mountains began to rumble and quake, my grandfather and his court decided to listen more closely to the rumors. That's when citizens of the City Valley flocked to the mediums, begging them to send their prayers to the Sirens and offering sacrifices to the angry Solan.

I had heard the story many times before: My father, who was a toddler at the time, was sent with his mother and a noble entourage on a pilgrimage to make offerings to the Sirens. Grandfather remained at the Overhang to handle the mayhem that was beginning in the City Valley. It was during that slow, ter-rifying journey on cable-lines that were plucked back and forth by the strange winds like a seasoned warrior playing with a child's bow that my father first heard the voice of Solan.

As soon as the royal cable-car came to a stop, his mother swept him up in her arms. The frantic pilgrims shoving their way around the cable station pulled his attention in every direction. But one voice was suddenly more distinct than all the other noises. The voice told father to look back over his mother's shoulder. From this vantage point, he could see out the bay doors of the Sun Point 1 cable station. It was late morning and the sickly Solan was almost at her zenith, the time of day when her light turned Gavina into a glowing obelisk that towered over the Midlyn Range. Sun Point Station 1 was two leagues' distance from Gavina, but Solan's light cleared all the clouds and shone so brightly that the striations and rock formations of the distant mountain were discernible.

Solan told father to look at her light shining all over his precious Overhang. He obeyed and saw that Solan's usual intense light was dulled by a dark flickering that strobed across Gavina. The entire cable station shook. Then the voice turned sour and told father to keep looking out the bay doors. He gazed at the distant Overhang, and just as a page lifted him from his mother's arms to better protect him from the throng of frightened people, he saw half the Overhang drop from the face of Gavina—his father along with it.

It had been more than fifty years since the Day of a Thousand Quakes and the death of Solan, but the trauma of what seemed like the entire world falling apart had not left father. Lately a few drinks of wine seemed to turn his sarcastic nature into stinging cynicism or a distant seriousness. Conversations became difficult because his attention tended to wander off as he gazed at the distant cloud banks. He had to be constantly reminded to pay attention, and one never knew what comment or question might trigger a violent outburst. His voice was still strong and his random tongue lashings were loud enough to echo through an entire floor of the Overhang.

But now father continued without any concern for the discomfort of his audience at the feast table. "Telios claims that the Austringer race is at its zenith, just as Solan once was."

He looked down at the table, lost in thought, and finally said, "But I believe he is a liar."

My father was not only having conversations with the sun, but he was forming opinions about Telios' apparent claims. These were not the actions of a sound mind. Embarrassed, I glanced across the table at mother. Her eyes were fixed on the back of father's head. Next to him, Aillil frowned and shook his head as though telling me not to pay father any heed. Beside him Lord-general Tuecyr sighed, but I thought I saw an odd gleam of satisfaction in his eye.

Father continued, undeterred. "We Austringers have lived just fine in these ice-covered peaks for centuries."

His tone became livelier and the crowd perked up, despite the fact that their king sounded as though he was about to declare war on our planet's only remaining sun. Austringers always enjoyed a little patriotism, especially when it was mixed with barley wine.

"We have heated our homes and halls for centuries without Telios' help," father said. "Even as this planet has cooled, we have mined these mountains to their core and used the molten heat to warm our homes. Never once have we needed Telios' help."

His gaze fell on me, and his voice grew gentle. "Tyrcel, on this eve of your first hunt, the Austringer elder council has agreed that you are ready for your first falcon. The Mother Siren knows you will treat the falcons she gives you with respect. We will need those gifts to secure our place here on Axis Solan despite what Telios might do. By the grace of the Sirens, we Austringers have always endured any threat, be it from man, giant, or sun. Enjoy the few weeks of freedom that the eyas hunt will give you. Be in the moment of the hunt because it will signify your transition into the next phase of your life."

The Lord's Hall erupted in applause, as much for me as relief that father's speech had ended on a positive note.

The partygoers began to make their farewells. The younger ones went off to find another party, while older wives and husbands headed home to their beds. Cony grabbed Aillil's arm and pulled him out of his seat. They rushed after a small group of other young men, and I was about to follow when father said, "Stay a moment longer, Tyrcel. I have more to tell you."

My head was swimming from the wine, and I was certain that I knew all I needed to know about hunting for falcons. What more could father possibly have to say?

Mother noticed my agitation and leaned over to kiss me on the crown of the head. "Don't worry, my dear, your friends will still be up when your father is finished with you. Be sure to say goodbye before you leave tomorrow morning."

"Remember, boy," said Lord Hengry as he rose to leave with mother. "Eyas hunting is as much trouble as not, but I look forward to meeting your new addition to the royal roosts."

After a quick bow to his king, Lord Hengry took mother's arm and left the Lord's Hall.

My father waited until they were gone before he began. "Hengry is right. The cliffs of Hunter's Bluff are not like those of the inner mountains of the Talliedes. Your training has taught you a lot, but nothing can compare to the winds off the Northern Straits that thrash against those cliffs. And nothing can ready you for an attack from a mother—"

"Father, forgive me, but I know all that."

He clenched his fist. "For once just listen to me. I know you are strong and I know you are one of the best climbers. But these things don't matter. My warnings from Telios have not been just about the end of the Austringers. Most of the warnings have been about you."

I was shocked into silence. I had never really understood my father's conversations with Telios. Like most of my friends, I spent my energy learning about warfare and hunting and did not devote any deep thoughts to what the mediums had to say. I was also not comfortable with the realization that my father was one of those crazy doomsayers and that he was dragging me into it.

"I do not know what is in store for you," he said. "Therefore, be cautious, Tyrcel."

He slouched back in his chair with the air of a man who was out of options.

"Telios is so stubborn," he said quietly. "Only speaking with me when it pleases him." In a sudden burst of energy, he slammed his fist on the table. "Damn him. His diminishing light has turned our world upside down. Abbo Doldra's northern horde wants to move into our lands as the country up there freezes to death. And now he makes threats against my family."

"But why mc?" I said, more baffled than afraid. "What do these voices... what does Telios want with me?"

Father's shoulders drooped again. "He told me you should ask him that yourself, when you speak with him."

2

My confusion did not abate through three days of hiking and riding the cables to the eyas hunting grounds, and by the time we rounded Wailen's Point, my father's odd rantings had not lost much of their grip on my thoughts. When he had told me Telios would be contacting me soon, I felt like I had to defend myself, but I wasn't sure against what.

I huddled in the back of our four-seat cable-car. A steady easterly wind pushed against the side so there was not too much swinging back and forth. Aillil, Markyn, and our mentor Marello were asleep in the other seats. I envied them. I couldn't stop my mind racing long enough to find a moment of sleep.

Wailen's Point was the last switch point on the cable line to Hunter's Bluff. It was named after one of the greatest Austringer generals of all time, Berrys Wailen, in honor of his defeat of the hill-giants in the last battle of the Shoulder Range Wars. The plateau was too rocky for any kind of farming or cultivation, no goats lived among its ragged outcrops, and it was barely big enough for a small emergency station and the cable switch port, but it was considered the gateway to the north, specifically Hunter's Bluff.

The car bumped around Wailen's Point and dropped. For a split second, we were weightless as our car left the tower and rolled a few quick feet back down into open sky.

Aillil sat up to look over the edge of the car, but the sight of the craggy, slat-like rock formations that grew out of the dark valley below made him sigh and settle back under his bedroll.

To our west were the Sawblades, a massive system of two ravines that came together in a canyon just south of the Shoulder Range, which was nothing but jagged rock formations that thrust up from an abysmally deep bottom. They were the weathered remnants of old granite mountains that had centuries ago been mined and stripped by ignorant hill-giants, and they signified the last long, open-sky section of the cable ride to Hunter's Bluff. But this section was a three-league stretch, and we were all ready to be back on solid ground.

I hadn't had a chance to talk to my brother about what father had told me, and I thought this long stretch of the cable ride would be a good time, especially with the others sound asleep.

"Aillil, I need to talk to you," I said as quietly as I could.

He grumbled from the seat in front of me. "Don't make me sit up and look at those loathsome Sawblades again. I want to close my eyes and not open them until I hear the clank of the Bluff station."

"A few seconds won't hurt you," I said.

Aillil did not respond, so I leaned forward and said, "I need to talk to you about father and his conversations with Telios."

Aillil sat up as though he had been jolted out of a nightmare.

"For the love of the Sirens!" he said in as much of a whisper as his anger would allow. He was wrapped tightly in his bedroll and had to untangle himself so he could turn and face me over the seat back.

"Now is not the time," he said. "I have enough trouble dealing with his rants and outbursts at the Overhang."

"But he told me Telios—"

Aillil leaned closer. "The types of people who claim to speak with Telios, or the rocks, or the falcons—" This slight sacrilege shocked me, but Aillil continued. "The types of people who claim to have these powers are more trouble than anything else. I'm not saying father will end up in a common stretcher cage, but he has been losing support in his court lately, and we don't need to give his opponents on the council any more ammunition."

I was shocked by Aillil's paranoia. He was talking about potential treason in our father's court. I felt the first bubbling of a seething anger deep in my belly.

Aillil misinterpreted my stunned silence. "Ty, I know the thought of treasonous activity at the court surprises you, but be glad I have told you now. It's better than learning it a month from now, when you're starting your own commission in the court." He settled back in his seat. "The things father said at the feast were just wine-induced rants."

I didn't like being dismissed in that way. "Thank you for my first courtly lesson, brother, but I wanted to talk to you about something father said after the feast."

Aillil did not appreciate the contempt in my voice. He reached over and grabbed me by the collar of my vest. "You little mountain runt. How dare you speak to me with that tone?"

I pushed back at his rock-like forearm. This was Aillil's oldest tactic when arguing with me. If a dispute or debate was not going in his favor, he did not hesitate to threaten me with a beating.

This time, however, I did not immediately give in. All my years of training dictated that young warriors must always respect their elders, but I was eighteen now, and this matter affected my family and the court. Besides, when

Aillil became king, I would be his closest advisor so sooner or later he would have to respect my counsel.

I struggled to push his arm away, but he kept a tight grip. He grabbed a bigger clump of my vest with his other hand and pulled me close.

"I suggest we end this conversation now, little brother."

I hated being called "little," so his subtle taunt hit its mark. I couldn't break his grip so I said, "I was unaware that this was a conversation."

He gave my cheek a quick rap with the back of his hand. "You will always be my little brother. Now sit back and close your eyes. You need to focus your thoughts on the cliffs of the Bluff. I can't cover your ass and find chicks for you, so make sure you're ready. If you come back empty-handed, your princely status will not protect you from the rumors that will spread throughout the court."

My face was flushed with heat, and my cheekbone stung. But I relaxed in his grip, letting him know I was not going to make any more trouble.

He finally let go of me and settled back into his seat. The steep, jagged points of the Sawblades in the distance created the dark silhouette that inspired their name. It would be hours before the southern bluff tower came into view. I pulled my bedroll over my shoulders and sank down into my seat.

As much as I hated to admit it, I knew Aillil was right. All my mental energies should be in preparation for the hunt. After we reached the bluff tower station, we still had a day's hike ahead of us to reach the campsite, and then the first climb would take place not long after that.

I grew excited as I thought about finding and claiming my first hunter falcon and tried to focus on what I had been taught: the best routes down the cliff face, the best ledges on which to rest, and what to do when attacked by a mother falcon. My mentors stressed that my first hunt wasn't just about owning a bird. It was about the hunt and about negotiating the steepest cliffs in the Midlyn Range while trying to stuff a young falcon into a rucksack dangling off my hips without snapping the bird's fragile neck, then climbing hundreds of feet back up the cliff without killing myself or my bird.

I had often trained by having one arm lashed to my side then being ordered to climb some random path up a cliff face with the use of just a single hand. By the time I was fourteen, I had mastered all the paths on Gavina. But where Gavina's crags were seemingly limitless in height, the cliffs of Hunter's Bluff had treacherous overhangs.

Lord Hengry would tell me, "No matter what you do on the cliffs, if the Sirens don't want to give you one of their children, then you won't have one of their children."

He would finish with a nonchalant yet chilling statement: "And if you are allowed to make it back to the top, you can try again next year. The Sirens do not hold a grudge."

Our cable-car swayed in the winds above the Sawblades, and in between my giddiness over the upcoming hunt and the subtle turn of my stomach whenever my thoughts slipped back to father, I tried to remember as much of my training as possible.

The route from the Hunter's Bluff cable tower to the base-camp location was a tiring five-league hike over rocky paths that we climbed up as well as down. Intermittent dirt sections ran through small fields of brown and green mountain grasses, and we passed a few small villages. These outskirts were where old Austringers went to live when they were no longer interested in hunting and dealing with the politics of the City Valley.

Walking was at first a relief from the stresses of the past three days of doing more sitting in cable-boxes than hiking. However, after we hiked through the night and the base-camp was still not in sight, I worried that Aillil would insist on starting the hunt at sunrise anyway, without even a few hours of rest.

Our hunter group was the last to arrive at the camp, just after dawn. Markyn and I had fallen behind, and when Aillil saw me rounding the trail-head stone, he called out, "It's about time, Ty."

He spoke with that fatherly tone that always dug under my skin. But this time I was too tired to argue with him, and I was relieved to see that he and Marello were busy starting a small fire to cook some groats and figs. Luckily, he only asked that Markyn and I set up the lean-tos while the food was cooking. That chore was easy enough that we would be done before the food was ready and would most likely be able to rest for a little while.

When we had finished eating and all four of us had picked our teeth clean, Aillil looked from Marello to Markyn and me. We knew it was time to head to the cliffs.

By Austringer law, a warrior was only allowed to own a maximum of two falcons. And by the time he was twenty-one, Aillil had already been successful twice. His young falcons were the talk of the Austringer court. Word among the officers was that he was the master of two of the greatest hunter falcons any Austringer had ever owned.

He turned his head toward the far southern edge of the bluff, directing my attention to the hunting path I would take. I choked down my last bite of groats, though my nervous belly wasn't sure it could handle any more food.

We had been divided into five groups of four hunters each—two novice hunters and two sentries. In my group, Markyn and I were the novices, and Aillil and Marello were the sentries. However, when I looked around, I realized that all the other groups had only experienced hunters with them and no novices. There were plenty of young warriors who were ready for their first hunt, but none besides Markyn and me had come along.

A sentry's job was to stand at the top of the cliff at an angle that afforded a clear view of the climber. He would watch the climber with a light-bow in hand, but his only ammunition was a relatively soft, sand-filled leather pouch tied to the end of a short wooden arrow. These harmless missiles would be used to scare away a mother falcon should one attack a climber. They were not intended to kill or seriously damage a bird—that was considered a high crime—but instead were used to buy the climber time until he got himself to a safe spot.

The sentries were also there to coach and instruct the hunters. From their vantage point, sentries might see things that a man who is clinging to the rock face could not. They were invaluable to a novice climber, and I knew I could trust my older brother in that regard. Markyn was also in good hands because Marello was our best mentor. He was also one of my father's oldest friends and the highest-ranking general in the Austringer army.

Marello, Jasko, Lord Rogell, and my father had fought side by side in the last battles of the Shoulder Range campaign. They were all curmudgeonly warriors with the minds of young falcons but the bones of old cliff goats. When father had offered Marello the lord-general position Tuecyr now held, he turned it down because he said his services were best used in the field and not arguing with all the fat barons who, he claimed, infected the Austringer court.

"Besides," he told my father, "who else is going to make sure our younger warriors know how to fight?"

There were few warriors—young or old—who could best Marello. To us young Austringer warriors-in-training, having him spar with us was both an honor and a guaranteed beating, but we accepted the important lesson of keeping our heads focused while in tremendous physical pain with humility and thankfulness.

We stood at the top of our climbing route as Marello gave us some last-minute instructions with the rising Telios behind him. From this point on Hunter's Bluff, Telios was brighter than at any other place in the Midlyn Range. It was so bright that I wondered how I was going to find good hand and footholds if I could barely open my eyes.

"You have been through this a thousand times," Marello said. "The cliffs below us are not too physically different from the training cliffs of Gavina. They do, however, offer you obstacles that Gavina does not, all of which you've been briefed on. I've chosen these particular cliffs as your starting points because they are the easiest to navigate and have the widest rest spots. That's why the other groups took the northern and southern-most faces."

Marello had been on countless eyas hunts and knew all the best routes to climb. He gave us a few more instructions, then showed Aillil the best spot to post sentry for me. Aillil had yet to handle a sentry duty, so he needed Marello's guidance.

They moved off to their posts—two high spots that had a clear view of the cliff faces—while Markyn and I stood at the top of the small pile of rocks that we had to climb over in order to start our descent.

Markyn looked at me with nervous excitement then smiled and gave me a sarcastic bow and a sweep of his hand. "After you, Prince Tyrcel."

I did not require any of my friends to address me formally, and I wasn't in the mood for joking, so I gave Markyn a quick slap against the back of his lowered head and stepped over the rock pile.

The glare from Telios was distracting, but the first few steps made the descent seem like it was going to be easy. When we reached the end of that relatively level section, Markyn took the climbing path to the left, and I headed to the right.

When I turned around on the slender ledge to begin the climb down, my nose was only inches from the cliff face. With my back to the sun and the warm rocks in front of me, I was swallowed in a heat the likes of which I had never felt before. I had heard about this, about how even with a single sun and at these heights, the southern face of Hunter's Bluff always remained warmer than anywhere else in the Midlyn Range. In fact, people said the rocks radiated heat for hours after Telios had set. But it was the first time I had experienced it.

I found a good handhold and officially began my hunt. My goat-skin rucksack flapped in the wind against my shoulders as I made my way down. When I found a secure foot rest, I let my weight sink into my feet. My arms shook from exertion, and I cursed Marello and Aillil for rushing us into the hunt after our long hike.

I continued climbing, and my palms were soon slippery with sweat from the warm rocks that I had to grip. I was irritated that I had not been briefed more on how to deal with the heat that radiated off these cliffs. It was an obstacle that should have been discussed more thoroughly in our training.

I swept my left hand down, searching for the next good spot to grab onto, and remembered my sentry. When I found a decent handhold, I peered over my shoulder. There up on the far ridge was Aillil. He waved to me then made a chopping motion up and down and swept his hand to the left. I felt reassured to see my brother keeping sentry and knew he was guiding me along the best path.

All the old warriors had said I was at the age when many Austringers died of rash decisions. Aillil had told me he took his sentry duty seriously, and he hoped my ego would not prevent me from heeding his instructions. I had laughed at the time, but now that I was hanging from the cliffs of Hunter's Bluff, I knew exactly what my brother meant.

I tightened my grip and shifted my weight to my right foot as I stepped down and to the left. I found a good ledge on which to plant my left foot, then brought my other foot down to it. After shifting my grip again, I caught a quick movement from Aillil out of the corner of my eye. He was motioning for me to stop and inspect something directly below me.

I had assumed that I wouldn't be on top of a falcon roost until I was halfway down the cliff face. I turned to look in the direction that Aillil was pointing, and my nose scraped against the rocks, reminding me that I wasn't as focused as I should be. A good climber keeps his hands and feet on the rocks and his torso as far away from them as possible. When a climber's body is pressed up against a cliff face, he loses maneuverability and his field of vision is reduced to nothing. When that happens, even a good climber might panic, and he would not be able to see, let alone heed, any instructions from his sentry.

I shifted my weight back and cocked my head over my left shoulder as far as I could. There, well within reach of my legs, was a ledge above which were the telltale signs of a roost.

The falcons made their roosts in the cracks of the cliff face, which were often deeper than a man's arm and nearly unrecognizable to the untrained eye. But I had been given detailed instructions on what a falcon roost looked like, and there below me was something that fit the description.

I gripped a small bump in the cliff and lowered my left foot down onto the ledge. At this point, the opening to the roost was directly in front of my belly. I looked up again at my brother. Aillil was making a slow up and down motion that meant I should remain calm, and he indicated that I should move a bit more to my left.

I shimmied a few feet in that direction, and when I saw a some twigs and feathers tucked into the crack right in front of my hip, I forgot the straining in my limbs and was overwhelmed by excitement at the thought of finding my first falcon.

But I could not gain a solid position that would allow me to use my right hand to search the roost. Again, I looked up at Aillil. He stood still, his light-bow in his hand, and didn't seem to know how to guide me from this point. That was fine with me. I decided to move on my own. I let go of both my handholds and let my body drop down past the ledge where I had just been standing. I fell a few feet and caught the ledge. My fingers dug into rock that was sodden with condensation and falcon refuse.

Aillil's heart must have jumped into his throat. It was an honor and a tradition for Austringer warriors to fall to their deaths, but mother would have hung Aillil from a stretcher cage if he let me come to such an end on my first hunt.

Aillil yelled curses at me, but the wind kept his words from clearly reaching my ears.

Meanwhile, that same wind whipped at my back, through every fold and pocket of my vest, chilling my skin as my sweat was whisked dry. I moved my feet back and forth across the rocks, scrambling to find a solid foothold. I could only last as long as my hands had the strength to hold me up, and I must have looked like a man trying to run up the cliff face.

The tips of my toes were finally able to find purchase, and I pulled my body up so my elbows could rest on the ledge of the aerie. After a few more blind scrapes, I found a deeper foothold that allowed me to stand solidly enough that I could carefully reach into the roost.

It was easy to crush a young falcon, so while I clung to the edge of the cliff with one hand, I had to maneuver my other arm with the utmost care. Luckily, the roost was not wide or deep, and my fingertips soon touched the back wall. Finding no signs of an eyas, I brought my hand forward and heard a high-pitched squawk. At the same moment, a warm clump of down slipped from under my palm.

"Damn," I shouted, and my hand blindly chased the squirming chick as gently as possible.

I slowly swept to the left, across the moist floor of the roost, and every time I had the chick in my grip, it wiggled out and disappeared into another nook of the cave. I had to act fast before I lost my grip or the chick's mother returned. I swept my hand to the right, and my fingers brushed soft feathers.

I quickly closed my hand over the bird and pulled it out. The wind caught at its feathers and whipped them from between my fingers. As I looked down, I realized that I was not holding a young falcon but the remains of a carrier pigeon.

Swallowing disappointment, I opened my hand to let the carcass blow away. As the wind cleared my palm of the dead pigeon bits, a piece of parchment was uncovered, which the breeze caught and yanked away from me. I reached after it and snatched it in midair, but the sudden movement caused my other hand to lose its grip on the rocks. I grabbed the ledge with both hands, crushing the parchment against the rocks, and stopped myself from plummeting.

I took a moment to catch my breath then secured myself with my left hand and held the parchment in my right. The edges were tattered, but it still had the remnants of an official Austringer stamp. I examined the parchment more closely and recognized the blue wax and scrawled signature of Lord Hengry.

Austringers only used carrier pigeons as a last resort because they rarely survived long in the Midlyn Range. Even more to the point, few Austringers cared to communicate with any foreign country. Finding fish, rodent, and bird carcasses in a falcon roost was common, but finding a dead pigeon with an official Austringer parchment on it was unheard of.

I began reading the brief note, and the hairs on the back of my neck stood up and added to the chill that was already running down my spine. I shoved the paper into my rucksack and began climbing back up, scrambling over any available ledge or bump in the cliff face. Aillil rushed down from his sentry post and reached the top of the climbing path just as I was stepping over the last pile of rocks. He grabbed my vest to steady me.

"You ignored my instructions the whole way up," he said. "Just because you've found a chick doesn't mean you lose your head and try and fly back up the cliff."

"Sorry, brother. I was a bit put off by what I found in that roost."

Aillil frowned and reached for my rucksack. "Let's have a look," he said.

"There's no chick in there."

He had the rucksack partway open and stared at me. "Then why aren't you elbow deep in that roost?"

"I found something strange," I said.

Aillil reached into my rucksack and pulled out the crumpled parchment. He scowled at it in confusion. "Tyrcel, there are more important things to do than read other people's long-lost communications."

"Normally I'd say yes, but take a look at it."

I turned the parchment over so he could see the signature and the remnant of wax. His expression changed when he realized the message had been written by father's closest advisor.

3

"Yes, brother, that appears to be Lord Hengry's signature and stamp," Aillil said.

"What does it mean?" I asked.

Aillil looked at me in frustration. "Isn't it obvious, Tyrcel?"

"This is Lord Hengry we're talking about," I protested. "He's father's oldest friend."

Aillil snatched the parchment from my hand and read the message again. A good portion of it was blurred from the elements, but what was legible caused us both great concern.

> jb mind gone.
> soon will be his body
> then the waves can crash
> within five moons' light
> and telios shines on different overhang

Aillil touched the wax seal with a fingertip and studied the signature. Then he crushed the parchment and pushed it back into my hand. I was livid that someone so close to father was plotting treason, and Aillil's slow response was driving me mad.

"JB!" I exclaimed, holding up the tattered parchment. "That has to be father's letters."

"Let me think for a minute, Ty," he said as he gazed out over the bluff. "Lord Hengry is conspiring with someone. But we don't know who. We also don't know when he sent this message."

I could barely contain myself. "And what about 'soon will be his body'? That can only mean one thing."

Aillil was distracted and didn't seem to be listening to me. "Those last few phrases," he murmured. "'Within five moons' light and Telios shines on a different overhang.'"

Suddenly I remembered something.

"Lord Hengry is the one who suggested we begin the hunt two weeks early," I said. He had insisted that a good hunt would be beneficial for Aillil and me, reasoning that we could use a long break from the court and our father's troubling behavior. "He obviously wanted us out of the way for whatever he's planning."

Aillil's eyes locked on mine. "The next five-moon night is tomorrow. I don't know what all this means, but we've got to get back to the Overhang and show this to father. I just can't believe that Lord Hengry would do something like this."

He collected his rucksack and bow, and we hurried along the footpath to where Marello was watching sentry over Markyn. When Marello glanced down from his post and saw us, he must have detected our urgency because he immediately signaled for Markyn to stop what he was doing. I didn't even consider that Marello might be in on the covert plot. He was like a father to me.

He came down from his post, and Markyn climbed back up from his hunt. When we were all on the footpath, I showed them the parchment. Markyn was confused and asked hurried and obvious questions. Aillil's eyes were on Marello. He was the senior member of our group, a general, and someone whom Aillil was groomed to obey. I watched as Marello studied the note and the expression on his face went from dismay to anger. I knew he would take action, and I was ready to do whatever he said to stop any traitorous bastards.

Marello finally looked up at Aillil. "Where are the other hunting groups?"

"Jasko's party is down past the southern plateau," Aillil said. "Wryn's is above them on the same path. Sir Levvyn's group is along the northern path, and Lord Rogell has taken the journey to the north cliffs."

Markyn looked frightened half out of his wits, and my mind was racing. The other groups had either departed before we arrived at the campsite or left for their hunt while we were eating. My stomach lurched when I remembered that there weren't any novice hunters among them.

Marello must have been thinking along the same lines because he said, "I'm not sure we can trust anyone else on Hunter's Bluff."

It was a chilling statement, but Marello immediately began to give instructions. "We have to move cautiously. Because we can't be sure of the loyalties of other members of this party, we can't let on that we know anything about the plot. We need to end this hunt and get back to the Overhang as quickly as possible."

The thought of my first hunt being canceled so abruptly because of traitors only fueled my anger.

"Tyrcel and Markyn, go rally Sir Levvyn's group," Marello said. "Aillil and I will head down the southern path and call those two groups back to the campsite."

Markyn and I nodded, and Marello added, "Be careful when you speak with the other sentries. Just tell them there's an urgent change of plans and they should gather the hunters and get back to the campsite. They'll be busy guiding any climbers back up, which will give you time to get back to the campsite before them. By the time we all meet up there, I'll have thought of a good excuse for the sudden change of plans."

We hurried back along the path toward the campsite. When we reached it, we dropped our sentry bows and other hunting gear and took off in separate directions.

We knew Sir Levvyn and his party were scouring the northern cliff face for falcon roosts, but being novices, Markyn and I had no idea where the hunting spots were. We ran to the edge of the bluff, and I dropped to my belly and peered over. Seeing nothing down below but distant treetops and clouds, I pushed back up to my feet and we continued farther north, where we repeated the process.

Then we noticed Austringer gear, ropes, and light weapons lying beside a small pile of boulders that sat in an arrangement similar to the head-stones on other climbing paths. I dropped again to my belly and looked over the edge. Thankfully, Sir Levvyn was not far below. He was busy watching over a high-ranking royal guard as he searched for falcon chicks.

Sir Levvyn's back was against the cliff face, and he held a heavy bow in one hand and a sand-filled arrow in the other. He was one of the surliest officers I had ever met, and it didn't surprise me that he was wielding a heavy-bow rather than the light training bows that sentries were supposed to use.

Markyn and I exchanged looks. "At least he's using the practice arrows," Markyn whispered.

I called down to Sir Levvyn. He startled a bit on his ledge and looked up at me. I was nothing more than a silhouette from his angle, but Levvyn recognized my voice. "What is it, Tyrcel?"

"Tell the men to climb up. There's been a change of plans. We are all meeting back at the camp."

Levvyn growled, "What change of plans, boy?"

I wasn't ready for such an obvious question. Markyn leaned forward and answered for me. "We want to discuss moving to the northern hunting cliffs, to join up with Lord Rogell."

I looked at my friend with admiration for his quick thinking. Markyn shrugged his shoulders.

"Why in all the Hells do I care where you and your group hunt, Tyrcel?" Levvyn asked. "Go on without us."

I tried to embellish by adding a bit of truth to the story. "I'm sorry, sir, but these orders are from General Marello. The other groups are already waiting at the lean-tos."

Sir Levvyn growled more curses as he turned back to his waiting climber.

I could not make out what he said, but he did motion for the climber to return to the top. I pushed myself to my feet. The wind was getting stronger, so Markyn and I snapped our masks over our faces and quickened our pace until we were running back to camp. All Austringer vests, for hunting or war, have a swath of padded leather sewn into the collars that can be pulled around the face to protect a warrior from the harsh winds that blustered on the tops of these mountains.

We passed the northern trail-head stones but saw no sign of Aillil or the other groups on the wide expanse of Hunter's Bluff.

We waited at the camp for half an hour before I told Markyn, "Stay here and wait for Levvyn's group to return. They shouldn't be much longer. Remember to play dumb, and don't tell them what we've found."

"Of course, Ty."

"I'm going to head down the southern path and link up with Aillil. They need to be back before Levvyn's group or he will know we were bluffing."

I scanned the campsite for any kind of weapon and found a small ax lying near the fire. I picked it up and slid the handle through my belt. Then I sped from the campsite, the lean-tos fluttering behind me. I ran along the southern footpath, which led down the bluff ridge and ended at a plateau that was an excellent hunting spot. As I ran, I could see the outline of the Overhang in the distance, framed against the peak of Gavina.

The sight of my home, so huge and yet so far away, made me falter, but then I heard men yelling. I picked up my pace and jumped over the last small switchback in the footpath in time to witness a man flipping a guard over his shoulder and off the plateau. The guard screamed a high-pitched bellow that faded away.

The man who had thrown him was Wryn, an officer in the Royal Guard.

"What in the name of all the Hells are you doing?" I demanded.

Wryn started toward me but someone shouted his name, and he bolted out of sight. That's when I saw Aillil grappling with an Austringer officer. They were almost immobile as they each tried to hold down the other man's arms. If one let go to strike his opponent, that opponent would also have a free hand. So they grappled and pushed each other back and forth. Occasionally one slipped a few inches, which brought them ever closer to the edge of the plateau, with the officer maneuvering Aillil between him and the cliff.

I yanked the ax from my belt and jumped over the last step of the footpath, using my momentum to hurl the ax at Aillil's opponent. The blunt side of the ax head crashed into the man's temple, and he collapsed at the edge of the cliff and lay still.

I was shaking. He was the first man I had killed, but I didn't have time to ponder it because Wryn was running toward me with a bronze-tipped spear in his hands.

If I moved backward, I'd fall off the plateau. I stepped to my left, back up the footpath, but forgot about the last step and fell onto my side. Wryn's spear was not far from my upheld arm when the ax that had just saved Aillil came down and shattered it. Wryn's momentum kept him moving forward, and he stumbled over the broken spear. Aillil gave him a good kick in the backside and sent him off the cliff edge.

"Thanks," I said, breathless and a little shaken. Then I noticed the skirmish behind Aillil.

"It's Marello," I shouted, pointing at the group of Austringers fighting at the other end of the plateau.

Marello was surrounded by three low-ranking members of the hunting party. One of them had a spear in his hands while the other two held the long, curved daggers that were standard issue for Austringer warriors. Marello was unarmed, save for a large stone. He dared any of his assailants to make the first move. None of them hurried to respond. All Austringer warriors knew the legends of Marello's actions in the hill-giant wars—how he was the only Austringer to ever be seen in hand-to-hand combat with a hill-giant—and that any challenge to Marello would be returned with a painful price. So they circled the old general, threatening one side if he moved to the other for an attack. It burned my heart to see these cowards taunt the best mentor they had ever had.

Aillil ran across the plateau and jumped into the air with the ax in his hand, but the warrior closest to him turned the long pole of his spear horizontal and Aillil's forearm crashed into it. The impact caused him to drop the ax. He turned on the guard, a man named Hektyr who had acquired an honorable reputation as a great tactician.

Aillil hooked his elbow over the spear handle, pulling Hektyr close enough to render the weapon useless. Hektyr pushed against Aillil's damaged wrist, and Aillil struck Hektyr's throat with his open palm. Hektyr staggered backward, dropping his spear, both his hands clutching his shattered esophagus. His face was blood red as he struggled to breathe. He dropped to his knees then fell over, writhing on the ground and hissing. Aillil kicked Hektyr's arms away and slammed his heel down on the man's throat.

I ran to stand behind Marello, both of us facing the attackers. The two remaining guards shifted left, then right, their eyes locked on us. Marello still held the stone in his hands, but I was weaponless. I scooped up a leather strap lying on the ground and wrapped it around the knuckles of my right hand.

"Don't worry, Tyrcel, these cowards don't know what they're doing," Marello said. He knew I was a fine fighter, at least in practice. But I was being forced to prove my worth for the first time in true combat—against my fellow Austringers. "They aren't seasoned enough to know that once you've gone to battle against a swarm of hill-giants, fighting pissant runts like them comes easy."

I knew Marello was trying to intimidate his opponents with his words. An enemy who cannot control his emotions is easily thrown off balance.

I joined in. "I'm not worried about these two. I know them well from our drills. They cower and stay at the back of the ranks like worried field mice."

Suddenly Aillil shouted, "Stop this madness. NOW!"

The boom of his voice made us all pause.

"Drop your daggers," he told the two guards. "You are outnumbered, and your only other choice is the edge."

He gripped Hektyr's spear in his left hand and pointed it at the guard facing Marello. Both guards stepped back but still held their long-daggers at the ready. Suddenly, from the bottom of the footpath, we heard men approaching.

"Sorry, Aillil, but I think you're the ones outnumbered here."

Captain Jasko stood at the mouth of the lower path with two long-daggers in his hands and a sneer on his face.

"In the name of your king and people, stand down, Jasko," Aillil said.

Jasko surveyed the situation and flicked a look at Marello, apparently one of the few men who had stayed loyal to my family.

"My king?" Jasko taunted. "I'm fairly certain my king won't care when I've thrown you off this plateau."

"You're mad," Aillil said.

He moved to face Jasko, holding the spear in his left hand ready for a thrust. Aillil was ambidextrous with most weapons, but Jasko could probably tell that my brother's swollen and bloodied right forearm was broken. Jasko turned his daggers with the razor edge facing out. He preferred to get in close to his opponents and slice them to shreds.

I exploited the distraction Jasko caused and slammed my leather-wrapped fist into the jaw of the guard across from me. Teeth flew, and he collapsed to the ground. My punch, however, set the melee in motion. Aillil flung the spear at Jasko, who twisted and shifted a few inches to his right. The spear flew past his ear and plunged into the chest of the guard behind him. The force of the spear lifted the man off his feet and pushed him over the edge of the plateau without a word.

Jasko sprinted forward. "Thanks for making this easy for me," he said as he jumped into the air with his dagger blades aimed at Aillil's chest.

I took the long-dagger from my unconscious opponent and met Jasko as he crashed into my brother, knocking him to the ground. From behind, I swiped upward deep into the meat of his upper arm. The blade hit bone and Jasko dropped one of his long-daggers, but he had already sunk his other blade halfway into Aillil's right shoulder. Both men screamed in pain.

I yelled, too. The sight of Aillil wounded in such a way was too much to bear. Blood gushed from his shoulder, and despite being seriously wounded, Jasko had one knee pressed into the pit of my brother's abdomen.

"I have another arm, prince," he said, and breathing heavily, he yanked the dagger out of Aillil's shoulder.

I looked to Marello for help, but he was at the other end of the plateau, still holding that huge stone and taunting a young officer, who took a swipe at him with a dagger. Marello dropped to a crouch and said, "Well, my man, I don't know what rotten hole you dropped out of, but I will make you wish you never did."

In a split second, he pushed upward and smashed the stone into his attacker's chin. Blood burst from the man's face, mixed with teeth and flesh.

"Your clumsiness shames me," Marello taunted as the man staggered backward. "What glory is there in killing such weaklings? I'm going to have to train our new recruits better if they can't even last a minute in a real fight."

Marello's face was flushed as his chest heaved, and in his eyes was a look that I had never seen before.

He brought the stone down on the top of the man's head. It made a dull thud and the guard dropped facedown in a pool of his own brains. Marello knelt and picked up the man's long-dagger. The remaining guard from Jasko's group was within arm's reach, but the man was so clumsy that Marello easily ducked the swipe of his blade. Marello pivoted and sent a lightning-fast swipe of his own long-dagger across the man's neck, ending the fight before it began.

"Marello!" I shouted.

Jasko was standing wide-legged over Aillil's body and swinging his long-dagger wildly at me. I stepped back, dodging Jasko's off-balance defense. Instead of attacking, I was hoping to tire him out. Blood streamed from his right armpit, and I assumed that the adrenaline surging through his body was making his heart pump faster. Fresh blood flowed over already dried blood and spattered in the air as we faced each other.

I knew not to get too close. Even with only one good arm, Jasko was a serious threat, especially while he was straddling Aillil.

Marello ran toward us. "Hold your blade, Jasko."

Jasko stopped swinging at me but kept the dagger up. He was breathing hard and growled from between clenched teeth, "It's too late for you Buteos. There are more men in this hunting party who share my opinions."

He scowled at Marello. "You're loyal to an insane man. It will be the end of you."

"No matter what happens to King Jorgen," Marello said, "the rightful heir is Aillil, and you've just stabbed him in the chest."

"Don't worry, Marello. There will be a new king soon."

"What has Hengry done?" I demanded.

Jasko looked up at the clouds moving fast across the afternoon sky as though trying to sear the image in his mind. His legs gave out and he stumbled to one knee, dropping his dagger to the ground beside Aillil.

Marello jabbed the tip of his long-dagger into Jasko's shoulder and pushed him off Aillil. "You did this the wrong way, Jasko. Now you're nothing but a dead traitor."

Jasko forced a smile. "I'm not dead yet. And I'm not the one you need to worry about."

He pushed the dagger away from his shoulder and gave a wheezy cough of a laugh. "Abbo Doldra's horde is coming. You can't change that." He struggled to his feet. His face was pale, and he stood unsteadily in front of Marello. "Funny, once the coup was over, I was to be the new lord-general."

"Lord-general?" I said, my mind whirring. "What about Landys Tuecyr?"

Jasko smiled, but he didn't address my question. "This is our last age, Marello. Axis Solan is cooling, and soon even the Austringer magnets and vents won't be able to keep us warm."

"That may be true, but why treason?" Marello asked as he moved toward Jasko, who put up his good arm in a weak defensive posture. "Why murder and a coup? What do you get out of it?"

"I get to live the rest of my days not taking orders from anyone, especially those Buteos," Jasko said. "Entitled princes who have never even seen a hill-giant. I could kill them with both my arms hacked off."

He scowled and stepped back a few paces. "The people are sick of the stagnant policies of Jorgen Buteo. They have little hope for the future, but they still need to be governed. They see many reasons for a change of leadership in the City Valley."

I was so shocked by the notion that my own people had turned against my father that it took me a moment to realize that Jasko intended to jump off the plateau. For Austringer warriors, it was more honorable to leap off a cliff than let an enemy have the glory of killing them. When there is no other option, it is the last act of an Austringer warrior. As a race that honors falcons as gods, we looked forward to the opportunity to take what we called our "last flight."

I moved forward to stop Jasko, but he was already teetering on the edge of the plateau.

"You have nothing to lose by telling me," I said.

"Telling you what, runt-prince?" he sneered.

My mind raced. I had so many questions, but I sensed I would only have the chance to ask one.

"When is Doldra's army invading?"

Jasko shook his head. "Sorry, but they're already halfway to the City Valley."

"That's impossible. How could they get so far without the alarms being raised?" Besides, I thought, the parchment said the invasion would happen within five moons' light, and that wasn't until tomorrow.

Jasko raised his eyebrows in a gesture that told me there were more traitors within the Austringer court and army than I ever could have imagined. And no alarms had been raised because anyone who wanted to raise them was probably dead.

He swayed a bit, and the wind at the edge of the plateau slapped his face mask around like a leaf. "Doldra will have no problem moving his people through the Range. And Tuecyr will be a wealthy man without me."

I remembered Markyn waiting back at the camp with the other hunters.

"Who else in the hunting party is in on this?" I asked.

"They all are," he said.

Then he leaned back and dropped off the edge of the plateau.

4

I rushed over to Aillil and crouched down beside him. His eyes were closed, and though Marello stood next to him, he was staring off in the distance and made no move to help.

"Brother, are you all right?"

Aillil's eyes fluttered open. "As it goes, Ty."

I ripped the vest and shirt off one of the dead guards and began to fix a field dressing over my brother's shoulder wound, which seemed to have missed his lung. The blood had clotted and was not actively running. From the two broken halves of Wryn's spear, I made a splint for his shattered forearm.

"Jasko said Lord-General Tuecyr is part of this conspiracy," I said to Aillil, not sure how much of the conversation he'd heard. I glanced up at Marello. "And the rest of the hunting party is also against us.

"Don't look at me that way, prince," Marello said. "You're in no position to question my loyalty."

I stood up to face Marello, so full of rage that I did not care that the old warrior could easily break my spine.

"I haven't questioned your loyalty before," I said. "But I'm wondering if I should do it now."

"You do not want to challenge me, boy."

"Now you call me boy?"

Marello stepped closer, gripping the hilt of his long-dagger. "Yes, I called you a boy. Don't forget who just fought by your side. And don't forget who just saw one of his oldest friends take his last flight. You'd be lucky to end up as great a warrior as him."

"Now you side with a traitor?" I said.

Aillil was still on the ground by our feet. He struggled to push himself up.

"Tyrcel, come to your senses and see that Marello's on our side," he said. "We don't have time for this."

"He's talking like a traitor, Aillil," I said, my eyes still locked on Marello.

"No, he's not. He's talking like a man who just saw a comrade he knew and trusted betray his king. His opinions of Jasko's abilities don't make him a traitor."

I stared at Marello a moment longer, though I knew Aillil was right. And I was relieved that I wasn't going to have to square off with Marello. It wouldn't have been much of a fight anyway.

"Now that you're not going to let Marello snap your neck, do you think we might get a move on?" Aillil said. "Gather as many weapons as possible."

He tried to sit up against one of the trail-head stones that sat at the mouth of the footpath but couldn't manage it. Dazed, he took a deep breath and said, "But first let me rest a minute."

Marello already had the three remaining long-daggers in his hands. "There are no more spears. We've got nothing but these daggers and the ax."

"And all of our bows are at the camp," I added.

Aillil gripped the trail-head stone and pulled himself to his feet. "Don't worry, Tyrcel. Marello's pretty handy with a rock."

Marello smiled, though there was sadness in his eyes. "Aye, prince." He scanned the the plateau. "So many good men turned traitor, and for what?"

"We've no time for that now," Aillil said. "Who else is up on the bluff? And where is Markyn?"

"I left him at the camp," I said. "Despite what Jasko said, I believe we can trust him."

"Okay, but there's still Lord Rogell and Sir Levvyn. Those two will be the biggest threats," Aillil said. "Plus, they've got six guards between them."

"But Lord Rogell's party is half a day's hike north," I said.

Aillil pondered our options. "That's the best news we're probably going to get. We've no escape route that does not lead back up the footpath and through the camp. We could, however, climb down from here."

I shook my head. "That descent is half a league and a half straight down—a difficult climb even without a useless right arm."

They both knew I was right. Aillil's wounds reduced our options, and they rendered him almost useless in a skirmish. And to keep his wounds from festering on the journey back to the Overhang, he needed the mediocre medical supplies that were back at the camp.

"Perhaps Jasko was lying and they're not all traitors," I said, trying to inspire an optimism I didn't feel.

"Rogell is very close to the lord-general," Marello said. "So if Tuecyr has turned, Rogell will certainly follow his lead. And Levvyn is always looking out for his own advantage."

Aillil nodded. "You're right. We've got to assume that they're all traitors." He grimaced as he pushed himself away from the trail-head stone. "Let's get moving. It's already midday, and we need to sort out who's coming back with us and who's taking their last flight here."

We started up the footpath with me supporting Aillil. To our right was the bluff, and to our left was open sky. Marello held two long-daggers and had his face mask snapped over his nose so only his eyes were visible. He walked several steps ahead of Aillil and me in a slight crouch to react to any signs of an ambush before it had time to happen.

But we reached the top of the footpath without incident. Aillil and I dropped to our knees as Marello crouched behind one of the trail-head stones. Sir Levvyn's hunting party was moving about the camp, but Sir Levvyn was nowhere to be seen.

"We have to be prepared to do battle," Marello said.

With Aillil out of commission, it was up to Marello and me. But besides the skirmish back on the plateau, my battle experience was little more than the practice drills all warriors go through.

"We'll leave Aillil here and move at them head on," Marello said to me. "We need to deal with them quickly and directly." He smiled wryly. "Let's hope you are right and they are still on our side."

He moved his dagger blades behind his forearms and stood up. "Let's get this mess sorted."

Leaving Aillil out of sight behind the trail-head stone, I followed Marello out onto the bluff, a single long-dagger in my hand. Levvyn's three guards noticed us, and soon the entire camp was in motion.

Markyn walked toward us, and the smile on his face faltered as he got closer, making me wonder just how bad I looked after our battle.

"Thank the Sirens," he said in a low voice. "I was beginning to fear the worst, Ty. What happened up there?"

"No time to explain now," I said. "Have you had any trouble here?"

"It's been a bit uncomfortable. I'm running out of good answers for Levvyn's questions."

"You haven't told them what we found?"

"Not at all, Tyrcel."

Markyn had always been the easy-going one. Regardless of the situation, he never failed to find some humor in it. Nothing seemed to stress him, and I was grateful that he'd managed not to discuss the parchment.

"Thank you," I said.

I saw a flicker of movement behind him, but his body blocked my view. Suddenly, the bronze tip of a spear burst through his chest, and Markyn fell face forward onto the grass, a smile still on his lips.

Sir Levvyn stood behind him, holding another spear in his right hand.

"No!" I screamed.

Markyn lay so still that I knew he was dead.

I turned to face Levvyn. "You will pay with your head, you bastard."

Sir Levvyn glanced quickly to his right. I turned just in time to see a guard hurling a spear at me. Marello pivoted into my back and deflected the speeding weapon from its deadly path with a swipe of both his dagger blades, an improvised move that explained why he was still alive after so many battles.

"You'll have to do better than that, coward," Marello taunted.

The guard, a mid-level officer named Torryl Alystros, pulled his dagger from its scabbard. Marello moved toward him, and Torryl met him halfway, swiping his blade at Marello's abdomen. Marello feigned a move to his left, only to stop short and let the clumsy attack miss him. Torryl's momentum moved him too far past Marello, who quickly stepped behind him and thrust his dagger into the man's ribs. He screamed and dropped to his knees.

Marello twisted the dagger, and Torryl tried to reach around and pull it out, but Marello did it for him. When he yanked the blade from Torryl's back, it was covered with chunks of lung mixed with soupy, red blood.

"You spoiled little worm," Marello said. "Did you think I forgot the few moves you use? I've covered your ass in every skirmish we've been in. Now you know how it feels to be stabbed in the back."

Meanwhile, I was in a stand-off with Sir Levvyn as the remaining two guards rushed to his aid. But Marello ran between us and hurled a huge stone at the guards. It smashed into one of their heads, splitting it wide open.

The last guard came at Marello. My old mentor smiled in his enemy's face and thanked these so-called warriors for the opportunity to toss them off the edge of the world. He pulled out his daggers and lunged at his opponent with a blood-curdling war cry. The guard pivoted back and swung his long-dagger at Marello's left side, barely grazing him, and Marello countered by stabbing the guard below the collar bone. The guard fell to his knees, clutching his shoulder. Blood flowed between his fingers. With a swipe of his long-dagger, Marello slit the man's throat.

Sir Levvyn came at me with the spear in his hands, and I had no choice but to back up until he had me pinned between him and the edge of the cliff.

He cursed the Austringers who had just been killed. "Now I will have to finish you both off myself," he said.

Marello charged at him, but Levvyn swung his spear around. I took advantage of the momentary distraction to swipe at him with my long-dagger. Levvyn spun around in a circle and brought the spear tip around with him. I jumped sideways out of its deadly path, and Marello lunged at him from behind with both long-daggers in hand. As Marello lifted his arms for the attack, Levvyn didn't have time to turn the razor tip around and instead punched the butt end of his spear into Marello's diaphragm. Marello collapsed, momentarily unable to breathe, and Levvyn turned his focus back to me.

His spear was still pointed at me, causing me to shift to the right as I attacked, where there was nothing but open sky. I tried diving out of the spear's reach and away from the edge of the bluff, but Levvyn caught me across the shoulder as I fell. The shallow slice cut the outer layer of my vest, and down stuffing burst out into the wind. Levvyn kicked me in the ribs, and the impact sent me sliding until my legs hung over the edge of the cliff.

I could barely breathe as I struggled to get a handhold, digging my finger-tips into loose gravel and dirt. With one more kick, Sir Levvyn could send me on my own last flight.

He pressed the butt end of his spear into my forehead. "Jasko's dead, I assume."

I didn't bother answering.

I scrambled to pull myself up, but my legs were flailing in open air. I noticed a flash of movement to Levvyn's right, and suddenly a spear punched a hole through his chest. He spun around, his feet just inches from my face, and fell from the bluff without a sound.

I looked up to see Aillil standing beside Markyn's bloody body. He had used the spear that had killed my friend to save me. Aillil swayed on his feet and tried to steady himself, then collapsed to the ground.

Marello hurried over to me and yanked me up and onto my feet. I ran to Aillil.

With no more traitors to distract me, I was overwhelmed by my emo-tions. The sight of my badly wounded brother and dead best friend sent my mind into a frenzy. Tears poured down my face as the adrenaline from the skirmish subsided, but my heart still raced. I turned Markyn's body over, and small rivulets of blood drained from the corners of his mouth and out of the huge wound in his chest.

Marello grabbed my shoulder in his vise-like grip and threw me back-ward onto my ass. I looked up at him, stunned.

"You cry like a runt, boy," he growled. "Your friend is dead, but Aillil is still alive. Help me get your brother to the lean-to, then we'll deal with Markyn."

Marello scanned the plateau. "We should also throw these corpses off the bluff so there's nothing up here to alarm Lord Rogell when he and his group come back. And then we need to make haste back to the cables."

5

Aillil was unconscious until early the next morning. He awoke just as pink sunlight was pushing through a dangerously thick mist that had accumulated on Hunter's Bluff. These types of mists were familiar to Austringers. Although they were maddening to any other race, they simply forced an Austringer to be a bit more careful where he walked.

But these high-altitude clouds could lead to the white-blindness, when the fog became so thick that a man could not see his hand in front of his face. Unsuspecting travelers and potential enemies often lost their sense of direction and fell off the cliffs. That possibility paralyzed many an Austringer enemy as he waited in fear for the mist to clear.

But the white-blindness barely slowed Austringers down. In addition to the centuries-old cliff-to-cliff cable network, there was an elaborate guide-cable system that Austringer foot-travelers might use in case of the white-blindness. If they could get a hand on it, they could get anywhere in their territory.

I sat beside Aillil's bedroll in the lean-to and watched him lift his hand in front of his face. I could make out the faint silhouette of his fingers, which meant the white-blindness was dissipating.

"Tyrcel," he called weakly.

"Yes, brother."

"My arm hurts so much I can't see straight. And I don't remember our journey. Are we back at the Overhang?"

I paused but couldn't think of a tactful reply. "Sorry, brother, but we're still at the campsite on Hunter's Bluff."

"What? Why are we still here? We need to get back and warn father."

"You were unconscious," I said. "And then night set in, and the night mists came, and it's hard enough traveling under those conditions without an unconscious man in the party."

Aillil struggled to sit up, straining to see me in the white gloom. "Then you should have left me here!"

The effort was too much for him, and he fell back onto his pallet. Over the sound of his labored breathing, we heard thunder erupt in the distance.

A storm had been approaching for awhile, but I hadn't been able to see any lightning through the mist. At these heights, out on an open bluff, lightning was a worry, but Marello and I had agreed that once the white-blindness cleared, we would start the journey back to the Overhang. We couldn't afford to let the storm slow us down.

I rested my hand on Aillil's shoulder above the field-dressing clotted with blood. We sat without speaking for a few seconds, waiting for the next thunderclap. But only winds whistled across the bluff, creating the morning breezes. And that meant the white-blindness would soon be over.

"Marello and I considered leaving you here if you were not awake by morning," I said. "But Lord Rogell will be back soon, and I can't leave you to his devices."

Aillil didn't argue with me, and he seemed to relax, perhaps relieved that we hadn't left him behind after all. However, the way back to the Overhang was long, and it involved hiking in addition to riding the sky cables. Aillil had to know he would be a burden to Marello and me. He would have to choke back the pain as the three of us made our way home as fast as we could. I figured if we could get him as far as the first tower, he could rest on the cable ride.

Another thunder clap sounded somewhere out in the fog.

"Where is Marello?" Aillil asked.

"Over on the lookout boulder keeping an eye out for Lord Rogell."

A silhouette appeared at the foot of Aillil's bedroll, startling both of us.

Marello said, "Good to see you're awake, Aillil. I'd love to sit and chat, but I think you two need to see something."

His face was recognizable enough through the mist that I decided it was time to start our journey home. Aillil perched himself up on his good elbow while I gathered equipment and stuffed objects into various rucksacks. I was so consumed with the desire to get moving that I didn't immediately register Marello's last statement.

"Help me up," Aillil said.

Marello grasped Aillil's good wrist and pulled him to his feet.

"What is it that we need to see?" my brother asked.

"Come with me."

Marello's tone was urgent, and I stopped what I was doing to join him and Aillil. I grabbed a spyglass from one of the rucksacks and peered beyond the lookout boulder and the edge of Hunter's Bluff in the direction of the thunderclaps, which had been joined now by a distant hissing sound. But I still didn't see any lightning.

"There are odd ships out in the Straits," Marello said.

We walked to the highest point of Hunter's Bluff through the thinning mist and peered out over the dark-blue cloud tops. The mist and the distant clouds seamlessly joined at the edge of the bluff. Telios had not yet risen above the clouds, so random beams of light burst up from below the eastern horizon.

The boulder that formed the high point of the bluff stood out like a smooth gray mass in a sea of clouds. Marello and I climbed the boulder and helped Aillil up. At first all we could see were the tops of the clouds, but the winds were slowly dissolving the dense mists and soon we caught intermittent glimpses of the distant Straits—and a steady column of black smoke rising up from the Sentinel mountains that framed Port Tallion.

I held the spyglass up to my eye. "I have never seen ships like those. Where are their sails?"

I was familiar with what a war-ship looked like. Indeed, our own war rigs that dangled from the sky-cables were not too different in design from a ship that floated on the sea. These ships in the distance, however, had no sails, but they were so far away that I couldn't make out what structure was sitting on their decks.

As I watched, strange barrel-shaped objects flew from each of the ships as high as the bottom of the clouds then came down behind the Sentinels. The movement was followed by a thunderous roar that vibrated through the boulder beneath us. More smoke billowed up through the clouds, and black soot smoldered on the horizon.

So the thunder I'd been hearing wasn't an approaching storm. "That's why we didn't see lightning," I said.

Although I couldn't understand what the ships were doing or why, I felt the first stirrings of worry that an invasion of my homeland had begun.

Marello grabbed the spyglass from me and peered through it. "It looks like those barrels are exploding against the Sentinels."

The Sentinels were two of the tallest mountains in the Shoulder Range. They rose leagues into the sky and were typically dotted with lights and fires that signaled messages to incoming ships. But when the mist cleared, those beloved mountains were half the height they used to be. And beneath the black cloud that hovered where the mountaintops had been, more enemy warships joined the flotilla.

Austringers had long ago concluded that there was little we could do if a hostile force decided to invade the Midlyn Range from the north. The Shoulder Range was massive, but there were many lowland sections between them that any savvy admiral could exploit—not to mention that the biggest open section was Port Tallion, which was heavily under Doldra's influence. Austringers only kept sentry over the northern coast from the cliffs of the Sentinels to monitor what was going on. We retained no governance or control over the port.

Doldra's horde could easily enter Port Tallion, beach their ships, and then begin their siege of the City Valley with little or no resistance.

"This is a good sign," Aillil said.

Marello and I looked at each other, certain that pain was clouding my brother's judgment.

"You're delirious," I said.

"No, Tyrcel. Remember how Jasko said that Doldra was already halfway to the Overhang? Yet here is his fleet sitting in the Straits. They wouldn't be destroying the Sentinels if their ships were docked at the port. This is the start of the invasion, which means we might not be too late to get back to the Overhang and warn father."

Marello kept the spyglass to his eye as he spoke. "I agree, and I think we ought to get moving."

Marello was no longer looking at the ships in the Straits. Instead, he was focused on a path a couple of leagues away that wound its way down the northern edge of Hunter's Bluff.

"What is it?" I asked.

He handed me the spyglass, and I looked in the direction of the northern pass. There hiking up a long switchback were Lord Rogell and his three hunting partners. Every inch of my body was suddenly buzzing with an urgency I had never felt before. I looked one last time at the warships floating on the sea then jumped down from the boulder and hurried to catch up with Aillil and Marello.

At the lean-tos, Marello and I distributed Aillil's gear between our rucksacks. Each of us had a bedroll, several days' worth of food, the standard-issue long-dagger, a heavy-bow, a quiver of arrows of all varieties, and one bronze-tipped spear. But Aillil was in no shape to carry any of that. He sat with his back propped against a rock and watched us.

"If we move fast, we can stay ahead of Doldra's forces," Marello said. "And Rogell's if we're lucky. We've got to be out of sight by the time they crest the ridge."

"What about citizens fleeing inland to the City Valley?" I asked. "Not everyone in Port Tallion is loyal to Doldra. The cables will soon be clogged with refugees."

"We'll need to stay ahead of them as well."

Fortunately, the mist had almost totally dissipated. Marello and I swung our rucksacks over our shoulders, and the three of us set out on the footpath toward the southern-most cable tower on Hunter's Bluff. It was a long, arduous trail. I had barely gotten over my fatigue from the hike up to the camp, and now after all that had happened, I was back on the same trail, hiking at a faster pace and with a heavier rucksack.

My dream of a great eyas hunt had suddenly turned into a nightmare.

The cable route to Hunter's Bluff hopped from one Sun Point mountaintop to the next and circumvented the Hollow Valley. An outsider looking at a map would wonder why the Austringer engineers had designed such a circuitous route from the City Valley to Hunter's Bluff and why, if Austringers insisted on using the cables, they had not been extended directly over the Hollow Valley.

But our engineers knew Austringers would find all the stops on various mountaintops to be a much more pleasant traveling experience—not only because we preferred to stay at high altitudes but because Heike would be far below. A longer trip was a small price to pay to be clear of that monster.

We moved as fast as the weight of our packs and the wounded Aillil would allow. He was showing signs of strain with each passing minute and had to be lowered in his harness down some of the steeper sections of the footpath. I was worried but tried my best not to show it. I thought about leaving him in a cave or by a hot spring until we could get to father and come back with help, but the thought of Lord Rogell finding Aillil, wounded and defenseless, made that plan out of the question. Austringers were expert trackers, and Aillil wouldn't be safe no matter where we hid him.

As the day wore on, we all began to feel tired. Aillil's shoulder wound had clotted well, but the stress of our travels caused it to intermittently reopen. We were forced to stop often and change his bandages. Marello didn't say anything, but his concerns were apparent as he kept his eyes on the horizon behind us.

As Telios began his descent in the west, we were within a league of the first cable tower and decided to stop at the last trail marker and eat a little food and tend to Aillil's shoulder. In front of us was the southern path, which slightly descended down the back end of Hunter's Bluff. While I fixed a new bandage to my brother's wound, Marello climbed the highest boulder he could find and looked through his spyglass. He scanned the trail that we had just hiked down for any signs of Rogell's party. We had not seen them but knew they couldn't be far behind. Rogell was a smart leader, and as soon as he realized the rest of the hunting party was gone, he'd hurry back to the Overhang.

Not far away, at the bottom of a steep decline, was the cable port. We finished a few last bites of figs and goat jerky and moved out. We came to the final trail-head stone, and it was only a few hundred feet of easy hiking down to the cable tower. As we made our way along the foot-path, the wind hissed through the cables. Soon, we were on the last stretch of the path, directly above the cable tower stairs. From this vantage point, we could see the cables disappear into the clouds that hung over the ravine.

We moved as quickly as possible over the rest of the footpath and up the tower stairs to the topmost platform, with Marello and me on either side of Aillil and all but carrying him up the stairs. At the release port landing, we tightened the harnesses that were sewn into our vests. I helped Aillil with his, while Marello went to release a three-man cable box from its dock. As I waited for the car to swing around to the landing, I glanced at the trail behind us. The gray light of dusk made it difficult to see far, but I made out a few odd glints and shapes moving over the distant ridge. My heart jumped into my throat.

I called down to Marello on the tower landing. "Rogell and his crew are within sight."

I dropped my rucksack and pulled my heavy-bow off my shoulder. From the quiver I pulled out a half-pound arrow. Marello came bounding up the landing and saw me standing at the ready with the bow in hand and said, "Don't waste time, Tyrcel. Get Aillil situated. Fighting them is what they want, but it will only make our situation worse. We've got to stay ahead of them."

I wanted to protest, but I knew Marello was right. Reluctantly, I dropped my bow. The three-person cable-car swung up from the dock and stopped next to the landing. I helped Aillil into the middle seat, snapped him into the safety tethers, and wrapped him warmly in his bedroll. He slumped down and mumbled a barely audible, "Thanks."

I took the front seat, and Marello sat down behind Aillil, cursing the fact that none of the cable-cars had sails on them. These smaller civilian cable-cars needed only two magnetic wheels' opposing forces to create the motion that allowed them to roll along the cable lines, whereas the larger courtly and military cable-cars often hung sails below their hulls to catch the wind and speed up their movement. The blustery winds at these heights were always unpredictable, so sails were not used on the smaller cars because they were too light and would be tossed around too easily.

Although the civilian car offered us few defensive options, once we were moving, Rogell couldn't catch up—at least not until we were all on the next mountain trail.

The car clanked over the tower pulleys and dropped a few feet into the open air. The hum of the rollers mixed with the wailing wind. By now our five moons were up and casting enough light that we could make out the distant Sawblades. And with their light, an invasion of the Midlyn Range was supposed to start.

The jagged outcroppings were so vast that they created the illusion of stillness as we rolled along. Ahead of us, still hours away, was Wailen's Point. We would not be there until early morning. In the blue hue of the moons' light, the switch-point was completely covered in a cloud bank that looked like a vast black sheet stretched across the horizon, and I couldn't help but think that it was a bad omen.

6

Just before dawn, when we were almost in the cloud bank, Telios began to rise. He cast long beams of light across the four Sun Point mountains, giving us a clear view of the land below and the mountains' western faces, which were covered with evergreen shrubs and rocky outcrops. Falcons floated in the updrafts, and others sat in nests that were well out of reach of the hill-giants who inhabited the lower cliffs.

I studied the ominous Sawblades to the west one last time. Telios' early morning light did not reach the bottom of the massive fissure from which they grew. There was a line of perpetual darkness that ran the length of the mountains' western cliffs. From the pitch-black bowl of the deep ravine rose plumes of gray smoke. Hill-giants made their homes in the caves and hollows of these mid-altitude ravines and valleys—another reason we Austringers preferred to ride the cables.

As Telios rose higher in the sky, we finally reached the cloud bank, and within it, the white-blindness prevailed. This cloud sat like a big white boulder on and around Wailen's Point, and the ride soon became a slow jaunt through a gauntlet of sensory deprivation. With nothing to see and little to hear, taste, or smell, all we could do was endure the cold, blustery winds and wait.

It was hours before the cable-car made the slow curve to the east around the switch point and we felt the familiar bump over the switch tower's tracks. We dropped a few weightless feet down and back out along the cable line. The slow hum of our car's wheels was eventually swallowed by the vast emptiness that opened around us. We weren't out of the cloud bank yet, but we knew we had just moved past the Sawblade ravine and over the north edge of the Hollow Valley.

The clouds cleared when we were half a league past the switch point. Marello hunched down in his seat with his vest and cloak gathered around his shoulders, and I leaned against the side of the compartment and looked down into the rolling hills of the Hollow Valley.

The valley was so wide and lush that for a few minutes each day, when Telios was at its highest and the valley was under no shadow of any mountain, its hills would glow with an eerie green hue. In our earliest lessons, Austringers were warned not to gaze upon the valley during these radiant minutes because the glow was said to draw one's attention so strongly that soon the person will feel compelled to wander into the forest, never to be seen again. I've even heard tell of men who were so transfixed by the glowing valley that they were compelled to jump from their cable cars. I was glad it wasn't midday.

The hills rolled toward the southeastern edge of the Ringing Forest, which had become the de facto perimeter around the valley, surrounding it on all sides except where the Main Road lined its western edge. Somewhere past the hills, the Main Road met the forest just a league outside the gates of the City Valley.

In this section of the forest, so close to the Austringers' City Valley, Heike lived. Before the cables were built, the Main Road had been paved on top of a three-hundred-foot berm, with a ten-foot retaining wall on both sides, to avoid this evil sorcerer. The height and retaining walls only brought psychological security to a traveler because Heike was widely known to haunt most of the Main Road north of the City Valley. As a result, most of the City Valley's commerce was conducted with the southern city of Olos so merchants could avoid being anywhere near the Hollow Valley.

According to my mentors and lessons, Heike was the last of the sorcerers who were descended from a race of stunted hill-giants. His ancestors had reached heights of only eight or nine feet, whereas the average hill-giant stood over twenty feet tall. Because of this height difference, Heike's ancestors were bullied by the other giants. Being physically weaker, they had to learn to survive not by brute strength, as was the hill-giant way, but through what intelligence they had—that is, until one of Heike's ancestors came across a mysterious scroll on which a few magic spells were written.

These spells were derived from the Old Ones and were the foundation on which the eight-armed Shirk, who haunted Mount Ch'thull, built his sinister reputation. Like any good predator, the Shirk exploited the weaker hill-giants by planting the scroll where he knew they would find it.

The scroll seduced the dim-witted giants with promises of redemption and power, but they were nothing more than basic recipes for healing and long life. The Shirk made sure the spells were easy to understand and execute, and their efficacy delighted Heike's ancestors and gave them a power they had never experienced before. The foolish giants on whom Heike's ancestors practiced their medicine didn't realize that although the spells extended their lives, they also made the giants' joints and limbs slowly stop moving and eventually turn to stone.

The stunted giants rose in prominence as healers, but they did not forget the treatment they had received and chose to live away from the hill-giant communities and take up residence in the lower valleys and ravines. Stories circulated about the strange sounds and voices that could be heard around their dark dwellings, and soon their magic was so strong that no other giant, no matter how desperate, would deal with them.

The strangest of these stunted giants was Heike. He preferred to live in the deep seclusion of the woods and hills of the Hollow Valley, where he practiced only the darker elements of his ancestral sorcery. In his first act of madness, Heike poisoned his entire family. Then he moved to the Hollow Valley, where he dug his lair under the largest oak tree he could find. His evil presence caused the oak to change to a poison tree, and it created a new breed of deadly sap that he used in his recipes.

Reports had always been confusing, but most stated that he looked like a cross between a massive insect and a lizard. They agreed, however, that the creature could leap extraordinary distances with the help of shiny, leather-like wings under the topmost two arms. Other victims who survived described Heike's gruesome face as a long oval visage covered in brown hair and with two stone-like black eyes that never blinked, while others said he didn't look much different from the average hill-giant.

He and his minions of blood-drinking, slime-covered, winged creatures haunted the valley, allowing no man or giant to enter it without a life-threatening challenge. Consequently, animals and plants were safe in the Hollow Valley for no one dared to hunt or forage there. In fact, some of the only helpful spells Heike used were the ones that kept the valley lush, even as the colder days increased. Of course, the lush nature of the valley was that same eerie green glow that compelled men to lose their minds.

In addition to seemingly being able to change his physical form, Heike was a master manipulator of all the senses. He liked to lure unwitting travelers off the road and deep into the valley with spells that tantalized their senses: smells of flowers, cool valley breezes, and delicious foods cooking. Once off the road and down into the valley, he separated members of parties from one another—and then from themselves.

A few travelers had survived encounters with Heike. They returned with stories of how they were bound and forced to watch as hundreds of Heike's pets bit into them and drank their blood. They told of how he kept them alive just enough for their hearts to keep producing blood—blood that would be sucked from any available part of their bodies.

Other times they were bound for days without food or water until they were dizzy with thirst and starvation. Then Heike would invite them to join him for dinner. The smell of the food caused their starving minds to abandon rational behavior, and they gorged themselves on what they believed to be a delicious feast. However, once a captive had filled his belly, Heike would laugh hysterically and inform him that he had just eaten a meal made from the roasted flesh of one of his fellow travelers. This realization usually drove a captive insane. Those poor victims' bodies were tossed into the Corpse Crags because no falcon went near them if they were put in a stretcher cage.

Sometimes Heike was more subtle and allowed his captives to leave relatively unharmed. The travelers would be traumatized, weakened, and emaciated, but they would not have any limbs cut off or body parts rearranged. For this they were grateful, and despite being riddled with bites (bites that swelled their limbs to near immobility), they would find the strength to hurry as far away from Heike as possible.

But Heike was not the type to let any man live if he could help it, and what his released captives did not know was that a slow-acting curse was upon them.

A few days after they were allowed to leave, the victims began to feel weak. Days later, they would be unable to walk or use their muscles effectively. Next they lost the ability to speak, then the ability to ingest food, and finally the victims died a slow, delirious death. Their flesh blackened and rotted before they died and would emit a strange gas that could infect other people. After treating only a few of these unfortunate victims, Austringer healers realized that the only effective way to stop the spread of Heike's poison was to burn the bodies then toss them into the Corpse Crags.

However, when a few victims stumbled back to Port Tallion instead of heading south, there were no Austringer healers who knew what to do with them, and a scourge broke out that plagued the port for years.

I shivered and pulled my cloak up around my neck. It might have been late morning, but it certainly wasn't warm as we all hung on a cable several leagues above the ground. But I also shivered because I knew that the Hollow Valley sitting ominously below us was beautiful and lush only because of the madness that lived within it.

Finally the next cable tower came into view, on the fourth Sun Point terrace. After we dismounted from our car, we faced a three-league hike across the mountain's footpaths. While I helped Aillil out of the cable-car, Marello slung his gear over his shoulder then turned to look through his spyglass at the vast expanse behind us.

"Damn," he growled under his breath.

I glanced back and saw the dark speck of another cable-car in the distance. Rogell and his hunting party had rigged an impromptu sail underneath the car to increase their speed. I was angry that Marello or I hadn't thought of that.

"We've got to hurry," Marello said.

I felt a flash of impatience. I was struggling to carry my gear while helping Aillil, who was only just waking up enough to stand on his own. I didn't need Marello to add to my frustration.

The cable ride had been restful for Aillil. He told me and Marello to go on ahead, and he would follow as fast as he could. He assured us he could walk, and if he needed to rest, he would. I hated the thought of leaving him, especially with Rogell only a few hours behind, but I knew if the situation were reversed I would want the same thing. So Marello and I ran ahead. Aillil was able to move fast enough that we were never out of sight unless we were around a turn or behind a hill or boulder. This brought me a little comfort and made me feel as though I could move at a faster pace while still keeping an eye on him.

Besides a few small villages and groups of hothouses, the scenery on Sun Point 4 was nothing but grassy crags and one main dirt path to the next cable tower. Marello and I considered leaving Aillil with an elder in one of the villages that we passed, but we worried that Rogell would discover him. Besides, every village we encountered seemed to be deserted, as though these Austringer clans already knew about the invasion that was beginning on our northern shores.

A few leagues before the next cable tower, another path wove its way down the mountain through the northern edge of the Hollow Valley and finally met the Main Road. Marello and I didn't consider this path as an option. Heike's reputation kept even the most desperate traveler out of that part of the Midlyn Range.

We stopped for a quick rest at the path's trail-head stones and let Aillil catch up. Marello climbed to the highest point he could find and checked the path behind us. I helped Aillil change his field dressings and was alarmed to notice a grayish hue to the skin around his shoulder wound.

"They're getting closer," Marello said.

Aillil had slowed us down too much. The next cable tower was two leagues—and several small climbs and switchbacks—away. Marello jumped down from his lookout point, grabbed his gear, and hurried up the path.

A few hours later, we stood at the base of the cable tower. Marello climbed the steps to prepare a cable-car, while I waited for Aillil to appear around the last switchback. I heard a loud curse from inside the tower.

"What is it?" I yelled up to Marello.

He leaped back down the steps four at a time. "There are no cable-cars."

"How can that be?" I said, growing agitated. It hadn't occurred to me that we might have to wait for a cable-car to return, partly because, as a prince, I had never had to wait.

"That's where all the villagers must have gone," Marello said. "They've fled their homes and moved back to the City Valley, and now we have no cars to ride."

"Did you check the cables to see if any cars were returning?" I asked.

My question only seemed to aggravate him more. "Of course, prince. There is nothing coming back this way."

The news increased my anxiety, and I turned around and scanned the footpath through my spyglass. There was still no sign of my brother.

"Don't waste your time with that spyglass," Marello said. "We're going to have to head back up the path anyway."

"But what about Rogell?"

"If we move fast enough, we can link up with Aillil and get to the path that moves through the low altitudes before Rogell's party has a chance to know what we're doing," Marello said. "Perhaps they won't suspect that we'd take that route."

We both knew that no Austringer would suspect anyone would take that route.

"But what about—"

Marello cut me off. "We can do that, or we can wait here for Rogell to overtake us. His hunters are not just simple guards. They're seasoned officers. We won't stand much of a chance in a head-on fight."

"What about an ambush?"

Marello slung his rucksack over his shoulder and started back down the path in the direction we'd just come. When I caught up with him, he said, "Rogell's too smart for that. And I don't think the terrain will allow for a decent ambush anyway. We've got to get down that path and out of their sight before they are upon us. This course is our only hope."

We hurried back around the switchback, toward the footpath that descended an entire league down the side of the mountain. The whole time we watched for Aillil but did not find him until we were in sight of the intersection. He was lying on the ground.

I rushed to him and knelt beside him. I moved to wipe the sweat off his forehead, but his skin was cold and dry. I lowered my ear next to his mouth and heard nothing but faint, raspy breaths. Despite all my training, the thought of losing my brother broke me. While tears spilled down my cheeks, Marello stood above us.

"I don't mean to make light of the situation," he said. "I trained Aillil since he was a child, and he was a good warrior, but I fear he doesn't have much time left and neither will we if we stay here mourning him. We have to get back to the Overhang and rally whoever we can to stop this treason before it's too late. I suggest we wrap Aillil in his cloak and move him behind that outcrop, then carry on down this cursed path."

I stood up, my fists clenched. "He's not dead yet, Marello, and I'm not leaving him to be skewered by Rogell and his traitors."

Marello's expression was hard. "You don't have to worry about Rogell killing him. He won't last another hour."

My stomach twisted in an angry knot. I knew Marello was right, but this was my brother we were talking about. I had to do whatever I could to help him. I started digging through the medical kit.

"There's no medicine or magic that can save him now," Marello said. He looked down the path we would soon be taking. "We can come back later and recover his body for a proper ceremony. And even if his wounds weren't fatal, he would be a liability in the lower altitudes. We've got a lot to worry about before we reach the Hollow Valley. If we are that lucky."

I wiped the tears from my eyes, and Marello helped me wrap Aillil in his cloak and move his body behind some large boulders. I took my own cloak off and wrapped that around him as well. I knew I wouldn't need it once we were in the lower, warmer altitudes, and I thought it might help Aillil be more comfortable as he drifted off into his next phase.

I knelt by his side one last time and said a choked, whispered goodbye to my brother. Anger boiled inside me, and I felt like I could take on Rogell's party all by myself.

Marello was checking the path above us through his spyglass. "Dammit, they're closer than I thought," he said.

I looked through my spyglass. Rogell's party was silhouetted on a ridge barely a league away, staring back at us through their own spyglasses.

"And now they know what direction we are heading," Marello said. "We've wasted too much time."

My anger flared. "My brother's death is not a waste of time."

"It will be, boy, if those traitors catch up with us. Get your gear on your shoulders and your legs under your ass. There's still a small chance that they won't follow us down this path."

I seethed with anger. I was a prince, and no Austringer—not even a general—had the right to address me in such a tone. But I knew I didn't have time to feel sorry for myself or even mourn the loss of my brother right now. Instead, I told myself to be grateful that my old mentor was with me. I would need his skills and experience to survive the perils we were about to face.

7

The first few leagues of the descent were easy running along gravelly switch-backs. Halfway down the mountain, the path became steeper, and we slowed our pace to negotiate the rocky, steep drops. Sometimes we climbed with the smallest of handholds or had to jump over deep crevasses. We knew that this rough terrain signaled that we were entering the altitude at which giants lived.

It was best to meet a hill-giant on an open plain or plateau, not among the rocky outcrops and deep ravines. Hill-giants were naturally camouflaged, and if not moving, they could blend in perfectly with the surrounding rocks. In fact, some of the older giants had ivy growing on their shoulders and backs.

A giant's usual method of attack was to toss massive rocks down on unsus-pecting travelers. But they were stupid and clumsy and always announced their presence with loud growls and slanders of their enemies, coupled with brag-ging about their ancestors.

Marello had experienced many an attack by hill-giants and hoped that their clumsiness and noise would alert us in time to take defensive action. So we moved as quickly as possible while keeping an eye on our surroundings. By the mid-altitudes, the path was overgrown with ivy, and huge footprints could be seen in the crushed foliage. Some of the ivy was so old and thick, with roots that clung deeply into the cracks and fissures, that we could use it as hand-holds. But the broken leaves and torn bark were further evidence of travelers we did not want to meet.

Then the path became a thin, hard-packed trail that wound between boulders and through slots in the rocks that a man could barely fit through. At times we had to climb up rock formations then climb back down the other side. It was tiring and took the better half of a day to descend just a few hundred feet.

When we were almost out of the rocky mid-altitudes, we climbed down a sandstone cliff and stopped to catch our breath and have a sip of water. We were in a wide corridor of stone that rose hundreds of feet high on both sides. It felt safe here, and we hadn't seen or heard a sign of Rogell's party or any giants. Our bodies were well past tired, so we took a few extra minutes to rest.

Ahead of us, the footpath opened out into a vast plain that swayed in a gold and green grassy wave. We sat speechless with fatigue as we sipped from our water skins, enthralled by the warm, glowing landscape ahead. Out on the plain, the footpath was a dusty, brown trail weaving for half a league through a sea of grass, colorful wildflowers, and a few boulders. Trees began to take the place of the boulders as the path descended to the Ringing Forest.

Marello and I cinched our water skins to our packs and moved forward down the long corridor. About halfway through the pass, a large stone thunked into the wall to our right, sending dirt and debris flying. We spun around only to realize to our horror that it was not a stone at all. It was Lord Rogell's head.

We heard a roar from somewhere above us. The voice rose to a volume that could not have been from the mouth of a man. It carried down the stone corridor and raised the hair on the back of my neck.

The hill-giants spoke in a mixture of their ancient Dyrollgoth tongue and a broken growl of words that barely resembled common Austringer.

Puny pinklings. You in hills of Chorn. Splitter of Boulders. I Chod, his oldest son. You must know that this day you die.

A second voice, equally disturbing, followed. *And I Dosh, Son of Dolor, descended from greatest line of Tree Rippers. I have uprooted an ancient oak tree and want to show it to you.*

Marello cursed. "Dammit. There's two of them."

And where there were two giants, there were most likely more not far away. We broke into a dead sprint toward the open plain.

As we shot down the corridor, another dull thunk sounded behind us. Judging by the tone, it was not a stone but another head from Rogell's party. Despite being grateful that the giants had relieved us of our pursuers, I couldn't help but shudder at the thought of how they must have died. Debris flew against our backs as a third head careened onto the path behind us.

"Will they follow us?" I asked, breathing hard and not slowing for an instant.

"They will," answered Marello, "but those big boulders will give us shelter to devise a defense."

We sprang out from between the rock faces and onto the open plain just as the last head clunked behind us. We made a dash for two large boulders that sat on either side of our path.

"Why not just run for the cover of the forest?" I asked.

"Too far," huffed Marello. "They can outrun us in an open field. We're going to have to stand and fight."

Hill-giants couldn't move fast high up the mountain because the freezing temperatures slowed them down, which is why we Austringers were able to build our cities and halls so high up. Giants did not mind, however, moving down into the valleys and forests at the base of the mountains if it was for a good reason—like killing an Austringer or two.

The giants dropped down into the corridor with a loud thud, and the ground shook as Chod and Dosh ran after us.

My grandfathers were right.

And mine as well!

They told us stories of how easy the puny pinklings cower and run.

Yes, and how easily you are squashed by our fists.

Out of decapitated heads to toss, the giants now threw large rocks at us, but they didn't come close to hitting us and instead bounced beside us or thunked into the ground.

"We're lucky this Chod fellow can't seem to aim," Marello said.

A wet, gurgling roar blew from the mouth of the corridor like a thunder-clap.

Slygoth pinkling! You run like little pink coward.

Chod and Dosh arrived at the mouth of the corridor at the same time. In their eagerness, they both tried to fit through the opening, but it was not wide enough and they became jammed shoulder to shoulder. Marello and I reached the shelter of the two boulders as Chod roared, *Grorym Dosh ahshok ahshok,* and tried to push Dosh behind him. *Ahshok Dosh ahshok nullrogoth.*

Dey Chod, mothuk ahshok mal. Dosh swung at Chod, but lost his balance and stumbled backward.

Their struggle gave us time to take cover. When both giants finally made it out onto the plain, they couldn't see Marello and me, and they stopped short. But they knew that we couldn't be far.

Don't worry, pinklings. Chod will find you and crush you.

Dosh, too.

Hill-giants' egos were bigger than their physical stature, and Chod scoffed at what he saw as Dosh trying to out-thunder him. He pushed Dosh back against the rocks. Dosh growled and swung the massive oak tree he was carrying into Chod's head. It was carved down on one end so his hand could get a good grip, but the rest of it looked like a dead tree with a few large stubs of thick, old branches long ago beaten off the trunk. Toward the top end, the bark was worn and chipped deep where it had crushed many an enemy. It was also covered in fresh blood.

Chod fell to the ground with a huge thud. *Mallass y'deyss non, Tree Ripper.*

Mallass y'nondeyss atun atun.

We could hear the feud between the two giants, though we had no idea what Chod and Dosh were saying and poked our heads out to see what was going on. I looked on in amazement.

"Maybe they'll do our job for us," I said.

"They won't kill each other. These types of scuffles never last long. But it will buy us some time."

"There are arrows stuck in them," I said, "and one has a broken spear in his backside."

Marello nodded. "Looks like Rogell and his traitors gave them a good fight. Let's hope those shafts will slow them down." He looked out from behind his boulder. "Well, at least they're not as tall as they could be."

I looked back up the hill at the giants, both of whom stood over twelve feet tall.

Marello grabbed his heavy-bow and as many arrows as he could carry. In his right hand he also carried our last spear. A few feet from the boulder, he dropped his bow and pushed his arrows into the soft ground. I knew exactly what he was doing: setting up his arsenal for a rapid volley. I moved out from behind my boulder to do the same. Meanwhile, Chod and Dosh were wrapping up their power struggle.

Marello cupped his hands around his mouth and yelled, "Hey, dolts! You can shove this up King Chorn's ass."

At the sound of Marello's voice, Chod and Dosh stopped wrestling and looked up just as Marello took a step and hurled his spear. It flew straight at Dosh. He saw it coming, and with uncanny speed and dexterity for so massive a frame, he swatted the missile in midair with his oak-tree club. The spear split in two. Those ash poles were stronger than a man's femur, and I was a bit unnerved to see one break so easily.

Marello spat then picked up his heavy-bow and arrows. I had finished setting up my own arsenal and was already sighting down a half-pound arrow aimed at Chod.

Chod and Dosh lumbered down the path. Out on an open plain, hill-giants usually just rushed their enemies, taking as many arrows as they had to until they got close enough to smash their enemies' brains out. It was a stupid strategy, but hill-giants could take a lot of arrows before being put down.

Marello saw my arsenal sticking out of the ground. "Good to see you remember your training."

I was happy to have such a compliment from Marello, but I was immediately forced to take cover behind my boulder as Chod hurled a huge stone at me. The stone smashed against the boulder and rolled down the path. I peered around and saw that Chod had no other weapon, so I leaped back out for the attack. Now that he was not carrying any huge rocks, Chod was a bit lighter on his feet. He lumbered ahead of Dosh, who was heading for Marello.

The best way to kill a hill-giant with a bow was to send an arrow directly into one of his eye sockets, penetrating his brain—a difficult if not impossible shot to make when the giant is moving, especially since their brains were so small.

"How are we going to stop them?" I asked Marello, trying to keep the panic out of my voice.

"We're going to have to hit them with as many arrows as possible," Marello said. "Most likely we won't be able to stop them, but we can slow them down. Aim for the face, the throat, or the knees. If we slow them down enough, we can get in close and pierce their throats with our daggers."

The giants were charging at us full-tilt. I tensed for the first volley.

Marello readied his bow and said, "A strong thrust up through the chin is the best way to stop them. And don't forget to pull your dagger out of their skulls before they turn to stone."

I was glad for the advice, but I didn't like the idea of having to get in closer than a dagger's length to a hill-giant's chin. Each of us aimed at our own giant, and Marello sent his first arrow into Dosh's shoulder. His shoulder jolted back, but the giant barely broke his stride.

Good shot, pinkling. But arrows don't kill Tree Ripper.

"Hit their knees," Marello ordered.

Chod bellowed a gruesome war cry that opened up his throat to an attack. I noticed the sudden vulnerability and sent my first arrow toward this target—a hard one to hit on a running giant. The arrow careened to the right and smashed into the cliffs behind him.

"Dammit, boy! What did I just tell you?" Marello growled.

I was ashamed of my missed shot, but there was no time to dwell on it. I fired my second half-pound arrow. It flew directly into Chod's left knee. His leg buckled, and he crashed to the ground. I took a few steps closer, but the giant was quickly back on his feet. Marello's second arrow found Dosh's thigh, right above the knee joint. He slowed down to yank the arrow out, and his war cry thundered across the plain.

Chod and Dosh continued closing the gap while Marello and I sent a rapid volley of arrows at them. As expert marksmen, we were trained to know that arrows shot from a nervous bow rarely hit their targets, and I was finally learning the point of all my training. Keeping one's emotions in control was absolutely necessary if another arrow was not to be wasted.

After Chod and Dosh were each hit with five arrows, they started moving at a more cautious pace, but that only made it easier for Marello and me to aim. With a few hits close to their eyes, both giants slowed down even more, flailing at the air to slap any incoming arrow off its course.

Marello and I dropped our heavy-bows and spread out into the knee-high grass in a double flanking maneuver. The giants howled at us, and Dosh swung his oak tree wildly at Marello, who easily danced out of harm's way. The giant's swinging arm had pink gashes in skin that looked like the hardest granite, and one of the half-pound arrows had gone through his biceps. It stabbed at his ribs as he tried to swing his oak tree.

"A bit slow today, Tree Ripper?" Marello taunted.

Y Dosh d'yur pinkling!

The giant raised his arms in an attempt to bring the oak down from above his head. Marello dodged the blow by leaping toward the giant. In close, he'd be out of the effective use of the oak tree but well within the reach of a hill-giant's favorite weapon: his fists. Marello had to get his long-dagger into the underside of Dosh's chin before the giant had time to crush him in an inescapable hug.

Marello leaped into the air and wrapped himself around Dosh's torso. He kicked one foot into the giant's belly, where pink viscera bulged from a deep arrow wound. The shock slowed Dosh down, but for only a few seconds. Pain was a stimulant for hill-giants; it increased their rage to berserker levels. Dosh roared as Marello brought his left forearm up against the giant's right arm that was cocked and ready to crush him against his chest. Then Marello pounded his long-dagger hilt-deep through Dosh's chin and up into his brain.

Dosh flailed, throwing Marello clear of his fists. The giant dropped to his knees, his gray, granite-like hand grabbing at his throat. Marello rushed back to Dosh and yanked his long-dagger from the giant's throat. Dark, thick blood spattered and soaked the grass and instantly morphed into small piles of gray pebbles. Dosh growled, but it was nothing more than a few gurgled grunts, and collapsed with a thunderous crash.

Meanwhile, three half-pound arrows had pierced the thick hide of Chod's left thigh, while two more were sunk into his hip and belly. In shock, Chod had pulled each arrow out as he ran toward me, doubling the arrows' damage. After the third arrow to his left leg, Chod dropped to his knee. He was breathing hard as he pressed his left hand into his belly, trying to keep his bowels from spilling out. His curses changed to a quick whispered, *and the Halls of mighty Chorn!*

He growled through clenched teeth that were as big as fists and yanked a massive fistful of his own innards out in a fit of rage and tossed them on the ground, where they changed into stones of various sizes.

Chod not need guts, pinkling.

His deep voice still resonated, but he was moving more slowly. As I rushed into dagger range, Chod flailed a bloodied fist, and I jumped backward, dodging the blow but tripping over the pile of rocks that had been his guts. I fell, hitting my head on a stone. It wasn't a bad hit, but it dazed me.

My clumsiness inspired Chod to get up and rush toward me. His wounds energized him, and blood and pebbles flew from his mouth as he growled curses. I scrambled backward. Chod raised a fist that was as big as my head and was about to bring it crashing down on me when the tip of Marello's broken spear appeared through his eye socket. He flailed at the air then dropped his arms to his sides and fell directly toward me. I rolled out from under the giant's shadow just in time to avoid being crushed. He landed facedown, forcing the broken spear handle back out of his head and raining blood and brains that spattered across my face and quickly turned to rocks and pebbles.

"You're going to have to do better than that against Heike," Marello yelled from up the path, where he stood by the pile of boulders that was Dosh's corpse, holding the other piece of the broken spear shaft. He glanced back up the path. "There will be more of them here soon. We better move inside the forest line."

I got up and kicked at the collection of small pebbles on the ground. I knew what happened when a hill-giant died, but seeing it was as surreal as seeing the giant had been.

"Won't they follow us into the woods?"

Marello walked past me, heading for the boulder where he had left the rest of his gear. "Perhaps. But Heike hates the hill-giants, too—they say even more than he hates men. Maybe that will be enough to keep them off our trail."

Marello and I hurried into the Ringing Forest, but with Telios getting lower in the sky, we did not want to move too deeply into the trees. Heike didn't haunt that edge of the forest, but he had spies everywhere. We lay on our bellies inside the first several feet of the forest line, peering through our spyglasses at the two massive new collections of boulders that lay along the footpath. Six giants were inspecting the remains of Chod and Dosh.

One of the giants walked a few paces toward the forest. He stopped and stared in our general direction, and soon all of them were gazing toward the tree line. But after a few minutes of consideration, they seemed to unanimously decide that pursuit of a couple of pinklings into the Ringing Forest was not something they wanted to do. The six granite men disappeared back up into the hills and cliffs from where they had come.

"Perhaps Telios is on our side tonight, Tyrcel," Marello said.

The hill-giants' departure was a mixed blessing. I was glad that we were now safe from having to do battle with them, but as I looked over my shoulder into the forest, I wondered: What's in there that the giants are afraid of?

Marello got to his feet and grabbed his rucksack, bow, and quiver, and headed back out onto the plain. I scrambled after him, perplexed, and asked, "Why are we heading back toward those giants?"

Marello didn't even slow down. "We're getting out of the forest for the night. I don't want to be within that tree line after dark."

"But what about the hill-giants?"

"It's dark enough now that we won't be seen. They don't see well in the dark." Marello stopped at the two trail-head stones that marked the entrance to the Ringing Forest—perhaps the remains of two other hill-giants who had perished long ago—and dropped his gear in the grass.

"We won't make a fire tonight," he said, "and we'll switch watches every two hours. We'll leave at first light."

8

Throughout the night, whenever I was on watch, I sat entranced by the smells of all the flowers and grasses. I soaked in the scents of these lowland plants—so different from the cold, mossy odors of the snow and rocks where I lived. Crickets, locusts, and other strange insects chirped through the night, mixing with the sounds of Marello's snoring.

I was amazed at how easily Marello fell asleep once he lay down on his bedroll. I could hardly close my eyes, and I watched as Telios finally rose and cast a long swath of light across the grassy plain. The dew on the thousands of wildflowers magnified their colors and glimmered where any hills and boulders lay in the path of the sunlight. I gently pushed Marello's shoulder. He awoke instantly with his long-dagger in his hand.

"Marello!" I said. "It's me. It's Tyrcel."

For a few frightening seconds, he gazed at me with the emptiness of a man who had lost his mind. But he soon gained his bearings. "Sirens, Tyrcel. I'm getting way too old for this."

I smiled. I needed Marello to be in good spirits. It made me feel a bit more relaxed. "Don't worry, old friend, we'll be back at the City Valley before we know it."

Marello didn't smile back.

"What's in that valley is like nothing you've been trained for," he said. "I've never told you this, but I almost ran into Heike once. It was during the last hill-giant purge, when the giants moved east of the Main Road and blocked access to Port Tallion. At the time, I was serving with the sentinel guard. There were so many wounded and so many supplies being transported that the cable lines were at maximum capacity at all times. So we were forced to use the Main Road. I had been wounded in the Twilight Campaign and was lying in the medical cart. For some reason we had stopped. We were on the berm-road."

I knew this area well. It was right outside the City Valley gates and was the only section of the Main Road that Heike had been known to terrorize. It was assumed that he haunted this section of road because it was under the cover of the Ringing Forest. Whenever the Austringer engineers tried to remove the trees that surrounded this stretch of the Main Road, they found them to be impervious to their hatchets and saws.

Marello continued. "The cart was covered, and I couldn't see over the sides or out the back. To move was excruciating. One of those bastard giants cracked a few of my ribs, right before I skewered his brains with my spear. I was delirious from the pain, but at some point, I began to hear a growing murmur among the surgeons, guards, and the wounded. The cart began to move and suddenly the whispers turned to shouts. Terrible screaming began, and men yelled to their comrades to run for their lives. In the mayhem, my cart was overturned and I ended up underneath. I was in and out of consciousness, and I have no idea how long I laid under that cart. If it weren't for the pain in my side, I would probably have died there on the road. But the pain made me restless, so I hauled myself out from under the cart and staggered to my feet."

Marello looked away. "What I next witnessed was the worst thing I've ever seen. Even worse than the purging of the North Guard prisoners who were butchered by Sy, the Hill King."

I had heard of that slaughter. When the remnants of the Austringers' North Guard were defeated in the crags of the Shoulders, more than two hundred warriors were taken prisoner. The ones who did not immediately lose their heads were crucified. While still alive, they were eviscerated and left to rot with their entrails dangling in the wind because the Hill King thought it was clever to leave the prisoners' innards open to any ranging bird of prey.

That incident compelled my people to move upon the hill-giants of the Shoulder Range. There was no mercy; Austringers made it a point to prove that they were in control of the entire Range.

"At first, I thought my eyes were deceiving me," Marello said. "I couldn't make sense of what lay on the road. As far as I could see, lined up along its edge, were the dead surgeons and guards. They looked like they had been butchered and hacked to pieces, but I couldn't see any blood or gore. Just piles..."

I shifted uneasily, wishing Marello would stop.

"But then, as I stumbled down the road, I came upon the first corpse. Well, it wasn't a corpse. Or, I should say, it wasn't dead. The poor bastard was under Heike's sorcery. His limbs had been rearranged. Removed and put back together." He wrestled with his memories. "Arms where the legs should be, and without the slightest scar on his contorted body. When I passed him, his eyes opened and he started screaming at me. Begging me to kill him. My ribs were throbbing in pain, but I managed to find a long-dagger and send it deep into what was left of his chest. But he did not die. His screams just grew more awful. I stabbed again and again, and each thrust of the dagger only awakened the others who lay along the road. Growing desperate, I found a good-sized rock and smashed the man's brains out."

"Sirens, Marello."

"That's not all."

I couldn't believe there could be more.

"After mercy killing that Austringer, I had to stumble past all the other moaning, mangled people who called out to me, begging me to kill them. Their screams only quickened my pace. Once past them, I found myself on a stretch of road that was under the canopy of the cursed forest. Not far into the trees, I noticed what looked like huge piles of some sort of yellowish ooze on the road. I stood over one of these piles, and I could see that it was like a clouded liquid suspended in a membrane, and floating within the pod was the decaying form of one of our warriors. These oozing pods were scattered down the road, and in that maddening last stretch of forest I saw them hanging from the trees. Some of the pods still contained a living victim who squirmed helplessly, trapped within. Fortunately for me, our guards were on full alert and moving so many supplies and troops that I was soon picked up by a supply caravan and transported back to the Overhang."

He started to gather his gear. "The surgeons back at the City Valley told me I was lucky Heike hadn't noticed me—probably because there were so many other men to distract him. That's the only reason they could think of, caught as I was in the Ringing Forest, alone and unarmed."

Marello could see that his story had an effect on me and quickly changed the subject. "What foods do you have left?"

I rummaged through my rucksack while Marello pulled out what was left of his own provisions. I had half a loaf of stale bread, two strips of jerky, and a handful of figs. Marello had about the same.

"We've got to eat as much as we can now, before we head into the forest," he said. "Don't eat everything we have, but most of it. The last bits of food we will eat as we get closer to the Main Road, at which point we will just have to keep moving toward the City Valley."

We piled our food supplies on top of his rucksack and started eating.

"Heike is a master of sensory manipulation," Marello said between bites of jerky. "He knows that men are base creatures who are ruled by their senses, and he exploits our weaknesses by tantalizing our senses with delicious aromas and beautiful fields of colors unlike any hill or bluff we have ever seen."

Marello shoved a handful of figs into my hand. "One of his tactics is to use his sorcery to cast spells that lead us to believe we're hungry. That's why you need to eat as much as you can. If you're actually hungry, you won't be able to resist following some delicious aroma that will lead you right into his hands."

He handed me another strip of jerky. "He will also try to manipulate our eyes and ears, so we have to be absolutely diligent about moving swiftly on the trail. Don't be distracted by all the new sights. Any pause in our pace will give Heike a chance to strike."

Telios had begun to appear over the horizon, and Marello looked toward the forest and said, "At heart, he's nothing more than a giant—as disgusting to our eyes as those we've just slain. But he has been infected by the dark magic of the Shirk, and like that vile monster, Heike can take the form of any other creature, such as goats or spiders. Or so they say. I've never actually seen the beast."

I found it difficult to eat after what Marello had told me, but he insisted that I force the food down. I noticed how unevenly he was distributing the last few strips of jerky, and he insisted that I eat all of the bread. As I chewed on the figs, I thought about the rest of our journey. My heart broke when I remembered Aillil alone up there on top of the mountain, and I was so eager to get home to rally my father and fight the traitors who had caused Aillil's death that I worried little about Heike. The chance of an encounter with him was not absolutely certain. What was certain, however, was that Abbo Doldra was invading my homeland.

When we had finished eating all but a few scraps of our food, Marello told me to gather up my gear and get ready to move out.

I tried a bit of bravado, saying, "I have never been more ready. It is not long to the Main Road, and if Heike wants to play, I've got a blade that will be happy to oblige."

Marello smiled at the determined look in my eyes. "You remind me of your father," he said. "You are still young, with a great deal to learn, but he would be proud of you."

I smiled at the unexpected compliment.

"But if at all possible," he added, "I'd rather not cross Heike's path."

Marello was quiet as we moved into the forest. He gave me a worried look and put the back of his hand against my chest, stopping me. "Remember, Tyrcel, Heike will try to divide us. He'll use sorcery to trick us into arguing. He loves to watch his prey struggle with confusion."

"Spells and magic are a trickster's weapons," I replied, trying to sound tough and fearless though my heart was pounding. "As long as we run on the footpath, we'll get to the Main Road in no time."

The forest was not wide at the point where the footpath intersected it. Marello and I kept a quick pace through the small, dense stretch of trees. The huge glow-maples and feather oaks of the prairie side of the forest soon became interspersed with old, white-willow birches. The path led down to a stream that was lined with more birches, and a dense ground cover of moon-ferns lazed up the slope above the water line. Thick red ferns lined the stream, and their roots sloped over the edge into that ever-flowing source of water. Their fronds rustled against each other in the breezes, accompanied by the buzzing of the dragonflies that hovered about them.

We stopped just inside the forest, where the path turned abruptly west, toward the Main Road. Through the trees we could see the vibrant colors of the first few grassy hills on the other side of the footpath. Even before we left the forest we could see how the hills in front of us were more striking than the prairie we had just left—more striking, in fact, than anything we had ever seen in the lowlands. Austringers had hothouses and summer gardens on the Market Bluff, but they were solely for food production. The colorful wildflowers were captivating.

The hot temperature was new to us as well. Tiny insects buzzed all about our faces and flitted through the branches. Rodents and small song birds moved about, rustling through the leaves. Marello warned that any of these creatures could be a spy for Heike. There was a constant hum and subtle vibration to this small stretch of woods, a strange ringing that made us nervous.

"You hear that?" Marello asked.

"Yes," I whispered, despite no one else being near us. "The Ringing Forest."

Our eyes went back to the valley and scanned the distant hilltops. One of Heike's tricks was to cast a spell that would compel a traveler to want to do nothing more than wander aimlessly through the beautiful hills and deep grasses of the lush valley where he would never be seen again.

"Let's get this over with," I said.

We passed through the small stretch of forest in just a few minutes. The path was bathed in sunlight. We broke into a run with the forest to our right and the open valley on our left. Once we reached the brightness of the valley, a sense of relief washed over me. The scent of the flowers carried on the warm breezes calmed my nerves. My lungs, which were so used to the thinner air of the higher altitudes, expanded, and I felt light on my feet.

Our sprint to the Main Road became a comfortable trot. Then we forgot why we were running. A subtle fog descended over our minds, and we slowed to a walk. Marello began to mumble about being hungry. At several points, we stopped to drink a bit of water.

During the last rest, I noticed Marello acting drowsy and distant. I gave him a drink of water and offered him the last of the figs. I was still full from the meal we had eaten earlier, but Marello grabbed the figs from me and shoved them into his mouth, hardly chewing before swallowing.

He gazed at me with a fierce look in his eyes. "What else do you have to eat? I'm famished."

I was taken aback. "A few more figs, Marello. But we should save them for later."

He cursed and hunched down on the grass like a spoiled child. The sight of him acting this way unnerved me, and I had to plead with him to get moving. After another sip of water, we were trotting along the path again. Soon we were halfway to the Main Road, and we could see the foothills, vividly lit by Telios, that sat on the other side of the West Prairie. However, to the north a cloud hung above the point where the road left Port Tallion and the Sentinels.

I walked with my eyes fixed on that cloud.

"That's the Main Road on that ridge-line, right?" I said. "Looks like we're going to be running in the rain."

But no storm cloud took that particular color, nor did a cloud that brought rain rise from the ground. With alarm, I realized it had to be the dust kicked up by a huge vanguard moving along the Main Road.

I turned to Marello, but I found myself completely alone. The hairs on the back of my neck instantly stood up, and I desperately scanned my surroundings. And then I noticed that I was standing in the middle of an open, grassy plain.

I had strayed from the path. From lack of use, it was overgrown with weeds, flowers, and grasses, and I didn't even realize that I had left it.

"Marello," I called. I tried to retrace my steps, but there were no signs of footprints heading in any direction. I called again and again, each call louder than the last. I was so desperate that I was taking the chance that Heike would hear me.

I took a deep breath. I had only stories and myths as a guide and no idea what to do if I encountered Heike. Then I heard Marello screaming my name.

"Tyrcel! Run!" His voice was full of terror and seemed to be cut short.

But instead of running away from the scream, I ran toward it. I couldn't turn away from my old friend and mentor, even if it meant we both died.

I reached the top of a hill with a view of the Hollow Valley below. I did not see Marello anywhere, but I heard his desperate voice call from different corners of the valley. As I searched through my spyglass, I noticed a familiar aroma floating on the breeze. It was the smell of freshly baked honey bread and goat stew steeped in Talliedian thyme.

Marello's voice came one last time from somewhere in the distance, begging for mercy. It was a horrid, heart-wrenching sound.

I ran as fast as I could toward Marello's voice, but within minutes I tired of running, and my legs began to feel heavy. And then his screams stopped.

I stood for a long time trying to decide what to do. I had no way of knowing where he was or what had happened to him. And though I hated to leave him behind, I knew my old mentor would want me to head for the City Valley gates without him. I consoled myself by vowing to gather a large contingent of the bravest warriors to come back and find him, and eliminate Heike once and for all. I took a deep breath. The air was rich with the smell of wildflowers, and the breeze seemed to carry the distant aroma of a stew pot.

My heart raced. There is no aroma, I told myself. Keep your wits about you, Tyrcel.

I distracted myself with brash thoughts about meeting Heike head-on. Then I took a sip of water, ate the last two figs, and started off again for the City

Valley, leaving the rucksack and empty water skin behind. I still had my quiver, heavy-bow, and long-dagger. Running kept me focused, and I decided that at the first sign of anything out of the ordinary, I would take the offensive.

But Heike wasn't showing himself. Instead, he sent terrible screams over the wind. New haunting and agonized voices drifted past me—not Marello's, but other voices begging for help. The voices were coming from the eastern edge of the forest. I considered changing direction to chase the sounds, but I remembered that I had to get back to father.

I continued toward the south edge of the Hollow Valley, where the Main Road met the Ringing Forest and then the City Valley. It seemed to take longer to reach than I had expected. This began to worry me because Heike had a firm grasp on the valley and the ability to warp one's sense of time.

I finally reached a point not far from the Main Road. In front of me was the southern tree-line of the Ringing Forest, and to my right rose the berm that, centuries ago, Austringer engineers made from all the excavated rubble of the homes and buildings of the City Valley and the Overhang. On top of this berm was the Main Road. The berm was originally hundreds of feet higher than the trees around it. But century after century the trees grew, unscathed by the hands of men. Nourished by Heike's sorcery, they grew so massive that their branches created an eerie tunnel over the road, a dark gauntlet through which any poor merchant or traveler had to pass. Many a terrified traveler had come running out of the trees, begging to be let back through the City Valley gates.

I wiped the sweat from my brow and moved to the base of the berm. It was a hill of boulders almost a hundred feet high covered by loose gravel. The climb would have been easy if every step I took didn't entail the risk of slipping back down. As the berm rose higher, it also became more vertical, and I had to lay flat against the side of it to not fall backward, and the random weed or root that I was able to use as a handhold was never secure.

I dug my knees and feet into the hillside and pushed my fists deep into the gravel. I reminded myself to focus on just getting to the top, where the Main Road waited.

I finally reached the top of the berm, but I still had to scale the ten-foot-high side wall. Luckily, it was composed of old dried mud and stones, which made for easy hand- and footholds. I pulled myself up bit by bit, swung my legs over, and dropped down onto the road. I stumbled when my legs met the ground and sat down with my back against the wall, my weapons scattered across the road. To my left was the dark opening of the tunnel that the tree canopy created. I fumbled around, searching for my water-skin, but it was on the other side of the wall with my rucksack.

I tried to gather saliva to slake the thirst that grew with each passing second, but it was pointless. Then I felt a pang of hunger deep in my belly. I wasn't sure if it was legitimate hunger or part of Heike's work, but I decided not to remain long enough to find out.

I sniffed the air and was relieved that there were no signs of goat stew. That meant my hunger was real and not an illusion. But just as I was enjoying a small sense of relief, the enticing aroma wafted over the side wall.

As I lifted my chin to breathe in the smell, I noticed that a big branch on one of the nearby trees was swaying in an odd manner.

The branch fell from the tree and lay in the middle of the road. Its tiny offshoots and leaves fluttered. But there was no breeze, and the leaves were moving back and forth as if they were searching. I watched in confusion as the tips of two of the topmost twigs touched the road and stopped moving. All the other shoots instantly jammed their ends into the dirt. The limb then shook with a quick vibration, and all the leaves fluttered one last time, then flattened themselves against their branches.

My heart filled with fear as the branch, which had to be over eight feet long, rose to stand up on the twigs that had stuck themselves into the road. And then it began to turn, its branch-like legs clicking against the hard-packed gravel. I pushed myself to my feet. When the beast finally faced me, my knees almost gave out. It gazed at me from two pitch-black eyes. They were arranged crookedly, with one a few inches above the other, and sat on either side of a black slit that pulsed with some evil rhythmic breathing. A shiny ooze dripped from the bottom of the slit.

Then the black slit opened, and the creature barked out a quick sound. I gathered my wits and walked to the center of the road, and just as I positioned myself in my best defensive stance, several more branches in the forest began to shake. Creatures of all sizes dropped from the trees and climbed over the walls. Most of the beasts were unrecognizable. Some looked like giant insects, while others looked like lizards with long, leathery wings.

The largest of the winged creatures fell from the side wall and righted itself. It had six arms growing from its back ribs that squirmed and reached aimlessly in the air as the beast turned its gaze to me. All the winged creatures headed in my direction.

As they passed the huge stick creature, it skewered them through the back, jamming its branches between the larva-like stubs of arms. The whole time, it never took its black eyes from me.

I readied my long-dagger behind my wrist as the large, horrid stick began to click its way toward me. All the creatures moved behind their leader, hissing, clicking, and taking pains not to get ahead of it. When the stick creature reached me, it reared back on its smaller hind branches and prepared to run me through with its large top branches. But before it could touch me, I swiped it across the midsection and chopped it clean in half.

The ensemble of monsters stopped as the two sections of the branch fell to the ground. The beast clicked out some strangled sounds, and ooze ran from the severed halves.

The ease with which I had stopped the beast gave me hope. But I still faced the army of smaller enemies. I only had my long-dagger and a few arrows left. I realized that I probably could not win this fight, and I hated the idea of dying in these stinking, humid lowlands. I doubted running away would do me any good, and this berm was not high or steep enough for a final flight.

The swarm of beasts began moving toward me again, but just as I raised my long-dagger, a loud snapping noise came from the forest, followed by low barking. The creatures scattered back toward the trees.

Where the road entered the tunnel of trees a few hundred feet away, something large was sliding down a drooping branch with careless ease. It clung to the end of the tree limb with one hand until it could place another hand on the road. Then it let go, and the branch whipped back up with a swoosh.

I reached into my quiver and pulled out my last five arrows. I kept four in my left hand and nocked one on the string of the bow. As I sighted down the arrow, I was stunned by the image in front of me, so stunned that I lowered my bow.

At first I thought it was a huge spider because it had too many arms to be a giant. But it was not the shape of any man or spider. What stood in front of me was bigger than a horse and looked like a full-grown example of the small winged creatures. The eight arms finally caught up with the stories I'd been told as a youngster. The eight-armed Shirk never left Tallies Harbor but used his favorite toy, Heike, to do his dirty work, collecting his victims from the travelers on the Main Road.

All this time I had thought they were just stories my instructors used to scare me into paying attention to their boring lectures.

The monster's body was covered with brown hair that stood out like needles. Its arms grew from points along its back ribs, each set growing consecutively smaller. The shoulder set was the strongest and looked long enough to wrap completely around a mature marble pine. But the last set of arms, nearest the creature's tail, looked like atrophied deformations. And below these lowest arms were two twisted and sinewy back legs.

The creature pushed its chest up by way of its forward arms and moved its back legs underneath its frame. Its head was longer than one of the leaves of a mature shore-palm plant, and its eyes were black discs set wide apart at the top of the cranium. The face stretched down into a tuft that seemed to be a mixture of the beast's hair and two long fangs. The fangs grew straight down from the opposite ends of the beast's mouth, then ended in an abrupt inward curl that mingled with the long hairs. A yellowish ooze dripped off the tips, the same strange ooze that had dripped from the stick creature.

The beast stared at me, completely still save for the ooze that bubbled and spattered out of two tiny slits of nostrils. Along the creature's jaw line and the top of its snout were stains that could only be fresh blood.

While the larger beast sat staring at me, its minions crawled closer to it. Some clambered onto its pelt and climbed up to its shoulders and back, while others darted in and out between its arms and back legs. They made various clicks and barking noises as they vied for space. But their small turf wars ended when the large beast gurgled out a hiss that made them all stop moving and sent a shiver down my spine.

I choked back my fears and called out, "Heike, I know it's you."

At the sound of my voice, Heike tilted his head as if trying to hear me better, and the smaller creatures repositioned themselves, darting their gaze back and forth between me and their master.

"I also know you have my friend," I said.

Heike started toward me. I pulled my bowstring back.

"I warn you, beast. I rarely miss my target."

Now that the mysterious Heike was finally in front of me, I was not as nervous as I thought I would be. I remembered all that Aillil and Marello had taught me and vowed to keep calm.

I took a few steps forward and called out, "Understand, beast, that I am a prince."

When he reached the remains of the stick creature that I had chopped in half, Heike stopped and nudged the two pieces as if hoping they would come back to life. I seized the opportunity and fired. The arrow flew in a blur and struck Heike's shoulder, its fletching wobbling to a quick halt. The creature didn't flinch and hardly seemed to notice it had been struck. That was a half-pound arrow, shot from close range, yet it had barely sunk deeper than the beast's pelt.

I armed my bow again and continued with my taunts. "Trained by the master warriors of the Austringer clan," I said and let the next arrow fly.

It thunked into the front of the beast but again hardly sunk deeper than the arrowhead. This time the hit did at least attract Heike's attention. He tilted his face to one side, ooze dripping from his mouth and nose, and stared at the arrow shaft sticking out of his belly.

I nocked my third arrow and called out, "I have plenty of arrows."

I remembered the most effective way to stop a hill-giant and aimed for Heike's eyes. The arrow flew with deadly speed but did nothing more than skid against the side of Heike's head and ricochet into one of the smaller creatures clinging to his back. The force of the arrow yanked the smaller monster up, and it screeched as it was skewered into the side wall. When I looked at Heike, I heard a strange whisper, then a sensation of time slowing down washed over me.

Heike slowly turned and looked back at his skewered pet for a long moment, then with a few clicks of his teeth, he turned back to face me. He hissed out a long wet breath, and more ooze fell from his mouth.

A strange delirium had washed over me, making me feel heavy and tired. I shook my head to clear it. Despite the threats I had made, I had only two more arrows, and I didn't want to have to get in close enough to use my long-dagger. I struggled to control my emotions and fought with the urge to lie down and sleep. Luckily, my racing heart kept me awake long enough to nock my next arrow.

I wished desperately that Aillil or Marello was here. But they were not, and the more time I wasted wishing, the closer Heike got.

I released the arrow, but it landed hardly an inch deep into the beast's side ribs. I immediately nocked my last arrow and let it fly. It struck Heike in the side of his neck but again made no damage.

All the while, Heike continued crawling forward, and I could hear the scraping noises of his legs in the gravel. The smaller beasts hissed and clicked in response to their master's movements. With no more arrows to shoot, I threw my heavy-bow at Heike. He paused, but the bow merely bounced off his chest and clanked onto the gravel.

I decided that running was now a good option. But Heike dug in his fore-arms and swung his legs forward, closing the distance between us with a single movement. I drew my long-dagger and scrambled backward as Heike launched himself into the air. He flew at me with all eight arms outstretched. I had the tip of my long-dagger pointed out, but when the blade met the monster's under-side, like my arrows, it could not penetrate his dense hair.

Heike fell on me, pinning me to the road. The hairs on his body were like thousands of needles piercing me wherever they touched. Pain engulfed me, but I managed to get one hand up under the pit of Heike's first arm. The beast hissed and thrashed, but my hand dug deep into the dense coat of hair while I tried to push the long-dagger through the hair and into his belly with my other hand.

The blade got stuck in the hair. I let go of the long-dagger and grabbed another of Heike's forearms just as he pulled himself off me. The hairs that had pierced my skin yanked out and doubled my agony.

When I tried to release my grip on Heike's arm, my hand did not budge. My left hand was stuck, and the thought of this made me desperate with fear, so I struggled even more to pull my hand away. I finally wrenched it free, but I left behind a patch of flesh from my palm. The pain sent a wave of panic through me, and I shoved my hand into another section of the beast, thinking that I might still defend myself. Now both my hands were stuck, my right on one of the beast's arms and my left burning in pain and thrust deep into the hairs of Heike's abdomen.

As Heike held me to the ground with his front arms, the smaller creatures began to scurry over my body. I thrashed and kicked, but as soon as I made contact with Heike's body, my foot became stuck in the sticky, piercing hairs. I ripped my foot out, but my boots remained attached to the hair, and I stuck my now naked foot somewhere else.

I soon ran out of strength, and Heike subdued me by pressing me against his underside. Thousands of tiny hairs pierced my skin, and the slightest movement was agonizing.

When I stopped moving, Heike pulled me away and dropped me on the ground. Every inch of my body was burning, and I was unable to move. Some evil spell or oil in that hair had gotten into my bloodstream and begun to subdue my muscles. Heike leaned over and stared at me for a long time, never revealing any sign of emotion or change. He just sat and watched his latest victim slipping into paralysis.

Then he clicked his teeth and began spitting a slimy ooze into the palms of all his hands. His minions gathered in front of him, and he slathered them with the ooze as well. Then they slithered over my body, rubbing the translucent mess all over me. The slime soon hardened around my paralyzed limbs, and with each stroke of Heike's long arms, I became more and more encased.

With each exhalation, the ooze tightened around my ribs until the lack of oxygen numbed my mind. Pain subsided, and everything went black.

9

I awoke to air that smelled like soil mixed with the stench of death. Instantly, my stomach tightened. I tried moving my arms but couldn't. Then I realized that I was bound to a wall with the same hardened ooze that Heike had used on me on the Main Road. My torso, wrists, and ankles were encased in it, and I could not move anything but my neck.

The strange creatures that I had seen on the road slithered and jumped all around me. Others that I had not seen before flew and hovered in the air, randomly landing on me as if my sole purpose was to satisfy them. They crawled over my exposed skin and moved around the room with the relaxed air of a creature in its own home. I struggled to break free, but all I seemed to do was agitate the beasts. The braver ones raised their wings and clicked their fangs, nipping at my fingers as I tried to wriggle loose.

My entire body ached as though I had a strong fever. The slimy creatures stopped at random places and sank their fangs into my flesh. I had puncture wounds and swollen mounds from bites of all sizes. Some of them itched horribly while others stung or oozed a yellowish fluid. A distorted, six-eyed flying insect lit on top of the binding that held my right arm to the wall. I could do nothing to defend myself as it crawled onto my forearm and sank a single long fang into my skin. I gritted my teeth as pain seared through my arm. The creature drank its fill and flew away. Blood ran down my wrist, alongside other dried streaks of blood and crusty ooze, and spattered on the ground where it was not long before some other horrid creature lapped up any small drops or puddles.

I tried again and again to break out of the binds that suspended me, but it was useless. Soon, the struggle wore me out, so I stopped and tried to calm myself by getting my bearings.

I was in a large, dark, damp room that was dimly lit by candles. The room was round, and thin tufts of what looked like white roots dangled from the ceiling. The walls appeared to be hard-packed dirt, and as far as I could see, they were covered in strange carvings and demonic symbols. I focused on the wall directly across from me, but only a few of the symbols were familiar. I vaguely recalled from my earliest lessons the smaller elements of these symbols. The three circles in a triangle represented the three eyes of the Shirk and gave its eternal protection to any neighboring symbols. Other symbols that twisted and looped back on themselves represented horrors such as living while dead and were set between more intricate, and sinister, carvings in the mud-caked walls.

Those details had been cut with a hand unlike any master craftsman I had ever seen. The reliefs and carvings were of creatures not unlike the evil things crawling about the room, and they were mauling a helpless victim whose face had a look of dead terror. I shuddered to think of the evil that could conceive of these scenes.

At regular intervals, thick beams of wood were embedded in the walls. I had never seen such architecture. The intricate and horrible reliefs blended seamlessly between the mud walls and those beams, then rose up into the black abyss above me.

The beams were not uniform and seemed to spread out from a single point, like the spokes of a wheel, arching down from the high ceiling and disappearing into the floor in long, curving lines. Each beam twisted and turned in its own individual way. As I gazed at them, I realized that the beams were the roots of what had to be a huge tree. The cave had been dug from under and around the roots of a tree—similar to the Austringer practice of carving homes out of a cave or crevice in the mountainside.

In the darkness, I heard the scurrying and slapping of creatures that did not walk like normal animals. At times the carvings on the walls seemed to waver and breathe. Above my head, up where I could barely see, I heard strange clicks and short screeches that frightened me enough that I forgot how tired I was. The leathery, winged creatures clung from the large roots and in almost every dark corner of the den. Many were sleeping with their heads tucked under their wings, while others watched me. Dust filled my nostrils, carrying with it a stench that made me want to retch.

To my right, along a straight wall that was obviously constructed as a divider between this room and whatever lay on the other side, there was a round hole several feet off the ground. Shelves covered the wall and were filled with dusty hide-bound books, scrolls, and parchments. Some of the books' spines had symbols similar to those carved into the walls, and the shelves that weren't littered in wax, dust, and dry insect carcasses were covered with similar images.

Down the curving wall to my left was another large, dark hole, like the end of a tunnel. It seemed to be almost directly across from the hole opposite it. Instead of shelves and books, however, this doorway was framed with more demonic carvings. It was trimmed in an ebony wood that was bent into a perfect circle, and at four equidistant spots there were plinths, each of which had its own horribly distorted face carved into it. What worried me most was how the bottom edge of the hole was worn into a rounded slope, a testament to how much this entrance was used. It would take hundreds of years or something very large to wear a thick slab of ebony down like that.

A white grub worm fell from the ceiling and landed with a slap on the ground. The worm struggled to right itself just as one of the creatures pounced. It wrapped the grub in its winged arms and sank its fangs in as the prey writhed. Another creature rushed forward, but the first one lifted its forelegs and clicked its fangs. The second creature backed off. Heike's pets looked well nourished and content; anything that crawled through the walls or ceiling must have just been extra.

In the center of the room was a dark table that looked like it too had been made out of planks of ebony. The table was the cleanest surface in the room and shared none of the twisted imagery that covered every other surface of this hovel. In the table's center sat several candles, some burning, others smoldering or almost completely melted. Surrounding the tray of candles were knives, dried bones, and several stones, worn smooth, like river stones.

I had learned the geological formations of the Midlyn Range, yet the stones on the table were like none I had ever seen. Greenish light pulsed from inside them, and the surfaces also had carvings of strange symbols and images. It was difficult, even in my captive state, to take my eyes away from those green stones. Just past the strange stones, heaped in a pile on the table, sat my weapons.

The sight of my weapons made me struggle to break free again, despite my fatigue, but then I heard a familiar voice.

"Marello!" I called. But I got no answer.

The voice sounded far away, and it was soon accompanied by a more sinister sound—a terrifying high-pitched gargling that might have had a few words mixed in. I tried again to break free while I listened to what sounded like a conversation. The voices were coming from the tunnel on the wall to my left. They grew louder, and the high-pitched voice dominated while poor Marello sobbed.

The noise worked Heike's minions into a frenzy. They began scurrying across the walls, and the larger ones made awkward attempts to fly only to land with a splat on the table or floor. They knocked over candles and parchments before flapping back up into the dusty air. Some circled the tunnel entrance while others disappeared into it.

At last, a man's head appeared in the opening. He was looking down so I only saw the bruised top and side of his head, but I knew it was Marello. My old friend was covered in bloody wounds and dirt, as if he had been partially skinned by some savage butcher. Soon, the rest of his body followed. He collapsed with a groan onto the floor. He tried to pick himself up but had a hard time of it. When he finally got to his feet, I noticed a hide collar wrapped around his neck. Attached to it was a long leash that led back up into the tunnel, vibrating and swinging as the strange voice in the tunnel grew louder. Marello wore only the torn remnants of his pants.

He stood next to the tunnel entrance and waited. Soon a large bundle of twigs and tinder fell out of the hole, followed by bunches of freshly cut herbs and plants. Marello hurried to pick up the bundles. I watched in dismay and horror as one of the strongest warriors of the Austringer clan struggled to lift a simple pile of twigs. He carried his bundles across to the other round doorway and pushed them through. The leather leash around his neck hung loose, its other end still in the tunnel.

Suddenly two small, gnarled hands clutched the rim of the hole. With a groan, Heike pulled himself through the opening. He resembled a man, but he was at least eight feet tall. His skin tone matched the dirt of the walls around him, and his head was too big for his body. He stood up and arched his back as if to stretch cramped muscles. Several of the winged creatures crawled over to him. He wore no shirt but only a pair of dirty, black canvas leggings.

He swiped the dirt from his chest and scooped up one of the smaller creatures then headed toward me, gently placing his pet on a bookshelf along the way. When he noticed the small fires that his excited minions had started when they knocked over the lit candles, he mumbled something and cupped the small blazes with his hands, smothering the fires. As he walked toward me again, his bald head brushed against the thin root fibers that hung from the ceiling.

He stopped in front of me and grabbed me by the chin, squeezing hard and forcing me to look into his wide-set eyes. After many long minutes, he finally whispered, as if talking to one of his pets, *Gorrumm, pest. N'slogoth rysown lallkathsh. The little pest wakes.*

His mouth was gapped and rotten-toothed, except for two incisors on his top jaw. His forehead was huge, and in its center, directly between the eyes, was a scar in the shape of the eight-pronged scythe of the Shirk. Heike had only a few faint wisps of hair floating over the two black pits of his eyes, and the skin on his face was wrapped tight over his skull, causing his eyes to bulge from their sockets. His arms were lanky cords of muscles, and his legs were as thick as a full-grown river birch. Every joint on his body looked swollen as if riddled with gout, yet his hands and feet were small and out of proportion to the rest of him. He held his right arm behind him, and that hand held the other end of the leash that was connected to Marello's neck.

Marello kept his eyes to the ground. His face was so gaunt that it looked as though he had no flesh left. I did not notice it at first, but his beard was also missing. Heike tugged at the leash and pulled Marello toward him. Marello stumbled and fell to his knees, his shoulder bumping Heike's leg. Instantly he dropped his head to the floor and began whining in the shrill pitch of a dog that knows it is in trouble. He scrambled back, but Heike slowly turned and looked down at him.

G'rrymm thollogth dysseus, he growled.

Marello froze, his eyes never leaving the floor.

Sillay syllah, Heike hissed.

He bent down, grabbed Marello by the neck, and stood him up, looking him right in the face, but Marello would not lift his eyes. Heike seemed to be amused.

We have another guest for dinner, he said to Marello, pointing over his shoulder toward me. *And I am sure you know this one, pest.*

He grabbed Marello's skinned chin and forced him to face me. Then I saw that all the flesh of his face had been skinned away, leaving his muscles, tendons, and teeth visible. Even his eyelids had been removed so that his eyes were huge, horrific bulges that couldn't close, and the rest of his body was covered in bruises.

I realized Heike's sorcery was the only thing keeping Marello alive. I was overwhelmed by a sense of pity and helplessness. My friend and mentor was lost, and I could do nothing to help him.

Heike smiled as I turned away from the sight of Marello's face.

Eeee, he laughed. *Yesu, Yesu. Something bother poor man?* He laughed at his own joke.

I didn't respond, so he snapped at Marello, *Ghrr'goth, pest? Get to kitchen!*

Marello groaned and cried as he pulled his butchered body through the doorway into the next room. The leash that was tied around his neck followed him through, seemingly without an end to its length.

Heike leaned in closer to me, the stench of rotting flesh emanating from his mouth and his deranged smile hovering an inch from my face.

Is pest scared?

Heike's use of the common tongue was choppy at best, but it still sent cold chills down my spine. I turned away and shut my eyes tight, but I could still hear Heike's raspy breath. He was silent for a moment, then repeated, *Is pest scared?*

The sickening sound of his childish voice and the stench of his breath caused me to gag. Tears of frustration streamed from my eyes, ran down my cheeks, and stung my cracked and bloodied lips.

Heike forced my head up so we were again face to face. Only this time his face was covered by a mask.

This make better for pest? he asked.

It looked like a human face stretched tight over the giant's huge head. The features were familiar, and just as I realized I was staring at Marello's face, the terror in my heart did me a favor and caused me to lose consciousness.

After a series of nightmares I thought would never end, I woke to a heart that was racing as if I had been running up the steepest paths of Gavina. As I regained my bearings and felt my heart slow down—indeed, as it sank into sadness—I noticed that the hovel was consumed in a dark silence. A few candles were lit on the table in front of me, but the handful of loathsome creatures I could make out in the dim light seemed to be sleeping.

After several minutes, I heard faint moans coming from the doorway that led to what I assumed was the kitchen. This moaning drew my eyes to the far corner of the room, where Heike had been sitting perfectly still.

But something wasn't right. Where I had expected to see an overgrown man, I saw the silhouette of a hunched creature facing the wall. Where its shoulders should have been were eight knobby protrusions. I instantly recognized the beast I had fought with on the Main Road. I confirmed my fears with the outline of the creature's head. It was elongated, with two bumps on the sides where I knew two round, dark pits of eyes sat.

The creature's knobby back lifted slowly up and down as it breathed, creating an ironic illusion of peace. I never knew a monster like Heike needed to sleep.

Another moan came from the kitchen, and I glanced away and then back at Heike. In that instant, he had transformed himself into the man-like, two armed hill-giant I had seen earlier. He peered over his shoulder at the kitchen, and when he heard another moan, he stood up, his five-hundred-year-old joints snapping and popping as he straightened his legs and stretched his chest high up into the air.

Heike met my gaze and smiled, the sight of his yellow-toothed mouth sending waves of fear through my body. Smiling, he gestured toward the table. Lying next to the few lit candles was his sinister mask of Marello's face. I closed my eyes.

Suddenly, without any sound of him moving across the room, Heike's voice was right in front of me. In a high-pitched whisper, he said, *It is good to see pest wake up. Pest was so hard to wake up. But Heike let pest sleep. So pest ready for dinner.*

He grabbed my chin, and I opened my eyes. *Pest see what Heike do? Perhaps you prefer own face better?*

I mumbled a desperate, "N...n...no."

Heike inhaled deeply, as if he was still waking up, but did not let go of my chin. *Arrrrhkkharu, gollonth te hessith, te hessith,* he whispered. He tightened his grip on my chin, and pulled my face close to his rotten nose, hissing, *Grror'ym. Perhaps I help you. Grror'ym, yesss. Perhaps Heike make it easy for pest to pay attention. For pest to stay awake.*

"Please, no!" I pleaded.

Yesss, this is how to speak to Heike. The contorted mouth smiled. *All pests pay attention.*

Heike let go of my chin and hissed out a list of rules.

Grror'ym dey pest yss sorrogoth lle.

It is rude for pest to ignore its hosts.

Grror'ym dey pest yss hat'umn lle.

It is rude for pest to refuse to eat.

Grror'ym dey pest yss hat'ull y'nthan lle.

It is rude for pest to try to run.

With each rule that Heike announced, his voice grew louder and his tone more angry. I squirmed and shifted helplessly in my bindings.

"Please," I moaned.

It's rude for pest to speak. Heike slapped me across the face.

He was about to slap me again when another loud moan came from the next room. Heike yelled a snarled curse and dove through the hole that led to his kitchen. I heard clattering and several dull thuds and then Heike yelling, *Grror'ym pest! You like all the rest.* There were more thuds then a quick squeal, followed by a steady, whimpering moaning. Heike's awful voice followed in what sounded like a rhythmic chanting, and the whimpering grew louder.

Mallass sirollgoth Ahkkharu sirollgoth! Mallass sirollgoth Ahkkharu sirollgoth!

I heard Marello's voice begging for mercy. But this only seemed to energize Heike. Marello's pleading grew more urgent, and my heart kept pace, until Marello was screaming a steady plea that ended with an abrupt, muffled cry.

Heike's sickening voice continued, *You pests beg and buzz and break Heike's house. Grror'ym! Grror'ym dey leessilligoth!* More sounds of beating came from the kitchen, though I could barely hear Marello's cries over what sounded like pots and pans clattering across the ground.

I was frozen with fear, and I did my best to keep my eyes from the table top. The thought of the same thing happening to me made me tremble in my binds. I looked around at the collection of winged demons that crawled about the room. My body ached and burned with the remnants of all the bites I had sustained.

As I suffered there, stuck to the side of Heike's hovel, I thought back to what Marello had told me—that Heike was a master of sensory manipulation. In other words, his sorcery depended on control of his victims' senses. That's why Marello had me eat most of our food and why he was so easily captured. By keeping me from becoming hungry at the first smell of food, he made himself more susceptible to Heike's sorcery.

Marello had assumed that Heike would find us, and he had sacrificed himself so that I might survive. I couldn't let his efforts be in vain, so I closed my eyes to think.

One of the first lessons of my training had been about controlling my emotions. I was taught that the mind instantly reacted to sensory stimuli and then made up stories that distracted a warrior from his ultimate goal of victory. The breath was a sign of emotional control. If a warrior could control his breath while under stress, he would be better able to control his emotions and mental activity, even when faced with a seemingly invincible enemy.

However, I could not move at all, so fighting Heike directly was not an option. In fact, it had already been proven to be a bad idea. Reasoning that I had little time left, I vowed not to beg or plead with Heike. Whatever Heike did, I would not give him the satisfaction of hearing me cry for mercy. I did, however, beg the Sirens to kill me before Heike had a chance to skin me alive—or worse.

My heart raced, especially as the sounds from the kitchen continued. I closed my eyes and focused on my breathing, forcing my mind not to react to the awful sounds coming from the other room and doing my best to ignore the stench of death that surrounded me. No matter what I heard, smelled, tasted, felt, or saw, I was not going to let it distract me. My breath and heartbeat began to calm. But despite the modicum of control that I found, my heart broke at the thought of dying.

My eyes were still closed when I heard Heike come back into the room. I didn't have the strength to lift my head and face my adversary.

Hmmm... no. What's this? Grrorym deyss? Pinkling pest sleep again?

I heard Heike place something on the table then he grabbed my chin. His face was just inches away, and the stench of his foul breath filled my nostrils. I desperately tried to not let the awful odor distract me, but I could not help gagging.

Aha! Heike knows pest not sleep.

He turned my head back and forth, trying to rouse me into opening my eyes. I did everything I could to keep my eyes closed and not react to Heike's taunts. He slapped me several times across the face. Blood swelled thick between my teeth and tongue, then ran out and over my chin. He dragged his coarse tongue up from my chin and over my cheekbone, lapping up the blood. My stomach turned again, but it was empty of anything to regurgitate. My jaw burned like a hot iron had been pressed against it, and my face felt as though it had been scraped raw by Heike's tongue. The room grew quiet.

Hmm, strong pest we have here, Heike said. *A quiet pinkling is good, but Heike talks now, so pest should not play games.*

He growled, but I continued to ignore him.

Heike will keep you alive long after you have no more words to beg me for mercy. He grabbed me by the hair, and said, *Heike will help open your eyes.*

He let go of my head, and the muscles in my neck strained to stop my head from dangling. I fought desperately to concentrate on my heartbeat and breath, but my natural instinct to defend myself was just as strong. I opened my eyes, just a hint, no wider than my lashes. Heike was gone, but the dusty, dark room was still there—the symbols, the books, the husks of dead things scattered about, the candles, and the table in the middle of the room with a human tongue sitting in a puddle of blood on top of the mask of Marello's face.

Then Heike pulled himself through the doorway with the litheness of a dancer, but instead of a human-like foot, he had a horrid, deformed foot that he used to grab hold of the wall above the hole, like a lowly insect. Indeed, instead of coming out of the hole and stepping to the floor, he clung to the wall above the door, then brought the rest of his body into the room. I was not sure if I was hallucinating, but I was certain that the searing pain and thirst that pervaded my body were absolutely real.

He held a huge cleaver in his hands and noticed that my eyes were now open.

He smiled. *The pest wakes, hat'ull. You are good pinkling for not crying so much. But Heike needs you to be awake. I will help you stay awake forever.*

He pushed my head back against the wall and pressed the tip of the cleaver next to the bridge of my nose. The tip dug in and began slicing the skin above my eyelid. I clenched my jaw but didn't utter a sound. I wouldn't give him the satisfaction. As blood ran down my face, Heike's pets suddenly became agitated. They flapped their wings and jumped in all directions. Heike paused and looked over his shoulder. At first I thought they were excited by the prospect of drinking more of my blood, but then they scurried and disappeared up into the darkness above or through the nearest cracks in the walls.

The larger of the creatures clung upside down from the roots and spread their wings wide, as if they too were agitated. One by one they reached the tiny claws at the ends of their wings up into the darkness from which they hung, then flipped over and pulled themselves up to some secret egress above them.

Heike watched his pets while he kept one hand on my chin. He wrinkled his brow and stared up at the ceiling, as if he was straining to hear some distant sound. Then thunder filled the room, and the walls shook with each thunderclap, sending dust into the air. A steady mist of dirt rained down from the darkened abyss above us. Heike slammed the cleaver into the dirt wall next to my face.

Grror'ym Heike dey Ahkkharu, he said, his voice rising to a higher pitch. He finally let go of my chin. Through the blood in my eyes, I saw Heike hurry back through the round doorway in a most terrifying fashion. He crawled up onto the wall and across the messy shelves and, with a single reach of his small hands and a push of his tiny feet, disappeared through the opening.

More thunderous booms sounded and shook the walls. A thick layer of dirt floated in the rancid air. Suddenly, Heike bounded back into the room. Within half a second, the demon was in front of me. Again, we were face to face, and Heike yanked my head up with a tight grab of my hair. I could only see out of my left eye—the right eye was swollen and sealed with clotted blood—but I could see enough to notice that Heike's head had lengthened into the long face of the monster I had seen up on the Main Road. As I watched, the face lengthened and began to sprout a thick coat of sharp and shiny brown hairs.

More guests coming for dinner, he hissed. *So Heike no longer has use for wasted pinklings.*

He parted his lips, revealing the two horrid fangs, and leaned in to bite my neck. I could not restrain myself any longer, and I screamed in agony as his teeth tore through my skin and dug through my muscles until they hit arteries. I felt the coldness of death washing over me.

Suddenly, a massive thunderclap shook the entire room. My eyes flew open. Heike, too, seemed surprised. He ripped his maw from my neck and cursed in his ancient language. At the same moment, I was deafened by a steady, high-pitched ringing. Heike was thrown off balance and braced himself against the table as the concussion shook the ground beneath his feet.

Another thunderclap boomed, so close this time that a wave of scorching heat shot out of the tunnel entrance across the room, pushing before it a thick cloud of dust. The heat grew more intense with each second, searing my already pocked and shredded skin. With the wave of heat came a light so bright that even with my eyelids closed tightly, it was blinding. It sent a wave of nausea up from my stomach, and just before I lost consciousness, I saw Heike pull himself to his feet then scurry across the wall and into the round doorway.

10

I was surrounded by an all-encompassing golden glow. It focused to a bright, white pinhole in the center of my vision. A soft voice spoke to me, and I strained to hear the words. My aching head pounded to a steady rhythm that I felt throughout my body. Was I in the white-blindness or possibly looking directly at Telios?

When I realized I couldn't see my body, I became nervous and the pounding in my head increased. I tried to move my arm, but I felt nothing and I could see nothing. When I turned my head to the right or left, the bright white spot in the center of the glow moved with me.

The pure-white center changed to a slightly darker shade, then back again. I no longer worried about my body. I was perfectly content to watch the white dot in the distance, like a child who follows the sparkling jewels of his mother's necklace. I knew the white spot had to blink again, and I would be watching and waiting the next time it happened.

The strange voice continued behind the glow. *Olos*, it whispered. The name of the giants' city. It repeated the word at random intervals. At times, it reminded me of my mother's voice and at other times my father's. There were other words that seemed to be giving me information, yet as soon as I understood them, I immediately forgot them.

I tried to speak, but my mouth didn't move. I tried harder, and the golden glow began to darken. As it faded to a deep gray, I could hear myself mumbling, and the sound of my voice surprised me into silence. Soon I was overwhelmed by the smell of burning wood and sulphur and a desperate, aching thirst.

I slowly blinked my eyes open. They were crusted and covered in dirt, and one was swollen from the wound Heike had started before the light consumed everything. But I could see where I was: in the dirt and filth of Heike's hovel. Only now there were glorious beams of light shining down from what used to be the dark cavern of a ceiling. The old smell of rotting flesh was gone, and a subtle breeze carried what smelled like burning wood. Many of the ornate walls in Heike's hovel had caved in and a huge pile of dirt and rubble sat in the middle of the room.

Instead of being bound to the wall, I sat slumped on the floor, my right arm held up against the wall, the only remaining limb still stuck in the strange crusted ooze that Heike used to bind me. With a twist of my feeble wrist, I broke the binds.

I felt more weak and hungry than I had ever been in my life. My limbs were as thin as the arms and legs of a starving man, and were almost completely covered in small red bumps and splotches where hundreds of those creatures had bitten me. I had somehow survived my encounter with Heike, though I wasn't sure if surviving was a good thing. Just moving my arms to wipe the dirt off my face was painful, and my throat begged for a sip of water.

I knew walking was not going to be easy, but I was emboldened by the light shining through the ceiling. That meant the only thing between me and freedom might be a little bit of digging. I forced myself to sit up straight with my back to the wall. Every muscle in my body ached as I moved. The exertion made my heart pound, and I suddenly remembered the dream I had had before waking up and the light that tried to speak to me. For a moment, I had thought it was Telios. I hoped my father's madness was not hereditary.

I had to move quickly because I had no way of knowing when Heike would be back. I grabbed my right thigh and pulled my knee up, then did the same with my left leg. By bracing my feet against the ground, I was able to slide my back up the wall until I was standing. My legs wobbled like those of an arthritic old man, but I was able to stagger forward and lean on the dirt-covered table. I was directly beneath one of the larger holes in the ceiling. I glanced through the round doorway into Heike's kitchen, which was also filled with debris and scattered pockets of daylight.

I was warmed by the light that shone down through the ceiling. But the pounding headache returned when I tilted my head to look at the hole above me. It was more than four feet wide. It looked like the massive tree under which Heike had dug his hovel had fallen over, yanking up soil and roots as it fell. But it was too high for me to reach.

I looked around at the piles of dirt, stones, and Heike's books. In the middle of the table was a mound of dirt that must have fallen when the tree collapsed. It was tall enough that if I could stand on it, I would be able to reach the opening in the ceiling.

I leaned into the mound with my chest against it and slowly began to pull myself up. Every muscle in my body screamed in pain and fatigue, but I eventually reached the top. I grabbed a handful of roots and tugged with all my might. They remained firmly stuck to the rootball above me, and I used them to steady myself as I stood up.

I poked my head through the hole, and a wave of fresh air washed over my face. I filled my lungs as if I'd been drowning. With all that remained of my strength, I reached both arms up through the hole and pulled myself halfway out. I could see the sky above and in the distance what looked like the foothills of the Sun Point Mountains.

Clumsily, I dragged myself the rest of the way out of the hole. I was on the side of a hill that had been created by the felling of a massive poison-oak tree. The trunk lying on the ground was charred black, and most of the smaller branches had burned away. The tree's rootball was as big as a small hill, and where the roots had once been, there was now a huge crater. The hole through which I had emerged was about eight feet from the top edge of the crater.

I pulled myself over the lip of the hole, and to keep from slipping down into the crater, I flipped over onto my belly. Like a fat skink, I slowly, painfully swept my arms and legs along the side of the pit. Gravity and fatigue tried to pull me back down into the root-pit, but sheer will gave me the strength to keep climbing. Finally, I reached the top of the crater and collapsed into the charred grass.

When I was able to lift my head again, I looked around the immediate area. I was certain now that I was in the foothills of the Sun Point Mountains, somewhere on the edge of the Ringing Forest, but when I looked to the right and left I did not see any trees. This forest was supposed to grow right up to the foothills that surrounded the Spring Sisters. I stretched my arms and crawled around the edge of the crater, then around the rootball of the poison-oak. The ground was covered with a crunchy black and gray ash. Where once there had been leaves and grass, there was now a charred, smoking surface. I saw trees in the distance, but a huge section of the Ringing Forest had been scorched to cinders.

Then I heard voices. I crept back around the rootball and peered out across the charred remains of the Hollow Valley. At the far end I saw a sight that unnerved me: massive war-cars, trebuchets, and thousands of men moving about.

They were not Austringers—I was certain of that. They had to be Abbo Doldra's vanguard. I wondered if his army had inadvertently saved my life.

I crawled along the crater until I reached the tree trunk and sat back against it to get a clearer view of the army. The edge of the charred ground, where black met grass, was back among the foothills behind me. The hills I could see had a charred northern face but a southern face with splashes of lush green grass. To my right, the burned ground faded to the natural browns and greens of the Sun Point foothills. Heike's den must have been right on the southern edge of the forest.

The sentries patrolling the battle-lines were hundreds of feet away, and none of Doldra's army was patrolling these hills. In fact, the entire contingent faced the City Valley. But I couldn't stay here for long. I had to make it back to the Overhang as quickly as possible. I looked up, and there in the distance sat the dark tip of Gavina, a massive landmark for any lost traveler in the Midlyn Range.

My original mission was still paramount, but I would have to do it without Aillil and Marello. I looked to the sky and based on Telios' location determined that it was midday. If I was healthy, it would take me the remaining daylight hours to make it back to Gavina, but in my present state, I knew it would take much longer.

I crawled to the nearest foothill, well out of sight of Doldra's sentries, and tried to stand up. It was not easy and instantly reminded me of how thirsty and hungry I was. My neck began to ache, and I instinctively put my hand to my throat and felt a large wet wound that burned when I touched it.

Directly south, on the other side of this mountain, sat Gavina. I reasoned that my best chance of survival was to get around the mountain and then access one of the many secret passages or covert assault-drop areas that the Austringer army used. I began stumbling up the low, sloped side of the mountain. I had to find water. My throat burned every time I swallowed, and fire consumed my neck.

By late afternoon, I had made my way into more familiar territory. I saw no signs of Doldra's scouts or patrols, so I allowed myself frequent rests. Gavina rose in front of me, so huge that it looked like I could reach out and touch it, but it was still almost a league away.

Like all Austringer warriors, I knew the secrets of Gavina. So I headed for the east assault-drop point, where a small fresh-water pool sat nearby. The pool was fed by an underground spring that flowed from the East Spring Sister. If the Austringer army was doing what it had been trained to do, there would already be activity at that point. In fact, there should be an entire contingent of Austringers gearing up to meet Doldra's army in the Hollow Valley. My hopes soared as I stumbled—and crawled when I had to—back to Gavina.

By dusk I was within the shrub and needle trees not far from Gavina's base. Halfway between me and the assault-drop point was the spring-fed pool. I tried to pick up the pace, and several yards before I reached the pool, I fell to my knees and crawled the rest of the way. It was hard to imagine that not far behind me, on the other side of the mountains, an army was preparing to destroy my homeland, while here, at this pool of life-giving water, nature sat undisturbed and serene. Every cell in my body seemed to soak up all the water I could drink. Finally satisfied, I rolled over onto my back, inhaling deeply. After a few restful breaths, I was thirsty again, so I took another long drink.

As I drank, I realized that I did not hear any sounds of activity around Gavina. I was within view of the east assault-drop point, and there was not one Austringer in sight. I took another long drink from the pool and lifted myself to my knees. The water had helped me regain a little strength, so I was able to walk slowly and clumsily to the footpath that led up the side of Gavina to the east assault-drop plateau. Like most paths carved by the Austringers, this one was no wider than two men standing shoulder to shoulder, and the incline was steep. I couldn't remember any other time in my life when ascending an Austringer path was so difficult, but I slowly made it to the plateau. The flat ledge of stone was big enough for ten platoons of warriors to assemble. Along the back edge that abutted the mountain were hundreds of drop-cables that reached down from the troop platform high up at the Austringer armory.

I stumbled to the closest cable. On each of the cables, at approximately ten-foot intervals, were loops with which an individual warrior could secure his harness and then ride the cables up or down. Hundreds of warriors could be dropped into assault formations within minutes using these cables.

My hopes were soon dashed when I realized that I was not going to be able to attach myself to the cable loop. Austringer warriors' vests and pants had harnesses that allowed them to quickly attach to or detach themselves from any cable loop—vertically or horizontally—that they might encounter. I, however, was no longer wearing any of my gear, only the torn remnants of an undershirt and what was left of my ripped pants. My heart sank as I watched the loops roll up one cable and down the other.

I leaned back against the mountain wall and slid to the ground. I was weak from exertion and hunger, and despite my determination to do whatever was necessary to make it up to the Overhang, my body could go no farther at the moment. The cables had been my best option, but now I would have to find one of the secret supply tunnels that ran throughout Gavina and walk all the way up to the Overhang. Those passageways were lined with tracks on which wheeled supply carts could be rolled down or pulled back up by cables. I knew of all of them, but because they were used so infrequently, my foggy mind could not easily recall their locations. I was also distracted by hunger, and my insatiable thirst had returned. But as I tried to calm my breath and think about all the supply tunnels I could choose from, I began to feel drowsy.

11

The glow was back. This time it provided a warmth I had not felt since I was a small child. I did not try to look in any direction or move my body, which had been erased by the brightness of the light. I no longer cared. I was safe and comfortable and could finally breathe easily. The pounding in my head seemed more like a persistent but gentle heartbeat.

I heard a new voice talking from somewhere behind the glow. It was a woman's, but not my mother's. The voice called out to me from different directions, but I had no idea which way was up or down. Somehow the light made me feel there was no reason to be nervous or scared. I also noticed a steady humming sound that reminded me of the chants the Austringer mediums and spirit guides sang during a prayer service, but this hum was never broken by the need to take a breath. It stretched on forever and mingled with the other strange words that echoed within the light. My heartbeat relaxed to the steady drone.

But voices grew louder, and a dark figure suddenly materialized. It had no distinct features and seemed to change shape. At times it took the form of a woman, while at other times, it looked like an eight-armed demon. The form moved between me and the light, and I was amazed that it could block such a bright glow. The dark figure spoke only a few words in the old Austringer tongue that I barely understood.

There's no more need to fight, Tyrcel. Your flight is on a new path.

Each time the swirling, ethereal voice repeated that phrase, the glow faded and the details of my surroundings returned. As the form disappeared, its voice changed back and forth between a soothing timbre and the sounds of young boys arguing. And just before the strange form finally disappeared, I noticed that the female shape in front of me had only a single arm.

When I opened my eyes, I was looking up a sheer cliff. The mountain rose so high that it disappeared up into the blue sky. Then a man's face came into view directly over me.

"We were wondering when you were going to wake up from your nap," he said.

I recognized his voice from the tail end of my dream. I grunted and tried to sit up, but the man put his hand on my shoulder.

"Whoa there, skinny. Better take it slow."

Groggy, I lay back and saw that I was still on the assault-drop plateau. Five Austringer warriors stood around me. One of them was kneeling on the slab and stringing up an apparatus that looked like a crossbow. They were dressed in extended-campaign gear.

"Wha... what's going on?"

"We just dropped down and found you lying here like a sack of bones," the first man said. "I'm Peytynn Jendyll. We can see you're wearing some rags that look like they could have been Austringer gear, but we all disagree about who exactly you are."

By this time the other four men had gathered around me.

"I'm Lyum Jendyll," the smallest of the men said. He had the voice of a child. "The real brains of this group."

The others pushed and jostled Lyum, and one of the larger men grabbed him by the neck and aggressively tousled his hair.

"I'm Teo Bromynn," he said and let go of the kicking Lyum. Teo added, "Master of falcon calls, camouflages, and glass and light manipulation."

With the sound of each voice, I realized that these were not men but young boys. The next one spoke up.

"I'm Destyr Peteys. Master of the metallurgic arts." He slashed his hand through the air as if it held a sword. "I can forge you anything from a shaving razor to the strongest spear tip in all of Axis Solan. I can make you cables that will last thousands of years, and curie the strongest magnets in the entire—"

Peytynn interrupted him, "Okay, Destyr, we get the point."

Finally the tallest of them said with a long, awkward drawl, "And I'm Morys Haggyn. Master chef and unfortunately big enough that I have to do all the heavy lifting in this group of runts." He sounded more nervous than the others.

"Yeah," said Peytynn, "when I was rounding those three up, I saw this massive lug standing in the mess hall skinning turnips. That's when I remembered the strong points of these three scientists"—he pointed at Lyum, Teo, and Destyr—"and thought to myself, 'This crew could use someone who knows how to cook.'"

"That's right," Morys said. "You'd all be nothing without me."

Destyr grabbed Morys' head-wrap and tossed it to Teo, then the two of them bolted off, fleeing the grip of Morys' huge hands.

I was still a bit foggy-headed and started to say, "I'm Prince—" but before I could finish, Lyum yelled, "Ha! I told you!"

"All right! All of you, keep your voices down," Peytynn said. "This mission is supposed to be covert." He looked down at me. "Please forgive my little brother. He's just happy because he was the only one of us who recognized you."

Peytynn stared at me from several different angles and said, "No offense, but are you really.... Well, you see...which prince are you?"

"Which one do you think I am?"

Peytynn looked around at the others. "I have no idea."

Teo, Morys, and Destyr nodded in agreement, but Lyum shouted, "He's Prince Tyrcel Buteo. Like I told you, idiots."

With that, he went back to tinkering with the strange tool shaped like a crossbow.

The four young men knelt down and gazed at me with eager eyes.

"The little one is right," I said. "I'm Prince Tyrcel Buteo."

Destyr and Teo hooted a victorious cheer.

"What did I just say about the noise?" Peytynn said. "Forgive them, but none of us have been in the presence of royalty before."

"Please help me sit up."

Peytynn nodded at Morys, who leaned over and with little effort pulled me up and propped me against the granite wall. Now that I was upright, I could make out their features better. They all looked like children, except for Morys.

"How old are you?"

"We're all fourteen years old," Peytynn said. "Except my brother Lyum; he's just twelve.

"Have you seen any Austringer platoons?" I asked, still baffled by the lack of military activity.

Peytynn shook his head. "It's just us down here."

"Has no one noticed the enemy at our gates?"

"Yes, they have, Prince Tyrcel. But it seems that not many people are worried about it."

"How can that be?" I asked, incredulous.

Peytynn glanced away and cleared his throat. "There's been a change of leadership at the Overhang."

I was stunned. "Explain yourself," I demanded.

Peytynn and the others shifted nervously on their feet. Finally Teo said, "Your father has not been seen for days, and Lord-General Tuecyr has declared himself the interim chancellor in his absence."

A seething heat ignited in my heart. "The traitor! And what about Lord Hengry?"

Destyr spoke up. "He hasn't been seen since Doldra's army arrived. People say he conspired with Doldra and has fled to his side."

Despite my weary and aching body, my heart sped up as I pondered the treasons that were sweeping through my Overhang. I focused on what was most important.

"Please tell me what you know of my mother, the queen," I said. "Where is she?"

"We have no idea where the Queen is, or any of the royal women," Peytynn said. "Shameful rumors have been circulating among the troops about you and your brother, Prince Aillil." He looked at me nervously. "If you don't mind me asking, why are you lying here like this?"

I wanted to strike him, but I knew he was not the cause of my pain. "My brother and I were on the annual eyas hunt when the rest of our crew turned against us. We fought our way out, but my brother was wounded. He soon succumbed to his wounds."

The four young Austringers looked at each other in amazement.

"What is it? Out with it," I demanded.

"I am sorry about your brother," Peytynn said, "but it would seem you're not a prince anymore." He continued as gingerly as possible. "What with recent events at the Overhang, you could very well be our new king."

They all dropped to their right knees and placed their right hands over their hearts in the Austringer sign of fealty.

"Get up," I said hoarsely. "My father is still king, and I intend to find him and restore him to his rightful place so he can end this treasonous invasion."

The boys stood up somewhat reluctantly and gathered their gear. Peytynn told Morys to help me. Morys was an overgrown fourteen-year-old who, despite shouldering a rucksack with the typical Austringer bronze-tipped spear and an atypical battle-ax, still managed to carry my dwindled frame in his arms.

They started walking down off the plateau.

"Wait a minute," I said.

They stopped and Peytynn said, "Yes, King—Prince Tyrcel."

"We can take one of the passageways back to the Overhang," I said. "I think I know where to find one."

"We aren't going back to the Overhang," Peytynn said. "There's nothing up there but cowards and traitors."

"No," I said. "I refuse to believe that."

They started back down the path, and I was carried along by Morys with no way to stop them. But the more they told me, the more I lost the will to argue with them.

"Since your father and Lord Hengry disappeared, the entire Austringer court and citizenry seem to have forgotten their loyalties," Peytynn said. "At first we didn't understand what was going on, but then we heard that the military had been ordered not to defend the City Valley or attack Doldra's army. Well, we Skirmishers did not agree with those orders because we were trained to defend our mountains."

The others gave a cheer.

Peytynn continued, "Any soldier who spoke up or defied the orders was deemed a traitor and has not been seen again. We assumed we were left alone because we are just kids, recent graduates of the lower schools."

I bounced down the path in Morys' arms. "You say Lord Hengry is gone?"

"Yes, my king—I mean, prince."

I remembered the parchment I had found in the falcon's roost. Lord Hengry's disappearance left me more confused than ever. Had Tuecyr done away with him to have all the power to himself? Was there no honor whatsoever among these men, my father's trusted friends and fellow warriors? If I made it back to the Overhang, who would I be able to trust?

Morys was strong, but carrying my extra weight slowed him down, and the others arrived at the bottom of the footpath ahead of us. Lyum waited next to a makeshift drag-stand fabricated from two thick birch limbs and several cross branches.

"I built this stand to not only accommodate my tools and gear, but also a wounded person," he told me. His voice was barely mature, but his speech revealed his intelligence. He pushed his foot against one of the side branches, hardly bowing the wood. "I didn't have time to bring any wheels, but these birch branches are flexible enough. Your ride shouldn't be too bumpy."

Morys gently laid me across the stand, then moved to the front and lifted the two thick side-branches off the ground. It was built to be pulled by two people—or a single person if that person was as big as Morys.

Destyr spoke up. "We're not going far anyway." He pointed toward the Sun Point 1 mountain. "Just in the foothills there, near the spring pool."

Peytynn said, "Yeah, we've got a well-established hideout on the side of that mountain. We can see as far north as the middle of the Hollow Valley and as far south as... well...Gavina."

My stomach growled, and I decided I wasn't going to do any planning until I got some food in my belly. "Peytynn, back on the footpath you called yourselves Skirmishers?"

"That's right, my prince. We are the Five Skirmishers. Or just Skirmishers for short. I'm in charge of this crew. Morys over there is the brawn, Destyr and Teo are expert bowmen, and Lyum over there is my little brother."

Lyum didn't like his brother's simple description of him. "I'm the brains of this operation," he said. His tone was more confident than any twelve-year-old I had ever met.

"Indeed," Peytynn said. "My little brother may be young, but he is a master of magnetic manipulation. He can make a magnet throw a pebble fast enough to kill a man."

"That's right," Lyum said.

I smiled. "Have you killed many men in your time, Lyum?"

"None yet. But I'm planning on trying out a few of my ideas on Abbo Doldra."

Peytynn rolled his eyes. "Yes, I am definitely glad my little brother is on my side. But anyway, that's who we are. The Five Skir... SIX SKIRMISHERS!"

I was touched that they wanted to add me to the roster. The other four raised their fists and cried, "Hoo-yah, THE SIX SKIRMISHERS!"

Peytynn stiffened. "All right, let's keep the yelling to a minimum."

The path we took was almost the exact one I had stumbled along after escaping Heike's hovel. At the spring pool, we replenished our water supply, and I had another long drink and splashed some cool water over my face and neck. Nothing seemed to quench my thirst, though, and the water did not cool the heat from the wound on my neck.

Despite the deflection of the fresh branches that made up the drag-stand, my ride was an exercise in misery. Every bump sent shockwaves of pain up my spine and across the scars on my neck. Bundles of supplies constantly threatened to tumble over my body, forcing me to raise my hands and use what little energy I had to prevent them from falling on top of me. The Skirmishers stopped several times to redistribute the supplies, but the effect only lasted a few steps before they were once again shaken loose.

"With all the geniuses in this group," whispered Peytynn, "not one of us remembered to bring any rope."

I did my best to rest as I bounced along the path and found it ironic that I had to put my safety in the hands of these youngsters. Morys' breathing was labored, but he had Austringer lungs, which were used to much higher altitudes, so he did not tire from his duties.

Eventually I drifted off to sleep. When I awoke, I was in the dark interior of a windowless cavern. At first I assumed it was another dream. Only this time, rather than a bright light and strange voices, I saw stark darkness and heard vaguely familiar voices. I rose up on my elbow and realized the cavern was actually a long cave. It was cool, but my thirst was immediately apparent. In the distance, I could see the dim light at the mouth of the cave and the silhouettes of the five boys milling about. Down near the entrance Morys' huge shadow sat hunched over a fire. He was stirring something in a stew-pot that filled the entire cave with a spicy, delicious aroma.

Near where I was lying, I noticed Lyum kneeling over a strange box-like contraption that was making a low humming sound. Lyum held something in his right hand and moved it randomly over the top of the box. In his left hand, he held thin, metal cables. When he touched them to the box, they sparked and ignited a light in a globe that sat by his side.

He was attempting to create continuous, artificial light in that small lantern using a relatively modern Austringer technology. However, artificial light was usually produced on a large scale throughout Austringer cities, which required massive magnets and long copper cables.

No one had ever made a handheld lantern glow for more than a few seconds because large magnets were needed to produce a bright enough light, and they were too heavy to be portable.

I was intrigued by the sparks that popped and jumped off whatever the wires were touching. But I knew they wouldn't be enough to make a useful light.

"Your magnets are too small, little man."

Lyum didn't look up from his project, but he did reply. "My magnets are fine, thank you." He jerked the wires away from the box and turned to face me. "I beg your pardon, King—Prince Tyrcel, but it is my humble opinion that the size of something does not dictate its efficacy."

I couldn't argue with him—his attitude was too compelling. "What's that you're doing with your hand?"

"I'm trying to find the point at which the magnet in my hand interrupts the magnetic moment of the conductors in this box."

Austringers were expert engineers, but I had chosen to study other subjects and didn't pay much attention during my magnetics classes. Young Lyum spoke as if he should have been the one teaching the classes.

"The magnetic moment, you say?"

"Yes. The most common angle at which all five of the magnetic conductors in the box are in a parallel field."

I was still baffled, but before I could ask him to explain, he shouted, "Got it," and immediately stuck the thin cables into the box. A few sparks shot out, but he kept his grip on the cables and soon the glass orb began glowing.

It was brighter than any portable artificial light I had ever seen. I expected it to burn out, but soon after that orb lit up, another one hanging from the top of the cave sparked on, then one on each side of it came to life and so on all the way to the entrance and deeper into the cave in the other direction. I was now awash in a flickering light that kept the entire cave bright enough to read in.

I was thoroughly impressed, but the other four boys didn't even look up from doing what they were doing to shout, almost in unison, "It's about time, Lyum."

Lyum ignored their teasing and carefully ran the magnet along the top of the box. The lights flickered as he traced the line of what he called the magnetic field, but once it came to rest, the light increased and steadied itself.

"How in all these lowland hells are you able to create such light with magnets that small?" I asked.

"Well, for one thing, I designed a way to curie cobalt into stronger magnets and had Destyr make me several prototypes. Then I designed a magnetic array that proved to be stronger and created more torque when allowed to cross fields. I just added these smaller magnets into our age-old array designs. It's all pretty simple really."

It didn't sound simple to me, but I didn't want to show my ignorance any more than I already had, so I was grateful when Morys knelt down beside me. He held a steaming bowl of stew in his hands with a huge end of crusty bread sitting in it. Nothing else in the world meant a thing. I ignored my weary muscles and sat right up. I grabbed the food from Morys before he had a chance to say anything and started shoveling it into my mouth. It was a simple broth of turnips and turmeric, but it tasted like the finest cuisine I had ever eaten.

"I made it light for you, Prince Tyrcel," said Morys. "You look like a sick pile of bones, and you don't want to eat anything too heavy for your first meal. That would only make you feel worse. But there's plenty when you want more."

I finished slurping down the broth and pushed the bowl back against Morys' chest. "Please," I begged, "I don't care what it is. Give me more."

Morys brought another bowl.

I ate that, too, and Morys told me to let it settle and he'd give me more later. I had no strength to argue. The food felt so good it calmed my heart and made me drowsy.

Peytynn came over and sat next to me, holding his own bowl of stew. "Don't worry, I won't keep you from resting. I just wanted to see if there's anything else we can do for you right now."

My eyes were heavy. "Nothing much now, thanks. I think I'm about to fall asleep." My pallet was made of several blankets piled on top of each other, but it felt like the softest bed I had ever been in.

When I turned to look at Peytynn, I saw that the light orbs extended so far back that they disappeared around a bend in the cave. Lining the walls were piles of crates and what looked like equipment and weapons. His form was backlit by the string of glowing glass lanterns. The lights reminded me of my recent dreams, and I thought of the voices that had spoken to me.

"I'm worried about my mother," I said drowsily.

He looked up from his bowl of soup. His face had a hint of sadness to it, and I wondered if he was thinking of his own parents and where they were in all this chaos. I decided to change the subject.

"What is this place?" I asked.

"A place we have made our own, Prince Tyrcel. A place the five of us have been coming to for a long while." He glanced at the equipment. "We come here to get away from all the bullies in the ranks, do a bit of lowland hunting, and test our latest inventions. As you can see, my little brother has provided us with sufficient lighting for as long as we want. Luckily, we don't need him to invent a way to heat this cave. Since it is the lowlands, it rarely gets cold enough to bother us."

"What do you mean, bullies in the ranks?" I asked.

"You may have noticed that we aren't the usual Austringer warrior types."

"Yes, but you're just fourteen—"

"I know, but even for fourteen-year-olds, we're all runts. Save Morys. Believe it or not, he's bullied for being too big and too nice. Apparently, that's an unusual combination." Peytynn leaned in close. "But I've seen him fell a foot-thick ash trunk with just one stroke of his battle-ax."

Impressed, I looked back at Morys, who was hunched over the stew-pot.

Peytynn continued. "It's not that we are not good at fighting. We are just more interested in other aspects of fighting. Like strategies and designing better weapons. I think that's why no one bothered with us when they started getting rid of anyone who was loyal to your father. No one ever really paid attention to us. That's how we were able to sneak all this gear out. They don't expect people our age to think for themselves."

"But why would you want to sneak down here to the lowlands?"

Peytynn swallowed a turnip chunk. "Because no one would think to look for us here."

"But what about your parents?" I asked.

He turned away. Toward the mouth of the cave, Lyum looked up from his bowl of stew.

"My parents disappeared a week ago," Peytynn said. "They were among the people who didn't agree with Lord-general Tuecyr."

I leaned my head back against the cave wall, overwhelmed by fatigue. How could the Austringers have allowed Tuecyr to take power? I looked around at the five young boys, and a deep sadness overwhelmed me. I had little desire to be the king of the Austringers. I did, however, want to get back to the Overhang and slash Tuecyr's throat.

12

I woke up from another night of busy, bright dreams that made me feel fatigued despite having slept. The string of lights were out, and the mouth of the cave shone with the grayish hue of a cloudy morning. Morys was again at the fire stirring the stew-pot. The smell of warm figs and oats emanated from it.

I sat up, which made my neck throb and my head feel like it was in a vise. I managed to get up, and though my knees were still wobbly, they seemed better able to bear my weight. I steadied myself by keeping one hand on the cave wall as I walked toward the entrance with a blanket draped over my back.

Morys handed me a steaming bowl of oat groats. "Eat this, Prince Tyrcel," he said. "It will be gentle but heavy in your belly and give you your strength back."

I took the bowl and spoon and stood beside the fire for a few seconds. I was a bit winded by my walk through the cave. "Thank you, Morys. You're a kind soul and a great cook."

I walked to the mouth of the cave, where Peytynn sat with several blankets wrapped around his body, looking like he too had just woken up. Lyum was still fast asleep with his head on Peytynn's legs.

"Sorry to bother you, Peytynn, but where does a man relieve himself around here?"

He pointed to the entrance of the cave. I put my bowl down and walked out onto a ledge that was no wider than a footpath. Peering over, I realized that the cave was not very high up the side of the mountain. To my left was a small bend in the footpath and then a sheer wall rose up. To my right the footpath sloped down and disappeared around another corner.

I walked to the edge of the footpath, relieved my bladder, and took a deep breath as I scanned the landscape. I had a clear view of the southern half of the Hollow Valley. I could see where the un-scorched ground met and blended with the charred remains of the rest of the valley. I searched for anything familiar, and as I thought of Heike, the wound on my neck heated up.

"Now you can see why we chose this cave for our headquarters," Destyr said as he came up next to me. "Forgive me, my prince, but you are currently pissing on the only path to our cave."

I leaned a little further over the edge to see that the footpath switched back, and its lower half was directly under us. Teo stood a few feet down the path from my newly made puddle. He was holding the drag-stand in his hands with various pieces of glass and other armaments piled neatly on it. He looked up at me and Destyr and waved with a big smile on his face.

"It's okay, Prince Tyrcel," he yelled. "I can wait till you finish."

Destyr leaned over. "No time for that, Teo. Get that stuff to the bunker."

"Sorry, Teo," I added.

"You go in and eat, and when you're ready Peytynn will bring you over to the bunker," Destyr said. "We'll meet you there." He turned back to the cave and yelled, "Peytynn, tell that little brother of yours that he can sleep when he's dead. We're setting up the glasses with or without him."

He looked back at me. "Lyum's a bit of a sour puss in the mornings. But he comes around eventually."

Peytynn gently roused Lyum from his sleep. "Lyum, let's get up now. Destyr and Teo are starting without you." He spoke in a gentle, fatherly tone. It reminded me of how Aillil used to talk to me when we were younger.

Lyum sat up slowly, rubbed his eyes, and yawned noisily. "Can't a man get his bearings for a minute?"

Destyr leaned into the cave. "First of all, you are hardly a man. Second of all, you know as well as I do that we only have a few minutes of light at the angle we need for this thing to work. Come on. Telios does not care how sleepy little twelve-year-olds are."

Lyum was still rubbing the sleep out of his eyes. "Despite being right, you are quite an awful, awful person."

He got to his feet and came out onto the ledge. "Good morning, prince. Good to see you standing upright." The morning light made him squint. "Destyr, why are you still standing there?"

Lyum walked around the bend to the left, toward the dead-end. Destyr pointed. "That, Prince Tyrcel, is where we piss around here."

"Thanks, Destyr." Although these kids called me prince, they talked to me in a way that was far from proper for royalty. I was glad for that.

Lyum came back, gathered a few things from the cave, and then disappeared down the footpath to the right. I sat down beside Peytynn and picked up my bowl of groats and figs. It was still piping hot and was surely the best thing I had ever eaten. My blanket fell off my shoulders, and I noticed Peytynn staring at my neck. The wound from Heike's bite had barely begun to heal, and with the slightest of movements, a yellowish fluid oozed from the scabs.

"How'd you get a wound like that?" Peytynn asked. "It must have bled like a hot spring."

I slowly chewed a mouthful of groats and didn't answer. I felt embarrassed and ashamed. My neck must have looked awful. Heike had not only bitten me but had ripped the flesh from my neck, and I had been powerless to stop him—or save Marello.

Peytynn studied my wound. "It doesn't look like it was made by any weapon I know."

"It wasn't," I said, still gazing out over the Hollow Valley.

"Well, whatever happened, I'm glad you survived and that we found you in time. You looked like you hadn't eaten in months."

"I'm not sure I have survived."

Peytynn looked at me. "What do you mean?"

I had begun to worry that I was only alive because of some spell of Heike's. *I made it so you will not die*, he'd said. Could I ever heal and get strong again, or was I cursed to be a walking, helpless corpse?

"He can use spells to keep his captives alive."

"Who can?" Peytynn asked, concern creeping into his voice.

"When he was about to kill me, he got distracted and didn't finish." The memory made me shiver and my neck throb.

"What the Sirens happened to you out there?" Peytynn asked.

"I did battle with a horrible creature on the Main Road, and when I regained consciousness, I was bound to a wall in Heike's foul hovel, with his gruesome collection of insect-like pets—his minions—crawling over me and poking their fangs into me as if I was a convenient meal."

Peytynn stared at me in horror.

"I believe he is somehow able to take the form of the Shirk," I continued, relieved to finally be able to tell someone about it. "At times he looked like a deranged giant, while at other times he had eight arms and his face turned into something that one should never have to witness."

I glanced over at Peytynn. He seemed to be deep in thought.

"What is it?" I asked.

"I believe, my prince, we Skirmishers have seen Heike's pets. But we've never seen a strange creature that took the shape of a man or had eight arms."

I was shocked. "Where have you seen these things? How are you still alive?"

Peytynn rose and stretched his arms into the air, yawning. "As soon as you finish eating, Prince Tyrcel, I will show you how we've seen them."

We left the cave and started down the footpath. It did indeed have a series of switchbacks, but it also led farther north along the edge of the mountain. We followed the path for almost an hour, and I was beginning to wish that Morys was with us so I might take him up on his generous offer to carry me.

He had given me an extra set of his clothes. The huge pants and shirt hung off my emaciated frame like empty turnip sacks hung on a hook. But with a few folds and tucks, I had been able to make them comfortable.

Peytynn came to a bend in the path and turned back to me. "Here we are, Prince Tyrcel. If my brother and the others have done what they set out to do, we should be in for a great show."

Around the bend, the path ended on a sunken, wide ridge that was lined with a low wall of natural rocks and berry shrubs. Behind the ridge, the mountainside was a low-grade incline of cedars that changed to aspens and rose up to another ridge that stretched in two directions around the northeast edge of the Sun Point 1 mountain.

Above the ridge, the top edge of Telios glowed brightly. The bottom part of the light remained blocked by the mountain, casting a lingering few minutes of shadow over our location.

At the end of the trail, Morys was sitting on the ground, resting against the slope of the hill behind him. As we approached, he said, "Beautiful view, isn't it, Prince Tyrcel?"

I looked back at the ridge. Lyum and Teo were busy turning bolts and adjusting levers on a large three-legged apparatus. On its top was a round, wooden box sandwiched between what looked like two large magnifying glasses.

"Yes, great view," I said, and walked over to the tripod. "What is all this?"

"This is the latest in modern weaponry," Destyr said. "What we have here are two receptor glasses affixed to both sides of a round-framed, glass-paned container."

Now that I was right next to it, I could see that the front of the magnifying glasses had a series of lenses that grew consecutively smaller as they were set farther away from the tripod. They were held in a long line by thin iron slats and formed a type of turret that was now aimed over the edge of the ridge.

I followed the direction of the glass turret out and over the plateau and for the first time saw what was below us. The Hollow Valley stretched as far as I could see. Directly below were the foothills that I had stumbled through after escaping Heike's hovel, and above that, on the horizon was the burned valley. And uncomfortably closer was the southern flank of Abbo Doldra's army with its trebuchets.

Halfway between our ridge and Doldra's army was the upturned tree that lay like a massive reminder of how far I had come. Even from this distance, I could see the huge rootball and long trunk of the ancient oak under which Heike had dug his lair. The sight gave me a cold shiver, and I touched my hands to the wound on my neck.

"You okay?" Peytynn was suddenly beside me. He had brought two small, handheld tripods, on each of which was mounted a spyglass that swiveled on a pin.

"Yes, fine," I said, snapping out of my daze.

"Take a look then," he said.

I took a tripod from Peytynn, set it up, and swiveled the spyglass so that it faced down into the valley. Peytynn set his up as well, then pointed toward the distant trebuchets. "At those trebuchets, look directly below them on the ground."

I looked through the glass and was amazed at how close it brought me to what was happening in the valley. I lifted my face away and studied the spyglass. "Where did you get this? This is stronger than any spyglass I've ever used."

Peytynn put a finger to his lips and leaned in a little closer. "Don't let Teo hear you say that. He already loves himself enough. He designed them. He won't tell anyone how, but I don't really care about that, as long as I get to use them."

We both looked through the spyglasses again, and Peytynn said, "You see those trebuchets? Look directly at the ground below them."

I shifted my gaze and saw men climbing over and all around the trebuchets. Below each, in orderly piles, sat strange ceramic barrels—like the ones I had seen from the lookout on Hunter's Bluff. "I see the trebuchets, but what are those vessels?"

"They contain whatever they've been using to torch the Hollow Valley. They load those things onto the trebuchets, light a fuse, then throw the barrels at a target. When they hit, they explode in a huge ball of fire."

"I have seen what they can do," I said, remembering how Aillil, Marello, and I had watched our enemies destroy the Sentinels. It seemed like a lifetime ago.

"Well, Prince Tyrcel, we have a hunch—"

"Actually, I have a hunch," Lyum called from back at the tripod, as confident as ever.

Peytynn continued, unperturbed. "We know that those barrels blow up when ignited with fire. So the Skirmishers here have designed a system of magnifying glasses—"

"Ahem," Teo interrupted.

"Okay, Teo designed the glasses," Peytynn said. "This system of lenses can concentrate rays of Telios' light into a small, super-hot beam. And at the right time of day, with a few adjustments to the pitch and angle of our tripod, we can place that beam of light anywhere we want." He looked through his spyglass. "And where we want is right on one of those barrels. I just hope Telios gives us enough time in one position to burn through the side of one of those things."

"It will," Lyum said.

The barrels were stacked on makeshift wooden stands in rows of five barrels each. I was amazed that things so small could do so much damage, but I understood what the Skirmishers had in mind and felt the excitement of finally gaining the upper hand.

I gestured at the big tripod. "What's in that center section?"

The wooden centerpiece was disc shaped, no more than a few inches wide, and filled with what looked like crystals.

Teo said, "Those are fragments of larger magnifying glasses that I've ground into millions of tiny magnifying glasses. You see, the sunlight is initially enhanced by that first, biggest glass orb. The enhanced light then hits the centerpiece, and in there it refracts through each micro lens, moving in every direction and consequently gaining energy that is then channelled through the front series of lenses, which have each been individually shaped to their own specifications for stronger light to be forced through smaller and smaller lenses."

He paused. "Basically, this thing can put a pinpoint of hot light on an object from almost a league away. And with enough time, this dot of light will burn a perfect little hole in whatever it touches."

"Except for granite," Destyr interjected.

"Yes, except for granite," Teo repeated. "Although I believe that's only because Telios does not stay in one place long enough for our beam to eat its way through any dense stone."

"How long have you guys been set up here on this ridge?" I asked Peytynn.

"We've used this ridge for years to spy on the Hollow Valley."

"So you saw what happened to the valley? From here?" I asked.

All the boys stopped what they were doing and looked at one another.

"Yes," Peytynn said.

"They burned it with those trebuchets?"

"Yes." Peytynn glanced at the others before continuing. "We could only see the distant mass of Doldra's horde setting up their camp in the hills of the valley that faced the city gates. We couldn't see what happened next for all the trees and such, even with our spyglasses. But we did suddenly hear men screaming in terror, awful screams that echoed through the foothills. Then came the fire. At first we could only see barrels flying up and down above the tree-line. And soon the entire Ringing Forest seemed to be burning. After the fires died out, there was no more forest. At least this section of it. And when the smoke cleared, we had the view you see below."

Peytynn scratched his chin. "The funny thing is, when they burned the forest to the ground, they took away the only thing protecting them from us."

I was not concerned with that irony. My mind was busy trying to piece together the timeframe. "Did you happen to see what was making Doldra's men scream, what made them burn the forest?" I asked.

"I did not, prince." He looked directly at me. "But we all just assumed it was the winged things."

"Blast it!" Lyum exclaimed. "We have no good shot at this angle."

Peytynn touched my arm. "Sorry, Prince Tyrcel, but you won't get a show today."

Teo spoke up. "We can just move to another hill, or move closer."

Peytynn scanned the distance with his spyglass. "Well, Teo, I am not one to get in the way of progress. If you want to move closer, I would say the best hill would be—"

"No hills," Teo said. "The best spot is the top of that big rootball over there."

My heart leaped into my throat. Teo was pointing directly at Heike's tree.

"That's a bit close, don't you think?" Peytynn said.

He turned back to discuss the matter with Teo, but the others had already broken down the turret and were carefully sliding the individual pieces into the rucksacks. They would each carry a pack, and Morys, of course, was responsible for the huge iron tripod.

"If we hurry," said Teo, "we can get there before Telios' light hits it."

In a low voice, I asked Peytynn, "Do you know anything about that tree?"

He looked confused. "Well, the unburnt side seems to have the bark of a poison oak, but other than that...."

His voice trailed off, and he stared at me with concern. The subject of Heike's tree had made the wound on my neck heat up. I pressed my palm against it until the pain subsided.

"Maybe we should get you back to the cave," he said. "Your wound—"

"I'm fine." I said. "I'm just a little hungry. I want to help you destroy those weapons. And then I need to get back to the Overhang."

He nodded. "We can eat as we're walking to that tree. Then we'll just have to stay behind it to keep out of the enemy's line of sight."

"What about Doldra's scouts?"

Peytynn shrugged his shoulders. "These guys don't really think about that sort of thing. They just want to play with their inventions. Any scouts will have to be handled by Morys and us."

As we walked, I chewed a few bites of bread and some jerky that Peytynn had handed me.

"How do you know about the winged creatures, Heike's pets?" I asked him.

Peytynn swallowed a mouthful of bread and said, "From that ridge back there, we often got glimpses of some pretty strange beasts crawling around the trees. Knowing all the old stories, at first we were nervous, but they never seemed to leave the forest, so we just kept our distance. A few times, though, I swear one of those things was looking back at us. Like it knew we were here but just didn't want to come out of the forest."

"Have you seen any of them since Doldra's fire-bombing?"

"No." He handed me another bit of jerky. "With any luck, they're all dead."

"Luck indeed," I said, full of dread with every step we took and unable to shake the feeling that I hadn't seen the last of Heike.

Soon the uprooted tree was directly between us and Doldra's army. Peytynn and I kept a vigilant eye on our flanks for any scouts. But Lyum, Destyr, and Teo scuttled around the pit below the rootball and were about to climb up to find the best spot to stand the tripod in direct view of the enemy. Peytynn fussed about their seeming lack of care for staying hidden, but he didn't want to call out and attract any unwanted attention.

Meanwhile, Morys was studying the ground around the edge of the huge pit that had been created when the tree fell over, the same pit that I had dug myself out of. Destyr and Teo climbed up the tree's massive tangle of roots, and Morys handed them the tripod without taking his eyes off the ground. His full attention was somewhere down in the pit.

Peytynn and I arrived at the edge of the hole. A wide swath of what looked like pebbles trailed around the fallen tree trunk and down into the hole. They had not been there when I escaped, and they were uncharred, unlike the rest of the surrounding soil and rubble. It reminded me of the pebbles I had seen when Marello and I killed Chod and Dosh.

Morys grabbed Peytynn's arm and put his other hand in front of my chest to stop us from getting any closer to the pit.

"You hear that?" Morys said. "I think there's something down there."

The three of us stood silently, while behind us Lyum and Teo argued over how to set up the turret. Under the sound of their voices, we heard hisses and moans emanating from the pit. My skin crawled. It was Heike's high-pitched garbling, only this time there was no evil joy to his timbre. He sounded like he was in pain. But he was still alive.

The thought gave me courage—and the hope that he could lift this evil curse and give me back my strength.

I leaned over the edge of the pit, and the wound on my neck began to burn. But I saw no sign of his pets, and the fact that he had let the Skirmishers walk right up to this spot without interference made me sure he was in a weakened state.

"I'm going down there," I said. "And I don't want any of you to follow me."

Morys stared at me. "That's Heike's hole, isn't it, prince?"

"Yes, it is."

"You don't have to go down there," Peytynn said.

"Yes, I do." I was compelled by something stronger than I had ever felt before. And I didn't have time to argue with them.

I reached over and pulled Peytynn's long-dagger out of its scabbard. "I'm just going to borrow this, Peytynn. I'll return it when I get back."

I looked down into the pit, then back up at Morys. I tried to make as light of the situation as possible, despite a worried knot in my gut. "If you hear any awful screams down there, feel free to jump down and help out."

Neither of them responded. Not even a laugh.

I started to climb down, then glanced back up at them one last time. Their faces were serious and full of concern. The light of Telios was crisp and bright behind them—a sharp contrast to the burned terrain that surrounded us.

13

I braced my feet on either side of the wide hole to listen to the moaning sounds coming out of it. Heike seemed to be in considerable distress. I gave a quick prayer to the Great Mother Falcon and let myself drop into the hole.

It was easier getting down than it had been climbing out. The loose soil slid out from under me, and I landed on a pile of dirt on the table in Heike's den. Only a little light filtered down from the opening above me, and as I struggled to get to my feet, a dark form hissed and scurried out of sight behind the table.

I leaped to the floor. The small room was even more cramped with all the dirt and rubble, which made me feel trapped. My heart pounded, so I took slow, deep breaths to control my emotions and waited, listening to the rasp of Heike's breathing. As my eyes adjusted to the darkness, I began to make out Heike's form in front of me. He was hunched over and groaning, no longer the terror he once was. My heart slowed down, and fear was replaced with anger. I wanted to crush his huge head under my foot.

"Show yourself, beast!"

He hissed. *Grrorym nolloth y'tullarukhat.* His voice was whiny, and there was no mistaking the fear in it. I walked around the mound of dirt that spilled off the table top. Heike growled and hissed as I came closer.

When I finally got a good look at him, I gasped and took a step backward, instinctively holding Peytynn's dagger in front of my face. Of all the horrors I had experienced since meeting Heike, this one was the most terribly strange. He seemed to be cut in half. Everything from his waist down was missing, and all that was left was the end of his spine and ribbons of flesh that dragged behind him. He appeared to be stuck between two different forms—his usual giant self and the horrid eight-armed Shirk. Three of his arms were intact, but five stumps had long since hardened into stone.

Barra! he snapped. *Barra pest, and let Ahkkharu alone. You are the pinkling who brought this to Heike.* But his breathing was laborious, and his voice no longer had the hollow depth that used to be so frightening.

I relaxed a bit but kept my hand tight around the hilt of the long-dagger. "I didn't bring this on you, though I wish I had. You have killed many good men."

Heike hissed as if the sound of my voice caused him pain. *Ahkkharu non lalasla. I not killed as easily as you worthless pinklings! Grrorym barra deyss!*

"Your sorcery doesn't seem to be working too well." I leaned closer and jabbed at one of the many wounds on Heike's arms. "You seem to be stuck in between tricks."

Heike screamed and flailed his arm at the blade. I leaned out of his reach and slashed at the tiny, deformed hand. The dagger sliced a long gash into the back of Heike's forearm. He screamed again, as a single streak of thick, dark blood ran from the wound, the blood pooling and then turning into a flat stone.

Heike groveled on the ground, blood and viscera twisting out of his waist. I moved in closer and kicked him in the face, sending him flying back against the wall. But my foot was just as shocked from the blow, and I tried not to wince out loud. Now I knew why Austringers were not trained to do weapon-less combat with hill-giants.

Heike rolled what was left of his body back onto his belly. He pushed him-self up by a half-petrified, brown-haired arm and looked me in the eye.

Just like me, you are stuck in the curse. But I can make your pain go away forever.

"How?" I demanded. "Explain yourself."

The beast smiled as best he could. *The spell I put on the pinkling was never removed. Heike uses it to keep a pest's heart making more blood. The blood for my babies.* He clenched his fist and pounded it against the ground. *But now they are all gone. GONE! Heike cannot last like this, Ahkkharu nall mallass,* he wailed.

He seemed to run out of energy and let his body collapse onto the ground. *Nall mallass, Heike hysst tull and sleep,* he drowsily mumbled between his ancient black magic tongue and the common Austringer language.

He sounded like he was falling asleep or maybe even dying. But I couldn't let that happen, not yet. I kicked him in the head again, not as hard this time, but he didn't respond.

"What about the spell?" I yelled at him, starting to panic. If what he said was true, the fastest way to get rid of the curse would be to have Heike undo it. Otherwise, I'd have to find an Austringer doctor who knew the cure, and with the whole kingdom in chaos, that might take longer than I could afford.

Heike hissed a few weak breaths that slowly petered out. I jabbed at him with the long-dagger, but nothing roused him. Then the three arms began changing, joint by joint, into a collection of granite stones. What remained of his torso and his huge head turned into boulders. I stared at the stones for a long moment, thinking of Marello and all the other men Heike had tortured and killed. Anyone who saw this pile of rocks now would never recognize the monster who had terrorized the valley for centuries, who had terrorized me.

Unfortunately, that meant I would have to find another way to undo the damage he had done to me.

I managed to climb up through the tunnel with less difficulty than I had the first time. When I neared the edge of the hole, I could see Peytynn standing where I had left him. The burned forest was surprisingly quiet, punctuated by Lyum, Teo, and Destyr's loud whispering. Morys leaned half into the pit to help me out.

My sweaty forehead was caked with mud, and as I reached for Morys' hand, a spasm of pain ran through my wounds. I clutched one hand to my neck, suddenly desperate to get out of that hole, and lifted my other hand toward Morys. He grabbed it and yanked me up.

I was exhausted. That last bout of pain had sapped my strength. Morys sat me down in the charred grass and leaned his big head over me. "It's good to see you in one piece, Prince Tyrcel." He shoved a small piece of goat jerky into my hand and added, "You need to keep your strength up."

I was glad to see Morys as well and grateful that he had stayed close. I smiled, feeling happy but weak with fatigue. "Morys, when they sing of this moment, I'm going to make sure you are remembered as the one who pulled the Austringer prince from the pit of the evil sorcerer."

Morys blushed a rosy red. "You would do that?"

Peytynn's face was soon leaning over me as well. "Good to see you, Prince Tyrcel. But if you two are finished with your reunion, we need to get back to the cave. It seems the smarties up there have revealed our location before we even had a chance to blow anything up. They couldn't resist taunting some of Doldra's men, and now they're headed this way."

I started to push myself to my feet, but the effort was too much, and I sat right back down.

"Given the state you're in, my prince," Peytynn said as gently as he could, "we'd make better time if Morys carried you. Don't worry about the tripod, Morys. I'll drag it back."

Morys scooped me up as if I were a child, draped me over his back with one arm over each shoulder, and began lumbering toward the foothills. Meanwhile, Peytynn shouted up to the three young Austringers, "Make haste. And leave your gadget up there."

Lyum continued watching the distant trebuchets. "Not a chance," he said. "We just need a few seconds."

Teo and Destyr were also transfixed by what they saw through their spyglasses. None of them seemed to care that three enemy guards on horseback were heading straight toward them.

"Lyum, I don't want to have to pull brotherly rank, but we are getting close to the time when I climb up there and drag you down."

"That's it," Teo said. "It's burning."

Morys paused, and we both looked back just as an explosion blasted through the foothills. He jumped and instinctively covered his head, jostling me in the process. Another explosion, just as loud, sounded off in the distance, followed by another and another until countless thunderous explosions grew into one massive shockwave that shook the ground.

Dirt puffed off the roots of the upturned tree, and Lyum, Teo, and Destyr struggled to keep their footing while a wave of scorching air blew past them. Peytynn was also shaken off-balance and for a second looked like he might tumble into the pit.

He stuck his fingers in his ears and yelled to Lyum, "I guess your hunch was right, little brother. That couldn't have worked out better."

Then the debris stopped falling, and we all stared at the scene in front of us. Where there had once been a mass of men and trebuchets, there was now a huge plume of black smoke billowing up from fires that spanned the entire front of Abbo Doldra's encampment. The screams of wounded men could be heard over the sound of breaking wood and crackling fires. Without any trees for the flames to attack, the only things that burned were the trebuchets and any bodies that hadn't been immediately vaporized.

"Holy mother of Sirens," said Peytynn under his breath. He looked up at the tripod that sat precariously on the rootball. "I must say, little brother, we Skirmishers are a force to be reckoned with."

Lyum grinned, his teeth glowing in a face blackened with soot.

I scanned the area where I'd seen the three Northerners making their way toward us. I spotted them about halfway to the tree, but they were all lying prostrate on the ground, where they had been tossed by the explosion's shockwave. I saw a few flickers of movement, but after a quick look, Peytynn put his spyglass in his rucksack and said, "I'm not sure how many of them know about us or are in any condition to chase us, but I think we should get back to the cave anyway."

We hurried back up the path. Along the way, Peytynn, Morys, and I stopped at the plateau where the boys had first set up the tripod that morning. From this vantage point, we had a clear view of the burned forest and the leftmost flank of what remained of Abbo Doldra's eastern contingent. The boys had successfully blown up one of the powder kegs, which had created a series of explosions that destroyed the entire encampment of soldiers and trebuchets.

I looked through a pair binoculars that pivoted on a small adjustable tripod. Doldra's scouting party had made its muster point at Heike's tree, and the men were moving out in different directions from there.

"It looks like they're splitting into groups of about four scouts each," Peytynn said. "They're all fanning out in this general direction. And there's a small group of three moving off in their own direction, which happens to be somewhat toward this ridge."

He pointed toward the small group of three northerners on horseback. "I think those are the same three that spotted us earlier. They appear to be officers, and I think the one in the middle was just now giving orders. And I am relatively sure it's a woman."

A woman? I didn't remember hearing that the northern forces used women in their ranks, but I did recall being told Abbo Doldra had a daughter who was the most feared warrior in the north.

"I think we ought to put the fire out back at the cave," I said. "Before they see the smoke."

Peytynn glanced at Morys, then back to me. "All due respect, Prince Tyrcel, but I'm not sure that's how the guys want to operate."

"What other way is there to operate? Do they want to bring the enemy to our doorstep?"

"Destyr, Teo, and my brother aren't finished with their new toys," Peytynn said in his usual diplomatic tone. "They want the smoke to be visible. They want to attract attention. They assume that we will have every advantage while hidden up in these hills, so they believe they can handle whatever comes our way. I think they're just eager to test their new weapons."

I shook my head slowly. "I admire their bravery." I hoped there were other small squads of warriors doing the same thing as I rubbed the wound on my neck. It pulsed with each beat of my heart and was hot to the touch.

"So you guys are going to stand your ground and fight?" I asked.

"Nah, the only one of us who's much good in a hand-to-hand fight is Morys. And, now...well...you." Peytynn smiled, but I could see the worry in his eyes. I must have looked a great deal better than when they found me, but I was still tortured by thirst and painful cramps in my belly, and Peytynn eyed me nervously whenever he saw me rubbing my neck.

"We're not going to do much fighting but just play with them for a while, then kill them," he said coolly, as though the thought of killing a man was no big deal. "Let's get back to the cave. Lyum and the others will want us to help set up and tell us what parts we'll play in this mess."

When we reached the cave less than an hour later, Destyr and Teo were loading equipment wrapped in canvas sheets onto the drag-stand. Lyum moved about inside the cave gathering supplies. The cooking fire was now a good-sized blaze, and the pot of oat groats from that morning's breakfast sat on the ring of stones that encircled the fire pit. I sat down and scooped a huge spoonful of the oats. The warmth of the fire eased the tension that constantly surged through my body, and the plain groats tasted like the finest food of the finest banquet. I chewed with delight, the food settling my stomach and relaxing my body.

When I reached for another scoop of oats, I noticed that the smoke was rising straight up from the fire. I lifted my gaze and saw a metal tube high in the shadows of the craggy ceiling that was acting like a chimney.

"So that's why you're not worried," I said. "You've got the smoke under control."

Peytynn came over to stand beside me. "Even more than you think. That chimney tube you see there comes out at the top of the hill. At that point, the geniuses attached various other pipes that run in three—"

"FOUR," Destyr shouted.

"Sorry, four directions around this particular foothill. So the tubes we close and those we leave open determine where an enemy sees our smoke. We can make them believe we are anywhere on this mountain. Or, if we blaze a big enough fire, we can leave them all open and make it seem like there are four encampments occupying this hill."

I chewed another mouthful of groats, dumbfounded, and stared up at the chimney tube. "Tell me again, Peytynn, how long you Skirmishers have been playing around down here."

"It doesn't really matter, does it?" He leaned closer and whispered, "Don't let the other guys hear you call this 'playing around.' No one here thinks they are playing at anything."

With my mouth full of food, I smiled and said, "No problem."

Morys came in and told us it was time to move out. Then he noticed that I was eating the old groats. "Prince Tyrcel! What are you doing? I would have made something fresh for you. Or at least warmed those groats. They have got to be hard as clay by now."

I dropped my spoon back in the pot and started to rise, but Morys ran over and grabbed me under the shoulders. The squeeze of his big hands hurt my pride a little, but deeper down than my pride, I was grateful for his help.

14

The little bit of rest and food made me feel stronger, and I walked with Peytynn and Morys down the footpath toward the base of the mountain. We met up with the other three Skirmishers along the way. They were hauling all their equipment on the drag-stand. Just before we reached the bottom, Lyum, Teo, and Destyr pulled the individual pieces off the drag-stand and hiked them up onto their shoulders. Morys took the iron tripod. Lastly, Peytynn pulled two long coils of rope off the drag-stand and handed one to me.

"Do you think you can carry this, Prince Tyrcel? I ask only because two ropes plus my weapons get heavy quick."

"I think I can manage, Peytynn."

I stuck my arm and head through the center of the coiled rope so that it hung over one shoulder and was draped across my body. Carrying it this way was easier and didn't slow me down much more than the pain in my gut did. Lyum and Peytynn discussed their plans as we walked, and I hurried to keep up, more grateful than ever that I had eaten those groats.

"We've got about six scouting groups of four men each heading in our direction," Peytynn said. "Which chimney did you leave open?"

"The one on the western side of the hill," his little brother said.

We stopped and looked up the hill to our right. A thin, steady stream of smoke rose from behind the shrubs and boulders.

Peytynn shook his head. "So you really want them to come right at us, huh, little brother?"

Lyum smiled. "Might as well get the thing started."

"So we're going to funnel them through the switchback?"

"That is the plan, since it is our most rehearsed strategy," Lyum said. "Plus, no matter which direction those scouting parties set out on, they all have to come through the switchback. It's our best bet."

The young Austringer smiled and pointed to the two coils that Peytynn and I carried. "Why do you think we've brought the ropes?" he asked.

I was trying my best to understand the strategy, but my brain was foggy.

"Where is this switchback?" I asked.

"Take a look about a quarter-league up ahead," Peytynn said, pointing. "You see that big pile of boulders sitting at the base of the hill? And directly across from it is the sheer rise of the next foothill, with another outcropping at its base."

I looked where Peytynn pointed and saw the bottleneck they were calling a pass. "Yes. Is that the switchback you're talking about?"

We all started walking again and caught up with the rest of the party as Peytynn explained.

"Well, those two points are not technically the switchback," he said. "They are the tail end of the switchback. Directly in between those two points, about another quarter-league back, is that other hill. So no one can enter this valley from a straight-on direction. They have to go around that foothill and all the various other hills that block the way, and then turn to get through that small opening. Granted, we Skirmishers have never fought in a war or done much more than classroom strategizing, but we believe that by forcing an enemy to go through that pass, we can control them."

"It's as good a plan as any," I said, looking at Lyum. "I don't suppose you're just going to stand in front of that pile of rubble and hack away at anyone who steps past, so what's the battle plan?"

"Look directly up above the two outcrops," Lyum said.

I did as he said and saw, about fifty feet above the outcrops that formed this so-called pass, a long cable stretching from cliff to cliff. It was far away, and the bright light of day made it flicker in and out of visibility. As soon as I saw it, I knew exactly what the plan was. It was a typical Austringer offensive. When enemy troops marched within reach, Austringer warriors would swing down from the cable on tethers, slashing the enemies' throats. If everything went according to plan, the Austringer warriors would be up and out of sight before the enemies could even figure out which direction the attack had come from.

I was impressed, but I found the boys to be a bit naive.

"Lyum, are you sure you are ready for such an offensive? A swing attack is not easy to pull off."

"Ask Teo and Destyr," he said. "They're the ones who want to try it. I was happy with just lobbing metal bearings at whoever walks by. Plus, Morys and Peytynn can handle whoever doesn't get their throats slashed." He paused and looked up at me. "And you can help, too, Prince Tyrcel."

Morys gave me a look that said he was grateful to have such a seasoned warrior by his side. But it also showed a trace of worry.

From about thirty feet up the hillside, Destyr called to us to hurry. He and Teo were nearly hidden from view by another, smaller plateau. "We can see the scouts coming, and we'd like to have things set up before they get here."

Lyum clambered up the hillside, and by the time I got to the plateau, the three of them already had the tripod set up. This time a strange array of magnets perched on top of it—two large, disc-shaped magnets in the center ringed by smaller ones. The larger base magnets sat side by side with barely an inch of space between them, into which was wedged a short piece of concave metal that ran into a long funnel.

When I arrived, Lyum was installing a third magnet on a long pin below the other two, so all magnets overlapped by about two inches. Lyum put the bottom disc on its pin but did not remove his hand. The first two magnets started to slowly spin in opposite directions—the left one spinning counterclockwise and the right clockwise.

"Where's the bearing sack?" Lyum asked. "It needs to be within arm's reach."

"It's under that pile over there," Teo said.

"Well, I can't just take my hand off this and go fetch the bearings, Teo. Do you think you can help?"

"You're a snippy one today, little fella," Teo said as he grabbed a rucksack. It must have been heavy because he didn't even try to lift it but instead dragged it over to the tripod. I could hear the dull sound of metal thunking against metal. Teo left the sack lying on the ground with its top flap open. It was full of iron bearings, the kind that were used in the wheel rotors of the smaller cable boxes.

"What are those for?" I asked.

"Those," answered Peytynn, "will be launched from this contraption that you see my brother holding. Basically, those three magnets are designed to repel each other. When just the two are seated, nothing happens, but when you add that third one, they all start spinning at tremendous speed. You see how the front two spin in opposite directions? When one of those bearings is dropped into that center gully, the edges of the magnets...well...throw it."

"Throw it?"

"It seems hard to believe, but I've seen it in practice, and I would not want to be on the receiving end of it."

"They don't look like they're spinning all that fast," I said, dubiously.

"That's because Lyum still has his hand on the third magnet."

Lyum looked over his shoulder at us. "This is the trigger magnet. Once it starts spinning, the other ones spin faster, and this whole thing tends to shake a bit." He smiled a little sheepishly. "Plus, once it starts spinning, it's really hard to stop it. We haven't quite figured that out yet."

"We?" Teo teased.

Lyum grunted and turned back to his work.

Destyr had been looking through his binoculars while we were talking. "I think we need to get in position. There's a party of scouts not too far away."

He and Teo grabbed the two coils of rope and started up the hillside toward the cable that hung over the pass. It took years of training to become an effective killer while swinging past an enemy, and I didn't think these boys knew what they were getting into.

"Are you sure you can do this?" I called after them.

Teo shouted back, "No, but it should be fun trying."

They trusted in their technology and strategy so whole-heartedly that it inspired me. These brave young Skirmishers had chosen to face an unknown number of enemies with a small supply of weapons by relying on the age-old Austringer tactic of surprising the enemy from above.

"We need to get down to the mountain pass," Peytynn said.

He, Morys, and I practically slid down the hillside in our haste. Peytynn handed me a short-bow with a small collection of arrows. He carried a spear, and Morys had his battle-ax. As I struggled to keep up, my heart pounded in my chest, increasing the tightness in my neck. But I was so excited about having a part in such a daring defense of my kingdom that I could ignore my aches and pains for a while.

We stopped about twenty yards from the pile of boulders at the mouth of the small valley.

"Morys, get behind that outcrop, and I'll wait on the other side," Peytynn said then turned to me. "And you can find a cozy roost up there close to that outcrop. There are plenty of places not too high up where you can find cover."

I smiled at him. "I am a good marksman, you know."

He looked at Morys' clothes hanging off my emaciated frame. "Of that I have no doubt, Prince Tyrcel. But with all due respect, our hope is that Teo and Destyr, and that contraption of my brother's, will be all we need."

It was a good plan but too open-ended for my tastes. I slung the short-bow over my shoulder and climbed about twenty feet up the pile of boulders to a comfortable ledge. The climb had sapped my strength, and I was glad that I would be able to lie down for a while and possibly even shoot arrows without standing up because I had no intention of sitting idly by if there was anything I could do to help. The ledge also had a few decent-sized rocks behind which I could take cover.

From this height, I could see all the other Skirmishers, including Lyum up by the tripod, and Teo and Destyr near the cross-cable. And not too far away I saw a light plume of dust rising behind the five approaching scouts. They were coming from the west side of the switchback and would be at the pass within minutes.

Peytynn stood behind the pile of boulders that lay almost directly below me, and Morys crouched behind the large outcrop on the other side of the path. Suddenly Peytynn scrambled around the rocks and out onto the path. The plume of dust was almost at the turn to the pass, and Peytynn walked directly toward it. This was not part of the plan that had been explained to me.

He was sandwiched between two cliffs, and the clumps of lowland grasses and shrubs along the path offered no cover.

The riders reached the gravel path just before the turn where they would have to move in single file through the pass. Peytynn stopped walking, and I realized what he was doing. He was standing in a spot that would hopefully compel the enemy scouts to halt within range of Teo and Destyr's swing attack.

The five horsemen came around the corner and immediately noticed Peytynn. They slowed down, but the path was narrow and as the scouts thinned out into single file, the horses jerked nervously at their reins. They spread out, a few of them walking through the grasses and thorny shrubs. When they were within about fifty yards of Peytynn, they halted.

The leader kept his eyes on Peytynn, while the others scanned the cliffs and hills, but the thin cross-rope was hidden directly above them by the glare of Telios' bright light. The five riders all had one hand on a sword hilt as their nervous mounts fidgeted beneath them.

"You there, Austringer," the leader called. "Identify yourself."

Peytynn yelled, "I'm Peytynn."

The riders looked at one another, obviously confused by the audacity of a young boy standing out in the open like this. I was hoping these scouts were second-wave soldiers who hadn't been extensively trained on Austringer battle tactics. However, it did not take a veteran soldier to know that they were in a risky position sitting at the bottom of this canyon.

The lead rider came forward and drew his sword. "All right then, Peytynn. You're going to have to put that spear down and come with us."

The rider stopped about ten feet from Peytynn. I was starting to get worried, but Peytynn coolly stood his ground. I looked around at the other Skirmishers, and Teo caught my eye. He motioned for me to wait. Peytynn shuffled a few inches back, but did not drop his weapon.

The rider leaned forward in his saddle and yelled, "Boy! Peytynn! Did you not hear what I just told you to do?"

Peytynn lifted the weapon and held it out toward the rider.

"Drop it on the ground, boy," he yelled.

Peytynn did as he was told, and at the same moment, there was a loud pop somewhere above our heads. The scouts pulled their swords out and scanned the hills around them.

I was guessing Lyum's contraption had no real ability to aim accurately because Peytynn began slowly backing up, as though he didn't want to be too close to the scouts when Lyum started shooting in earnest. Another pop sounded from up the hill, and Peytynn instinctively hunched his shoulders.

The lead scout saw Peytynn's reaction and opened his mouth to speak when suddenly there was another pop and his cheekbone spouted a burst of scarlet blood. He fell backward off his horse and landed on his spine across a large stone next to the path. His horse reared, jerked the reins out of the dying rider's fingers, and bolted back the way it had come.

Everything had happened so fast that the other four riders didn't react until their leader's horse was coming at them, causing their horses to shift uneasily. They tried to gain control of their mounts, but there were more pops and pieces of metal flying through the air. As they tried to pinpoint the source of the firing, a shadow swooped over them, and one of the scouts was pushed off his horse. The other scouts watched as he lay writhing on the ground with blood spilling from his neck. They frantically looked around but could see no signs of an enemy.

Another pop and then the next blur, and the third scout fell from his mount, blood gushing from his neck before he reached the ground. Both of the dead scouts' horses spooked and turned tail.

Teo and Destyr's swing attack had been a success. I looked over at them, but the smile froze on my face when I saw Destyr dangling by the rope only a short distance from the scouts. He must have misjudged the distance to the other side of the pass. The two remaining scouts had their swords drawn and were completely focused on him. I nocked an arrow and began to aim at one of the guards, but just then Morys ran out from behind the boulders. He was amazingly fast for such a huge boy, and his shoulders were almost as high as the first horse he came to. The scout glanced down just as Morys' battle-ax chopped him directly in the belly, knocking him from the horse.

The last scout looked from Destyr to his friend on the ground, whom some massive Austringer had just chopped practically in half. Destyr swung his legs back and forth to build momentum, and while the scout tried to control his horse and keep an eye above him, Peytynn hurled a bronze spear into the rider's chest.

I looked back at the plateau. From this angle, I could only make out the top of Lyum's head, but I could hear Destyr and Teo bragging as they swung across the gap and untied themselves from their rope tethers. Their attack had been better planned than I'd thought. I was reminded of what good Austringers they were.

Peytynn walked over and waved at me to climb down, while Morys cleaned his battle-ax blade on the pants of his kill.

When I reached the ground, I said, "I must say, for a bunch of fourteen-year-olds—"

"Twelve!" Lyum yelled from up on the plateau.

"For a bunch of kids, you guys are fearless."

Peytynn yanked his spear from the scout's chest and said, "Thanks, Prince Tyrcel. We may be young, but we know more than most Austringers twice our age."

"You're right," I said. I watched as all the riders' horses disappeared around the pass. "It won't be long before the other scouts see those horses. We should move quickly." I pointed to the five dead riders strewn about the pass. "Their weapons are too cumbersome, but they might have something else worth salvaging."

Teo called down from the ridge. "Looks like we have another group of them heading this way."

"It won't be easy to overpower a larger group of armed soldiers, no matter how good our strategy," said Peytynn. "Skirmishers, regroup at the plateau."

15

"There's a good forty men down there," I said.

I put the binoculars down and rolled onto my side to look back into the cave where the Skirmishers were gathering supplies and trying not to argue too loudly. "You boys need to do more hustling and less talking."

Peytynn's voice came from somewhere inside the cave. "Again with the *boys.*"

A moment later, he walked out of the cave with his rucksack over his shoulders and a spear in his hand. He looked out toward the pass where we had just made our ambush. It was half a league away, with some rough terrain between. The clamor of the soldiers could be heard echoing between the hills.

"It looks like we've made quite a stir," Peytynn said. "I don't think this cave is the safest refuge at this point, so we should head back toward the City Valley. We'll sneak in around the western foothills. There have got to be other skirmish groups we can join up with."

My gear was already packed, though I didn't have much besides a bit of food and a long-dagger the Skirmishers had given me. My own clothes were ruined, and I was still wearing Morys' hand-me-downs.

"I won't be joining you," I said.

Peytynn looked surprised. "You have other plans, Prince Tyrcel?"

"I've got to get back to the Overhang." I rose to my feet slowly. I was feeling stronger, but I was still plagued by stomach pains and a ravenous thirst. "I need to stop the lord-general and release my brother's falcons. Then I need to find out what has happened to my mother."

We stood staring down the valley at the dust cloud that was growing closer.

"I could use all of you Skirmishers back at the Overhang," I said. "I'm going to need trustworthy people. We've got to rally our warriors to defend the City Valley, if it isn't too late."

Peytynn smiled. "That sounds like as good a plan as any. You can count on the Skirmishers to be at your service."

"Not at my service," I said. "At my side. You have already proven your-selves in battle. You don't need me to order you around."

The rest of the Skirmishers came out of the cave with Lyum in the lead.

"Finally," he said, "I'm getting the respect I deserve."

"All right, Skirmishers," Peytynn said. "We're heading back to the Over-hang to help Prince Tyrcel clean out the scum who have been conspiring with Abbo Doldra. Plus," he added as he pointed over his shoulder, "we've got com-pany coming this way."

The footpath that led down from the cave initially headed north in the general direction of the oncoming soldiers, but we were down the hillside long before our enemies got close enough to see us. When we reached the valley, we headed south toward the Overhang. Again, I found myself on the path that I had stumbled along when I escaped from Heike. The wound on my neck throbbed with a constant, dull ache, as if it had a memory all its own.

At the spring pool, we filled our water skins and paused for only a few minutes' rest. We were all eager to keep moving.

Despite my fatigue and discomfort, the closer we got to the Overhang, the more determined I became. I set a pace that none of the younger men could match for long and gave short, curt answers to their questions. We reached Gavina and moved up the footpath that led to the eastern assault-drop landing. I reached the landing so quickly that I had to wait for the others to catch up.

The drop-cables whirred endlessly along the well-oiled pulleys. While I waited, I tightened the straps on the harness that was built into my pants and vest. But Morys' clothes were so big on me that no matter how tightly I cinched the straps, they were never as tight as I would have liked.

Morys came up and started hooking himself into the straps, and he was about to latch into a cable when he glanced over at me, taking in the situation with a worried look.

"It's okay," I said. "This will be tight enough."

He nodded, but he didn't look convinced. "Just to make sure, I'll ride below you on the same cable."

"What are you going to do, catch me?" I asked.

"If I have to."

It sounded ridiculous, and it reminded me of my weakened state. But it did make me feel better.

I waited while the others latched onto their own cables and began rising up the side of the mountain. Then I connected with a passing loop, and Morys waited a few seconds for the next loop to come by. I dangled off the cable, and my weight sank uneasily down into the straps that were sewn into the hips of my pants. It was not a comfortable ride, and I prayed I would not slip through the straps and need Morys to catch me.

These particular cable lines stopped at the main platform at the Austringer armory. The armory was over half a league high, in the very bottom of the eastern section of the Overhang. From halfway up the mountainside, I could see the small contingent of enemy soldiers who had been tracking us. They were at the base of Gavina leading up to the east assault-drop landing. I knew that, like most enemies who came upon footpaths made by Austringers, this group was thinking how difficult it was going to be for them to ascend. The path was carved into the side of the mountain in such a way that Austringers could get down without being noticed should they need to move to the lowlands for a ground assault. It was no wider than two men across and uncomfortably steep—two traits that an invading army would take seriously.

As the cable pulled me higher, my lungs tightened. I had been down in the lowlands for so long that I had started to become unacclimated to the thinner air of these heights. I took long, slow breaths and watched the platform come into view.

Clouds still covered the armory's platform holes, but I could hear the thuds of the other boys unhooking then landing safely on the metal platform above. A single cable had a descending side and an ascending side, and at a platform like the armory's, the cables moved through portals through which Austringer warriors, in full battle gear, could be dropped or lifted.

The cables moved slowly enough that an Austringer warrior was able to get his feet onto the platform and unhook himself without slowing down the next warrior.

I rose through the portal, lifted my feet to the edge, and pushed up and out of the cable loop with Morys right behind me. Luckily the armory platform was empty of any other Austringers. We were relatively safe here, but the sight of me was sure to raise eyebrows. I would have to act quickly.

Giving the others no time to rest, I headed for the platform steps that disappeared into a darkened corridor. They led to the armory's other offices, the War Room, barracks, and the mess hall. Above all these sections and offices—out on a veranda built with thick glass walls—were the royal roosts, where my family kept our falcons.

When we reached the mess hall level, we were no longer the only people on the steps. Officers of all ranks were moving in every direction. Some paused thinking they might have just seen a Buteo prince, but my baggy clothes must have led them to believe otherwise and I avoided making eye contact. I saw none of the rich barons who had access to these wings of the Overhang.

We kept moving, giving any potential enemy little time to register who we were. I had to find the lord-general fast, before any spies or traitors got word back to him. We continued up the steps to the level that contained the War Room and then up to the landing outside its east entrance. Silently we moved behind the large pillars on both sides of the rear entryway. Two massive

oak doors were closed on the opposite west entrance to isolate all the officers
and decision-makers from the outside world. Although the War Room had not
been used for a long time, I was certain that just outside those doors stood two
sentries.

"Let's move," I said to my companions. We stood up and hurried around
the massive central table. "We've got to get through those doors quickly so
we can be out of the room and facing the guards before they know what has
happened. They won't recognize me at first, and we'll use that to get close and
subdue them."

"Subdue them?" Peytynn asked.

"We don't know if they're loyal to my family or to the lord-general," I said
as we reached the doors. "Who knows, they might be happy to see me, but we
can't assume they will be."

I rubbed the wound on my neck, took a deep breath, and yanked the doors
open. I was right: Two guards were standing sentry outside the War Room. At
the sight of us so suddenly behind them, they jumped to attention. But they
quickly realized that we were not any type of officer or baron.

"Halt," one yelled, but he sounded more surprised than authoritative.

We looked like children. For once, my sparse beard came in handy. I stood
in front of the guards, just out of spear range, and the Skirmishers arranged
themselves behind me. Most common warriors did not see their royal leaders
very often, so these guards did not seem to recognize me as Prince Tyrcel Buteo.

Besides, everyone likely believed the traitors on our hunting trip had suc-
ceeded and the king's sons were dead.

"What are you doing in the War Room?" the first guard asked.

"We were down at the mess hall, having a bite to eat," I said.

The guards moved their spears in front of their chests. One of them
stepped closer. "If you were just in the mess hall, why didn't you take the west
stairs?"

Only officers and barons used the east staircase, a fact a bunch of kids
might not have known. Warriors used the west stairwell because it had direct
access to all the other facilities, and these guards expected us to know that.

The guard pressed the tip of his spear to Peytynn's chest, and the other
Skirmishers started to protest, which only made the guard angrier. The second
guard pointed his spear at me, and I lost my patience.

"Enough!" I said. "The Overhang is my home, and I will walk through
any room I please."

The guards looked at me in amazement. I stepped forward with my chest
and shoulders high and said, "I am Prince Tyrcel Buteo."

The guards snapped to attention reflexively, but then stepped back and
exchanged nervous glances before turning back to me.

"They told us there are no more Buteos," the second guard said.

"Clearly, they were wrong," I said. "Tell me what Lord-general Tuecyr has done with my father, King Jorgen Buteo."

The guards looked at each other again, and the first one shrugged. "He took his last flight nearly a fortnight ago. His body was found in the crags above the Lord's Hall veranda."

I stumbled backward, dazed, and almost lost my balance, but Peytynn put a hand on my arm. In my heart, I had known he was gone. How else could the traitors have been so successful? But hearing the words overwhelmed me. Aillil should have been there to take over. But he was gone, too. I seethed with anger at the lord-general and prayed that he had not harmed my mother.

The guards recovered their senses before I did. The first one came toward me with his spear drawn and said, "Tyrcel Buteo, under orders from the high council, you are under arrest."

"This man is your king," Peytynn protested, still gripping my arm. The other Skirmishers moved in closer, fierce looks on their faces.

The guard started to grab my other arm when the butt end of Morys' ax handle cracked against the side of the guard's head, dropping him to the ground. The other guard jumped back and raised his spear. He trembled slightly, likely having seen no combat outside the training drills and sparring courts of the gymnasium. But the doors to the War Room were now behind him, closed and blocking his retreat. With a swipe of my arm, I knocked the shaft of the spear out of my way then delivered a quick chop to the side of the guard's neck. He fell to the ground, alive but unconscious.

I looked back at Morys, who was now holding his battle-ax upright and ready. For all their technological breakthroughs, these Skirmishers had brawn, and I was grateful for it.

"Hold on, Morys, don't chop him in half yet," I said. "Drag them into the War Room, and let's keep going." I did not want my first act as a king to be the killing of two common guards.

We moved the guards' bodies and headed back to the landing outside the War Room.

"Down these steps is the west hall that leads to the main thoroughfare," I said. "Tuecyr's quarters are three floors up from there. We need to get there without being seen. I want to surprise him."

Peytynn interrupted, "Forgive me, but how do you suppose we're going to get up three flights of stairs without being seen?"

I smiled, excited to take my new friends through one of the many secret passageways in the Overhang, used only by Austringer royalty.

"Trust me. I know a few tricks," I said. "For the short walk to the inner staircase, just act natural." I brushed some dirt and dust off Lyum's shoulders. "And tidy yourselves up a bit. We don't want to look suspicious." I straightened the belt and harnesses on Destyr's vest. "And for the sake of the Sirens," I continued, turning and addressing Morys, "shoulder your weapons. There should be no reason for anyone to have their spears or axes drawn. That will only attract more attention."

As we started down the steps, I was blissfully unaware of the pain that throbbed in my neck. I only felt the excitement of finally avenging my father.

I knew there would be two men at the bottom of the wide staircase guarding the entrance from the outside thoroughfare to the War Room's stairs.

I turned back to the Skirmishers and said, "Keep the pace quick and natural, like anyone who belongs here would. We're just six friends walking around town. These men will assume we're important if we're coming out of the War Room."

They nodded. "After all," I added, "this is our home, too. None of us are doing anything wrong."

Halfway down, the two guards snapped to attention, and the guard on the right leaned forward and opened the wide door for us to pass through. The Skirmishers walked past the guards with heads held high, avoiding eye contact.

The doors opened onto another landing at the top of a wide set of stairs that disappeared down a long, curving hallway. The main thoroughfare of the Overhang was at the bottom of this stairway. I moved slowly down the steps, and once the guards closed the doors behind us, I crept back up the steps to the landing. At the far left side, I pressed both my hands against the stone wall. The Skirmishers eyed me nervously, no doubt wondering if I had lost my mind.

"Aha," I said, as my right hand touched a stone just below the ceiling. I dug two fingers into the top and heard a small click. Then I pushed the larger stones that were right in front of me. They moved back into the wall as if weightless, creating a new opening. I motioned for the Skirmishers to pass through.

From the other side, the door was a facade of thin stones with a metal backing attached to the side wall. This false facade moved easily and quietly on well-oiled hinges and was designed to automatically spring shut. I let go, and it swung to a close, leaving us in the faint, blue-white light admitted by the open windows carved into the wall that rose above us.

We stood at the bottom of a long staircase that wound up and out of sight around a high curve. The wall to our left was lined with windows that ascended with the stairs at a height of exactly five feet. As we took the steps, all of us, except Lyum, had a clear view out the windows. The higher we went, the breeze through the windows grew blustery, as if we were out on some mountain bluff.

The steps had been carved out of the huge stone column on our right. I looked back at the others and said, "Be careful. Some of the steps are loose."

They looked puzzled until we rounded the column and they saw a massive hole in the wall to the left, a remnant from the Day of a Thousand Quakes. The gap in the wall was as high as twenty men and came all the way down to the steps. At many points, there was nothing between us and the sky. Telios' light beamed in and mixed with the strong wind that howled as it got caught in the stairwell. A small group of pigeons flew up at our approach, and I reflexively grabbed the hilt of my long-dagger.

Outside the windows, clouds blew by, and in between, we could see the Spring Sisters and the City Valley. Abbo Doldra's army was somewhere close to those mountains.

As we passed the open wall, we felt the blustery wind at our backs. The climb seemed to get steeper with each step. Morys was the last in line, and he fell farther behind with each breath, but by the time we reached the top, I was just as winded. Along the way, we passed many small side landings that were carved into the center column. They were the secret entries to other passageways hidden throughout the Overhang.

As we climbed higher, the light faded, and we soon came to a landing so small that only one of us could stand on it at a time. I whispered for them to stop. The steps ended at a wall right in front of us. Again, I swiped my hand across the stones until I heard a pop. A small line of light appeared running down the wall in front of us. The light grew as I slowly pulled a door inward, which forced us to move back down a few steps. The Skirmishers whispered curses as they stepped on one another's toes.

I put a finger to my lips, and the Skirmishers promptly stopped talking.

"The door to Tuecyr's office is at the far end of this hallway," I whispered.

Like most halls in the Overhang, this one had been carved around a central column, so I couldn't get a clear view down it. I was hoping the lord-general didn't feel the need for a lot of guards, but things had changed since I'd left the Overhang for the eyas hunt. There was no telling how paranoid Tuecyr was now, despite the seeming success of his coup d'état. He also knew all the secret passageways as well as I did.

"I'm guessing that the lord-general is not out protecting our city, so he's probably in his quarters," I said.

"Trying to run the kingdom from his desk," Peytynn said with a sneer. "The Skirmishers are ready, King Tyrcel. Let's take back our Overhang."

I wasn't sure I'd ever get used to being called king, but I was glad to have such trustworthy allies. Trust mattered just as much as physical strength.

Because there were few actual ends to the hallways in the Overhang, we stepped out into the middle of it. Anyone could have been approaching from either direction, but I was willing to take that risk. I also reasoned that anyone who was in the lord-general's vicinity was most likely a co-conspirator, and I would have no problem quieting them with a fist to the jaw.

We hurried along the curve of the inside wall, moving as quietly as possible so we might hear any approaching footsteps. I pulled out my long-dagger and held it at the ready. With our backs to the central pillar, we crept until I knew we were near our destination. I motioned for everyone to stop and leaned forward just enough to get a view of the doors that led to Tuecyr's office. Two guards stood on the landing outside the door. In front of them was a flight of steps that led to the main thoroughfare on this level. I was hoping there were no more guards down those steps.

I looked back at my crew. "Morys and I are the biggest, so we'll take the lead. We've got to move fast, and we have no choice but to take these guys out. I don't trust anyone in the lord-general's quarters. The rest of you follow directly behind us. Understood?"

They all nodded.

Morys moved next to me, and we stepped into the middle of the hall. We began walking quickly, and the two guards must have heard us coming because they were looking in our direction when we rounded the central pillar. They had their spears positioned in front of them, but they looked confused at the sight of our dirty, youthful faces.

Nevertheless, they ordered us to halt. "Identify yourselves."

Without slowing my stride, I said, "I am Tyrcel Buteo."

As I approached the guards, I slid my long-dagger behind my forearm. The guards widened their stance and brought their spears down to force us to stop. But there was still about ten feet between us, and I continued moving forward as I spoke.

"I am now your king. I advise you to drop your weapons or pay the penalty for treason."

The guards did not budge. The one on the right was about to sound the alarm when Peytynn's spear crashed into his chest. Blood splashed against the other guard, distracting him enough that I was able to leap past his spear and get a clean swipe of my long-dagger across his throat. He dropped his spear and clutched his neck. Blood ran fast through his fingers. I jumped behind him and caught his body as it fell and laid him, wild-eyed, on the landing. I looked up at Peytynn. He had a look of grim determination on his face. None of us relished having to kill our own countrymen. I had accepted it as a necessity, but just the thought of having to kill Austingers filled me with sadness. I could only imagine the toll it was taking on my young friends.

We turned our attention to the doors leading to Tuecyr's office. I tried the handle and found that they were unlocked. When I pushed, they easily swung wide open.

"Move fast, Skirmishers," I said.

16

I charged into the room and saw a flicker of movement. My training reflex made me dive forward just as Tuecyr released an arrow toward the doors. I rolled clear of the arrow's path, but Morys was right behind me. The arrow bored its way through his shoulder. He screamed and dropped to the ground, and the Skirmishers crowded around him.

Except for Peytynn. He followed my lead, and we flanked the lord-general, weapons drawn. Tuecyr didn't have time to nock another arrow, so he dropped his bow and sat back in his chair. Peytynn cocked back his spear, ready to plunge it into Tuecyr, but I stopped him.

"Not yet," I ordered.

Peytynn lowered his arm, and I moved to stand in front of the desk. Tuecyr looked up at me with a mixture of surprise and contempt. His hair and clothing were disheveled.

Then he looked away from me and waved his hands in the air as if I was wasting his time. "Do what you came to do," he said. "Let's get this over with."

I stood silent for a moment. Now that I was in front of the man who had orchestrated this treason, I hardly knew where to start.

"My brother is dead because of you," I said.

"You were all supposed to be dead."

"Even my father, your king?" I asked.

Tuecyr smiled, but it was a wretched sight. "Well, young prince, I did have plans for him but he took care of things himself. I never laid a finger on him. I did, however, personally see to the disposal of his body."

I tightened my grip on the long-dagger.

"And my mother?"

Tuecyr's smile hardly changed as he said, "I wish I knew. She seems to have slipped away before I could find her. I've just been so busy these days."

"You mock me, traitor?"

Peytynn moved forward to strike the lord-general, but I waved him back. The wound on my neck ached, and I needed to get control of my emotions. Tuecyr's arrogance enraged me, but I was confident that my mother had escaped down into the Bellows of Gavina. These were the warm caverns that ran throughout the mountain and were home to countless supply routes and secret royal tunnels.

But I felt such sorrow for my father, a once-great man who had succumbed to madness. He hadn't been strong enough to save his kingdom from the likes of the lord-general.

And now I wasn't sure I wanted to be the new king. I had a sinking feeling that Heike's spell was permanent and likely deadly, but beyond that, I didn't think I had the stomach for the intrigue among the officers and the fat barons. Aillil would have handled it all better than I. I thought of him out there among the boulders, and then I remembered the parchment I had found in the falcon roost.

I scanned the lord-general's desk. It looked as unkempt as the man himself, but sitting in a few ceramic cups were piles of different wax balls and seals that were obviously not the lord-general's.

"Funny thing, Tuecyr," I said. "I found a message attached to a pigeon carcass in a falcon roost."

At first he gave me an impatient look, but then the meaning dawned on him. He gazed at me in disbelief.

"You forged Lord Hengry's seal, didn't you?" I said. "You've been forging any seal you needed to make your plans work."

I leaned forward and slammed my long-dagger into the top of the desk, making Tuecyr jump.

"Do you realize Doldra's army destroyed both of the Sentinels?"

The lord-general sat back in his chair and eyed me condescendingly. "Had everyone else played their parts properly, that would have been all that Doldra destroyed."

"You never can trust a traitor," I sneered.

"If Jasko had done his job, you wouldn't be pestering me now," Tuecyr said as he looked beyond me to the Skirmishers. "It was you and these...these children, wasn't it? You're the ones who destroyed a third of Doldra's army. I thought perhaps Aillil had survived, but you? There's even a rumor that Doldra himself died in your attack in the Hollow Valley."

"These Austringers were defending their homeland," I said.

The lord-general raised his voice. "Your defense has ruined an otherwise perfect plan and forced a passive invading force to change its tack." Tuecyr grabbed a chalice from his desktop and took a generous gulp of barley wine. "Doldra was supposed to wait outside the gates while I resolved the Austringer leadership situation. Then we would open the gates for him to pass peacefully through the city."

"What stopped you? Apparently, you had everyone bent to your will."

He looked up at me, wild-eyed. "It was not as easy as I thought it would be to sway our people to my point of view."

"Your point of view is treason and murder!" I shouted.

"We needed new leadership. The Midlyn Range could not wait while your father continued to practice his isolationist policies. Our City Valley would be overrun by migrants at some point. It was inevitable. I wanted to work with Abbo Doldra to make it happen without resorting to violence. Only then would we be able to avoid the in-fighting that always comes with the need for more space. Besides, you know as well as I that no invading horde of migrants would be able to survive up here."

I stared at him, amazed at his capacity for double-crossing people.

The lord-general took another drink of wine. "For the most part, the Austringer way of life would not have had to change much. But you had to interfere, and now the Spring Sisters and the City Gates are under siege. After your attack in the Hollow Valley, Abbo Doldra's horde is no longer waiting idly by."

"You bastard scum! Do you really think Doldra would have shared power with anyone? His army's trebuchets can bring down ancient mountains as if they were nothing but hills of dirt. He will make us prisoners in our own homes."

"Yes, yes, yes, I've heard all this before." The lord-general waved me off again.

"And yet you didn't listen?"

I moved closer to him, and he leaned over the other arm of his chair in an effort to put some space between us. He reached for his barley wine, but his nervous hand knocked the chalice off the desk. He watched as it rolled across the stone floor, avoiding my furious gaze.

"I might not be ready to be king," I said, "but I won't allow you to be the new Austringer leader. Your treachery cannot go unpunished."

I turned to Peytynn. "Bring your rope and follow me out onto the lord-general's balcony."

My dagger was still stuck in the desktop, and Tuecyr now lunged for it. But I was quicker and grabbed his wrist tightly until he let go. With my other hand, I wrapped my fingers around his neck. He gasped for breath while his face turned a deep red. I lifted him by his neck and slammed him into the wall behind his desk, then dragged him, kicking and gurgling, out onto the balcony. I threw him against the stone balustrade, and he rolled into a ball, spitting curses at all of my ancestors.

I turned to Peytynn. "Tie your rope to the balustrade."

As he did so, I leaned over the lord-general with my knee in his chest. "In the next life, you will never see the demons who rule the Hells as they torment you and eternally feast on your organs. Plus, my brother's falcons have a taste for eyes."

I pressed both my thumbs into the soft tissue of Tuecyr's eyes. He screamed and writhed in pain. I could feel the heat in my face, and the wound on my neck throbbed as my rage grew stronger.

Peytynn grabbed my shoulders and pulled me off Tuecyr. He gazed at my handiwork in horror and looked like he might be sick. I grabbed the rope from his hands, leaned back over Tuecyr, and wrapped the rope around his neck several times, then tied a slip knot that would tighten with his weight.

"You should be happy, Tuecyr. You will die before my falcons find you dangling in the wind."

I cinched the rope around his neck and pulled him up by it. The lord-general fought and spat as he was lifted, and he tried in vain to push my arms away. I forced him over the balustrade. He flipped backward with one last scream, the rope jerked to a tight snap, and suddenly all was quiet.

I leaned on the balustrade for a few minutes to catch my breath, adrenaline masking the pain in my neck and my fatigue. Peytynn was watching me with a mixture of respect and fear. We heard a sob from Tuecyr's office, and Peytynn suddenly said, "Morys!"

We hurried back into the room. The other Skirmishers were huddled around him, and I pushed my way into their tight little circle. Morys lay on the floor with his eyes closed and Tuecyr's arrow still stuck in his chest. Blood still trickled from the wound, but his skin was pale and waxy, and it was clear he was dead.

His friends had tears running down their cheeks. I was sad, too, and I remembered how I had cried for Aillil and how Marello had tried to make me act like a man and not show my grief. He had meant well, but I wouldn't do the same to these boys.

I walked over to Lyum, who was sobbing the loudest, and put my hand on his shoulder. "Morys will never be forgotten," I said. "His memory will be honored by all of us and by all loyal Austringers."

Lyum continued to cry as he wriggled out from under my hand.

"We should send him on his final flight. It's the honorable way for any Austringer warrior."

The boys nodded, and I looked at Peytynn. "I have more work to do, but you don't have to come with me."

Peytynn shook his head. "Now more than ever, we are with you, King Tyrcel."

I was glad to see the boys had not lost heart. They might be young, but they were true Austringer warriors. The wound on my neck began to throb and I tensed in anticipation of another bout of pain. Sure enough, a sharp pain in my abdomen echoed with each beat of my heart as the burning sensation in my neck slowly faded. I pressed my hand hard against the new ache in my belly as a loud clamor came from the hallway.

The Skirmishers drew their weapons and turned to face the door, making a tight perimeter around Morys' body. Through the open doorway, we could see a large group of Austringer warriors running toward us. I grabbed my dagger from the desk and pushed in front of the Skirmishers just as the approaching warriors reached the threshold and stopped.

I attempted a nervous diplomacy first. "Tell your men to stand down, commander. We need to talk."

These warriors were in full battle dress with their masks pinned across their mouths and their visors down to protect their eyes. Blood was spattered across many of their faces and arms. The leader raised his hand, and I tensed, my hand tight on the dagger. The Skirmishers shuffled behind me, and I knew they were closing ranks and ready to do battle.

The lead guard lifted his visor and said, "Prince Tyrcel?" I instantly recognized the voice. The guard removed his face mask. "It's me, Cony."

I stepped forward to clasp his wrist, and we shook hands and hugged like two best friends who hadn't seen each other in a long time.

"Cony, you old bugger. You have no idea how good it is to see you. What are you doing in the lord-general's hall?"

"We've come to take back the Overhang, Prince Tyrcel," he said, holding me out at arm's length. The other warriors began removing their masks and visors, looking relieved. I flushed with pride knowing that Cony wasn't going to stand down in the face of treason.

He expression grew serious as he took in my face, neck, and disheveled clothes. "What in all the Hells happened to you?"

"The other men in the hunting party were traitors. All except Marello."

Cony nodded. "I've heard rumors." He glanced around the room. "And Aillil? Is he with you?"

I cleared my throat. "He didn't make it. But he died an honorable death."

Cony startled, as if from a sudden shock. "Your brother was a good man and a good friend." He composed himself and said, "But I am glad to see you are still alive. And where is Marello now?"

"Gone, too," I said, regretting that I had to be the bearer of so much bad news. "Heike got him."

"By the Sirens!" Cony said.

Peytynn came to stand beside me. "Are you sure we can trust him?" he asked. "There have been a lot of surprises lately."

"This man is a good friend of my brother's, of mine," I said without hesitation. "He's a captain in the royal guard and a trustworthy warrior. Besides, if he'd wanted to kill us, he would have done it by now."

Cony's sorrowful face quickly turned back to that of a focused warrior. He peered around me to the empty chair at Tuecyr's desk.

"I take it the lord-general is not in?"

"Not anymore," I said and couldn't help smiling.

Cony's gaze trailed over to the rope hanging from the balustrade, and his look changed to one of surprise and respect. He cocked his head. "I don't suppose you and your men here are the ones who wreaked all that havoc on Doldra's army out in the Hollow Valley?"

"Indeed we are," I said, and the Skirmishers puffed out their chests with pride.

"Well done," Cony said, looking at each Skirmisher in turn until his gaze fell on Morys' body.

"Unfortunately, we lost a good man."

Cony nodded. "He needs a proper send-off."

The Skirmishers sniffled at that, and before they could break into tears again, I said, "Wrap Morys in some of those tapestries hanging in the lord-general's office. We're too far from the Pyre Hall, so just leave his body on the veranda and we'll retrieve it later. We're not going to just toss him into the Corpse Crags. While you're doing that, I need to talk things over with Cony."

They immediately busied themselves getting Morys wrapped as ceremoniously as possible and moving him out onto the balcony. The custom for the death flight of an Austringer warrior is to set the corpse on fire to release the soul to the sky and then throw the ashes to the wind above the Pyre Hall's balcony. But we had no shrouds, oils, or flame, and as I took Cony aside, I watched the young Austringers give heartfelt remembrances above Morys' corpse.

"What is the state of the Overhang?" I asked Cony.

"It is in an awful state. No one is sure where your father is, and the lord-general had installed himself as the interim chancellor, without the consent of the Baron Council or the High Court. Once I realized what was going on, I rallied as many loyal warriors as I could find, and we have fought our way to this staircase in hopes of putting a stop to Tuecyr's treason. Since the invasion, the Overhang has operated only by the sheer will of desperate people."

He paused for a moment. "Since your father disappeared, there have been rumors that the people have lost faith in the power of the Buteos to lead them."

I couldn't blame them. With my father gone and no Buteo to take his place, it was easy to see why the people faltered. I wondered if I had the power to restore the Austringers' faith, but there were more pressing matters at the moment.

"According to Tuecyr, my father has taken his final flight," I said.

Cony again looked shocked. We had no reason to believe Tuecyr had lied about it. I tried to keep our focus on the task at hand.

"What is the state of our defenses?" I asked.

"Our warriors are in disarray. Half of them have been misled by the lies of the lord-general, but the other half have taken action. I have commandeered the City Gate war rig and have ordered it moved into position over the entrance to the Main Road. Smaller skirmish groups are creating havoc for Doldra's encampments in the western foothills."

"The warriors who have believed the lies of the lord-general—are they deeply committed or just confused?" I asked.

"I believe most of them can be persuaded to return to our side. But there are many who had their hearts set on new leadership and, of course, their own promotions."

The Skirmishers came to join us. Suddenly, my mind was clear and I felt like a young hunter falcon who has finally learned how to make quick and sure decisions.

"Cony, take your men and head back to where our scattered troops are. Inspire them with the news of my return, and let them know that I've come to save our Austringer civilization. Gather all our warriors at the Rig Docks and wait for me and my Skirmishers there. That will be our new command center. It is closer to the central hub and the direct routes to the two remaining fronts. From there we will wage our assault on the northern horde."

With that, we dispersed down the steps and into a lower hallway.

"I've just got to take a quick detour up to the roosts," I said. "I want to release Aillil's falcons."

Cony nodded, his face a mixture of anger and grief. "Of course, prince."

Without regard for their rank or numbers, Peytynn turned to face Cony and the warriors who followed him and said, "He's no longer Prince Tyrcel." His eyes met mine. "He's King Tyrcel now."

Cony and his men began to kneel in a show of respect and loyalty, but I grabbed Cony by the vest and pulled him to his feet. "We don't have time for ceremony now." The warriors all rose together. "Let's take care of Doldra's army first."

Cony smiled, clasped my wrist like Austringer warriors do, and ordered his men to move out. As we hurried down the hall, my neck throbbed and my stomach tightened in a quick spasm of pain.

"You okay, King Tyrcel?" Peytynn asked.

"Fine," I said, trying to keep from wincing.

17

I headed down the hall toward the flight of steps that led up to the royal falcon roosts with the Skirmishers close behind me. We ascended a winding flight of steps and ran down another hall that led west, around the center sections of the Overhang. The roosts were on the western face of Gavina, at the height just below where the granite cliffs had a permanent cover of snow and ice. It was from these roosts that we Buteos trained our falcons and released them for their hunting excursions.

Austringer hunter falcons were never hand-fed. Instead, they were released on a regular schedule to hunt vermin in the lowlands or goats off the cliffs of Gavina, or to feast upon the organs of any unfortunate criminal who might be dangling below a war rig or, as in the lord-general's case, his own balcony.

We burst into the tack room, where we were met by Amanto and his son Remond. They were wielding long ash staves, with the tips pointed at us. The two roost masters were a force to be reckoned with. They were strange mediums well practiced in an even stranger, almost magic art of self-defense. They were loyal to my family, but these last two remaining masters chose to live up in the peaks of the Overhang with the royal falcons. I knew the men well and had nothing but respect for Amanto.

"It's me, Tyrcel." I said, with my hands raised.

Amanto and his son lowered their staves. "My prince! These old eyes of mine weren't sure it was really you. You look like you have been dried out like old goat jerky over the cliffs of the city bluffs."

It was comforting to be in his presence. His seemingly infinite knowledge of falcons and his not-too-subtle wit always made me feel welcome—even when I knew I must look like a weathered piece of leather.

"Thank you for the kind words, Amanto," I said with a smile. "It is good to see you and Remond are okay."

"My son and I have been up here since the lord-general took over." He glanced toward the wall at the other side of the stairwell landing. There in the darkened corner were two Austringer warriors, obviously dead. "As you can see, Prince Tyrcel, we have been busy keeping pests out of the roosts while making sure the falcons remain on schedule."

I didn't know what was more unbelievable—that two Austringers were foolish enough to try to overtake Amanto and his son or that two common warriors would have the guts to enter the royal roosts.

Amanto looked around at the Skirmishers and asked, "Where is Aillil?"

Again, I felt the pain of having to explain how my brother had died. "He was killed by the traitors in our hunting party."

Amanto pursed his lips the way he always did whenever he was frustrated with Aillil or me. This time I knew he was frustrated with all the traitors.

"Amanto, I want to release Aillil's falcons," I said. "I'm not sure what's going on around here and if things get worse...well...I don't think you and Remond can defend these roosts forever."

Amanto moved past me without a word, grabbed the thin rope that hung around his neck, and pulled a single iron key from under his shirt. Like two men with the same brain, Remond had the door open as soon as his father unlocked it. I followed them inside and had to stop as a wave of pain throbbed deep in my chest. It left just as quickly, and I took a moment to catch my breath and get my bearings.

The roost had floor-to-ceiling cages carved into the mountain wall with a wide walkway in front and a long wall that separated the room from the sky. I was happy to see that the room was as tidy as it had ever been, though I was not sure if it was because Amanto was loyal to my family or the falcons.

"Like I said, my king, your brother's falcons have been groomed without any change in schedule."

The first few cages were empty. They belonged to father's hunters, but lately those falcons had been allowed to roam the sky all day and night. We walked down the short viewing path until we came to the cages that belonged to Aillil's two hunters. I was a decent falconer, but I did not yet have any birds of my own, so I was not the best at handling a mature hunter.

The Skirmishers waited anxiously near the doorway while I took a moment to reunite with Aillil's female hunter, Stella. I wore a glove and held her gauntlet in my other hand, and she sat on my bony arm looking nervously around the roost. Of all the falcons in my family, Stella had always been the most accepting of me. I stroked the back of my free hand down her breast feathers. Every few strokes, Stella would reach down and grab at my fingers with her beak. She seemed uncomfortable around me, as though she sensed a change in me.

Finally I slipped a brown suede hood over her head. It was sewn with fine gold thread and decorated with cloth of various shades of indigo and green. On top was my family's double plume and dagger crest. I moved my face closer to her. I loved the musty smell of her warm feathers. It reminded me of the smells that bounced off the wind-scoured cliffs of Hunter's Bluff. She opened her mouth in protest, threatening whatever might be getting too close.

I called to Remond, who was just coming in from the balcony hall. "Take care of Rymeo while I release Stella."

The roost master moved over to the cage that housed Aillil's second hunter. His son, already a few steps ahead of him, held open the gate to Rymeo's pen. This fine falcon was a male and so well trained that myths had already been written about the massive rams it had picked up off the cliffs of Gavina. Rymeo was the younger of Aillil's two hunters, and Stella was the alpha of the flock.

I started for the doorway out onto the balcony, but I stumbled and had to brace myself with my free hand against the wall. Stella squawked and jumped up from my arm, flapping her long wings wildly, but the gauntlet kept her tethered. I was not myself, and it made her edgy.

As silent and certain as ever, Amanto grabbed my struggling arm, then the gauntlet, and gently moved Stella to his own gloved arm. He disappeared behind the balcony door.

Peytynn walked over to me.

"You're not well," he said.

"I'm fine." I took a few more deep breaths and tried to regain my composure.

"You need to rest," Peytynn persisted.

"There's no time for that. We need to meet Cony at the west docks."

Peytynn started to protest, but I waved a hand at him impatiently.

I said goodbye to Amanto and left the roosts in his good hands. We made our way back down the winding stairs. From the hall outside the lord-general's quarters, we moved west along the central promenade that was the main hub of all traffic and activity in the Overhang.

Suddenly horns began to sound all around us. Instantly, all the people—citizens and warriors alike—stopped what they were doing and hurried off. The horns were the highest of all the warning alerts and only used in times of imminent attack. I was glad to hear them; it meant the Austringers were getting ready to defend their city. And it meant that Cony had not encountered any resistance he couldn't handle.

We hurried toward the barracks, where we would take the stairs down to the west docks.

"At the beginning of the invasion, there were no alarms at all," Peytynn said.

"Yeah," Destyr said. "It has taken them too long to sound that alarm."

We came to the barracks and passed through the main hall that led to the west vestibule, then wound our way down the many levels of the Overhang until we came to the western assault-drop station and the war docks. I began to lag behind, overcome by fatigue and pain, and the others paused several times to allow me to catch up.

At the bottom of the steps, we were stopped by two guards with their spears in front of them. The Skirmishers were moving so fast that they almost bumped into each other as they tried to stop.

"Halt!" cried one of the guards.

Peytynn stepped forward and slapped at the spears with his own, saying, "Halt yourself! You better watch who you're giving orders to. We stand here with the king of the Austringers, Tyrcel Buteo."

The two guards looked nervously at each other, not sure what to make of this disheveled person who claimed to be their king. Luckily, Cony came forward and told the guards to stand down.

"I apologize, King Tyrcel, but they were just doing their job," Cony said. "You can't be too careful these days."

"I won't argue with any Austringers who are doing their job," I said.

We clasped wrists, but my grip couldn't match Cony's. He eyed me, no doubt taking in my weakened state.

"Forgive me, king," he said in a low voice, "but this does not seem to be the same arm that threw me in our recent game of slip. Perhaps you should give your orders and leave the fighting to us."

I gritted my teeth against another wave of pain.

"Are you injured?" Cony asked. "That wound on your neck looks serious."

I tried to smile. "Marello wasn't the only one to do battle with Heike."

Cony looked at me in wide-eyed shock. "We must call a healer."

He started to signal to one of the guards, but I reached out a hand and stopped him. "There's no time. We have to deal with Doldra's army first."

"The Austringers cannot afford to lose another king," he said.

"I'm a king in title only," I said. "Besides, with men like you in charge—"

But he cut me off. "As the king and the last Buteo, you need to think of your people first," he said. "And right now, they need a king. Not a martyr."

I stared at him, surprised by his frankness. His cheeks started to color as he no doubt realized his blunder, but he held my gaze. "I appreciate your advice, Cony, but I am capable of making my own decisions."

He nodded and said, "Forgive me. I didn't mean to imply otherwise."

Then he followed me as I moved through the mob of warriors who were gathering and securing their gear. They were packing assault gear only. This would not be a long-term campaign. The fighting was in our own front yard, so we could go to battle then return to the Overhang after dark to recuperate.

"How close are we to launching a full-scale ground assault?" I asked Cony.

"The vanguard will be ready within the next twenty minutes, and the Gate Rig has begun to move into position."

As we walked toward the west docks, the breeze picked up. There were few closed doorways in this section of the Overhang, and the massive openings that accommodated the war rigs let in a lot of wind. At the rig bay, we walked up a small flight of stairs that led to a central office at the farthest corner of the bay. It was set up as the forward command center, and on one side it overlooked the bay and the western horizon. From the other side, we had a view of the western assault-drop station.

As we reached the top of the steps, the gate-rig stern rolled slowly out of the dock. It looked like the tail-end of a sailing vessel, only this one moved along massive cables, and when it had its sails out, they hung from below the hull. The rig was so big that it had its own cable-car ports and enough space for thousands of men to do simultaneous drop assaults. The wind blustered around us as the rig left the massive warehouse and for a few seconds created a vacuum that sucked the air out after it.

"What is the mood of our warriors?" I asked. "Have they rallied to our cause, or are they simply doing their jobs?"

"The majority are loyal, King Tyrcel. And any who are not are being detained. There is a long line of traitors waiting for their own personal stretcher cages. In the meantime, we have over twenty thousand loyal warriors who are ready to fight."

He looked at me with satisfaction. "I told them that you threw Tuecyr on his final flight. That has brought great relief to them. Forgive them—they were confused under the lord-general's spell."

"Let's be careful who we forgive too quickly," I said and gripped the handle of my long-dagger as pain racked my abdomen. "My brother and best friends are dead because of those traitors."

"Aillil was my best friend, my king," he reminded me, and I saw that he shared my anger. But he was also watching me with concern. "King Tyrcel...?" he began, but I cut him off.

"I'm fine." I took a deep breath and steadied myself.

Then the Skirmishers appeared at the top of the steps and I motioned them over. We all moved to a table in the middle of the office on which was spread a large map of the Midlyn Range that showed the positions of all of Abbo Doldra's forces, from the City Valley back to Port Tallion. We all knew our first act would be to push Doldra's forces away from our gates and the Spring Sisters.

I pointed to the foothills to the west of Doldra's army. "Their one weakness is that the trebuchets are only effective on distant targets. " I said. "Move a third of our men to the west and flank his troops from that direction. If we move fast, we can surprise them and get close enough that the trebuchets will be useless against us. It will be close combat, but these northern fighters are not well seasoned."

"Aye, King Tyrcel," agreed Cony. "The West Prairie is where the biggest threat is. Doldra's Hollow Valley contingent is in disarray, and the Main Road trebuchet can only get close enough to destroy the gates of the City Valley. But the trebuchets in the West Prairie can hit the West Spring Sister. It's there we need to focus. If we can do that, then the war rig will be in place when it comes time to take the Main Road."

I looked at my small squad of Skirmishers who stood around the table and said, "Cony, we've seen Doldra's forces. They may be many, but they are a mixture of mercenaries and loyal soldiers. I believe their fighting skills will be lax because they are hoping to survive in the shadow of those trebuchets. That's why we have to start the assault as soon as possible. If we hurry, we can prevent the City Valley from being taken."

"Yes, but Doldra's army has nowhere to retreat. They may be average fighters, but even an average fighter who is backed into a corner will fight with all his heart."

"That's why most of them will have to die," I said. "My small skirmish group and I will drop with the first wave of warriors. As the others set up and wait for the rest of the contingent, we will head north and gather some intelligence and see if we can't neutralize those trebuchets."

Cony glanced at the four teenage boys, clearly skeptical that they were capable of what I was proposing. But he didn't know them as well as I did.

"Everyone has their orders," I said. "Let's get to it."

Cony left to gather his gear and rouse the men's fighting spirit. Like any good Austringer leader, he would command the battle from the front lines, though this would be his first real battle. As the Skirmishers and I hurried to load our quivers and secure our drop-harnesses, Lyum spoke up.

"King Tyrcel, it might not be so easy to take care of the trebuchets the way we did in the Hollow Valley. It's later in the day and Telios' highest light is long over, and besides, it only works if we have my magnification unit."

"I understand, Lyum, but I am confident that you and the guys will come up with something."

I was in nearly constant pain by now and plagued by waves of fatigue, but I managed to shove as many arrows into my quiver as would fit and secured two long-daggers over my shoulders. I also scrounged up a better-fitting vest than the one Morys had loaned me. As I gathered up my gear, my head and body pounded. I couldn't tell if it was because of the sickness Heike had set on me or the anticipation of battle, but the heightened energy caused the muscles in my neck to tighten around my airway. The wound on my neck began to burn and throb in time with my heartbeat.

It was the worst flare-up yet, and it made me drop my quiver and stumble backward onto a bench. Lyum grabbed my arm and helped me to my seat.

"King Tyrcel, are you okay?" he asked.

I bent forward and clutched at my belly as I tucked my head to my chest to ease the throbbing in my neck. I gritted my teeth and held my breath as the pain in my belly slowly subsided. Sweat beaded on my forehead.

Finally, I managed to say, "Between you and me, I'm not sure how to answer that question."

18

Thousands of Austringer warriors traveled along the cables that ran between Gavina and the West Spring Sister, heading to the war docks and the assault-drop station. To the east, a small platoon and sentry were posted to watch the Hollow Valley, but it was every commanders' opinion that the East Spring Sister was not in any immediate threat. Doldra's front lines in the Hollow Valley had effectively been burned to cinders.

The warriors' goal was to drop to ground level then move through the foothills around the western end of Doldra's troops, who were encamped throughout the prairie. Meanwhile, Cony's contingent of warriors had entrenched themselves into defensive positions around the gates of the City Valley.

The Skirmishers waited patiently at the assault-drop platform at the back of the western war docks. My current bout of pain had subsided, though I knew it was only a temporary reprieve, and I hurried to slip my arms into my vest and cinch the harness straps tight.

Lyum came over to me, looking downhearted. "King Tyrcel, I've been thinking about it non-stop, and because it is late afternoon and there are more shadows than light, we're going to have to use the more cumbersome method of something like a flaming arrow."

I hooked my vest loop into a cable hook that was moving behind me, and as I jumped off the platform, I mustered what I hoped was an encouraging smile and said, "I knew you'd come up with something."

I was out of my hook less than a second after my feet hit the ground. As I secured my vest straps, I looked up and saw the feet of the rest of the Skirmishers coming down right behind me. In the distance to my right stood the City Valley gates. At this point, there was no way of knowing how many of Doldra's forces waited on the other side. The foothills of the West Spring Sister were to my left. It was through those foothills that I hoped to sneak up on the forces encamped on the prairie.

We had to skirt around the base of the West Spring Sister to reach the foothills. From there I hoped to move from hill to hill and see if we could get a clear shot at any of the explosive barrels. Lyum was right: We were going to have to use a burning arrow to try to ignite the powder or wait until morning for the sun to reach the right angle. Unfortunately, both options would more than likely reveal our position. But all I needed was one good shot with a burning arrow, then we could disappear into the foothills and regroup with Cony to secure the valley.

I fought fatigue at every step, but I was still moving faster than the Skirmishers. I paused on the footpath and waited for them to catch up.

"Keep up the pace, Skirmishers," I said. "We've got to figure out our best options by morning. That's when the western flank and the ground troops in the City Valley will be ready."

In a few hours, we were around the Spring Sister and out into the foothills. Another league of hills and small valleys lay between us and Doldra's forces. We were no longer within the protective boundaries of the City Valley walls, but that did not bother us. We preferred to be out moving around the hills, using our wits to wreak as much destruction on the enemy as possible.

As we wound our way closer to the front lines, we kept to the shadows of the lowest paths, which were about ten or twenty feet up. Most Austringers knew those paths well, and we often found ourselves among friends. About halfway to the front lines as night was beginning to fall, we saw a plume of smoke wafting out of a small cave entrance. We crept to the entrance and saw a group of ten Austringer warriors sitting inside. I startled them with a click of my tongue and a quick whistle, imitating a night-owl in a secret greeting often used by Austringers.

The men grabbed their weapons and stood at full alert as I stepped into the light of the small fire that burned and popped in its pit.

"I am Tyrcel Buteo," I announced and paused before adding the news that I was still getting used to: "Your new king."

The warriors, who were not much older than me, looked infused with a new energy, and I swelled with pride to think I had inspired such hope.

"What are you doing here?" I asked.

An eager warrior stepped forward. "King Tyrcel, we have a few other men up on the ridge. They're on lookout for any of Doldra's scouts."

"Have you had any success?"

The warrior smiled. "Ah, yes. More than you'd think. Once we kill the first few scouts, another group comes looking for them. So we kill them, and more are sent looking for them."

"You'd think they'd stop sending search parties out for the search parties that never returned," another man said. "As I'm sure you can imagine, up in these hills, it's like picking off kid goats with hammer spears at close range."

I nodded in approval. "Are there more skirmish groups like yours out here?"

"Aye, king. Lots of us are strewn about these hills," the first man said.

"Who is your commander?" I asked.

"We don't have one."

My confusion must have shown on my face, and I heard the Skirmishers shifting nervously behind me.

"We were never onboard with the lord-general's plan," the warrior said. "Little by little, groups like us dropped out and led our own counterinsurgency."

Just like the Skirmishers. My hopes had not been for nothing. I touched my fingertips to the wound on my neck as a small ache shot through my throat.

"How long has your group been here?" I asked.

"About a fortnight, King Tyrcel."

"And you are not worried about the trebuchets?"

"No, my king. The northerners don't seem to be able to easily move them through these hills. The paths are too tight, and the loose gravel and foothills make it difficult for them."

That eased my mind a bit. "Have you lost any men?"

"We've lost many. This group started out as a full platoon. But we are still maintaining fighting strength."

I was impressed by their perseverance. I gave them one last bit of information to inspire them.

"Keep up the good work, and know that the entire Austringer force is not far behind us, ready to level those trebuchets and any northerner who stands in our way."

All the men inside the cave pumped their right fists in the air but kept the volume of their cheers low because the night winds carried sounds easily. The lead warrior told me of a quick and effective route to a ridge that overlooked the front lines of Doldra's forces. He offered to guide us there, but I refused because I believed we Skirmishers needed to keep our numbers to a minimum to avoid detection.

"Stay alert," I said. "If everything works out, my friends and I will soon be starting the next fight and you will have your hands full."

I clasped wrists with the leader and left the cave. It was dark now as we crept along the path. The moons were full, but the Midlyn clouds blocked most of the light.

Doldra's scouts were a noisy bunch, which explained how they were so easily killed. But now they traveled in groups of nothing less than twenty, so we thought it best to avoid them. Often we found ourselves a few feet above a group of enemy scouts, and if there were no boulders to duck behind, we had to stretch out flat and hope not to be noticed. There was more activity here than we had experienced in the Hollow Valley, and we were not prepared for it, so we were grateful for the darkness.

We finally reached a long ridge that overlooked the middle of Doldra's western contingent. Kneeling behind a cluster of boulders that lined the ridge, we scanned the enemy's encampment with our spyglasses. The reflections of the campfires glowed amber on the side panels of the tents set up throughout the prairie.

Teo used his custom binoculars. "They have arranged their trebuchets with more space between them," he said. "They're staggered and well in front of the troop tents and trenches. They are just within range of our heavy-bows, but it's hard to see any of the barrels, so hitting one will be lucky at best." He lowered the binoculars and turned to me. "Looks like they're not going to be fooled twice."

I had been hoping for a quick attack so the western contingent and forward assault force could move in quickly to finish the job. I looked around at the other Skirmishers.

"We are all Austringer archers, the best bowmen who have ever lived," I said. "We're going to have to rely on quantity to hit a barrel, as opposed to marksmanship."

They looked dubious, and Lyum said, "Let's not forget that I am half the archer that you guys are. I'm only twelve, remember? I haven't had as much time to practice."

"Okay," I said, "but that still leaves four of us. We'll use Lyum as our eyes. Once we choose a particular group of barrels, he'll keep his eyes on it and guide our shots. Destyr, get a small fire started behind those boulders. We need to get as many burning arrows in the air all heading in the same general direction before the fire is spotted."

My friends looked at me as if I was a lunatic. "If one of you has a better idea, I'm ready to listen."

The plan was far-fetched but not beyond the realm of possibility. Besides storming directly into the camp and igniting a barrel, which would be a suicide mission, this was our best option.

Destyr gathered a small pile of kindling for the fire while the rest of us set out all the half-pound arrows. These arrows had more than enough weight to pierce the ceramic barrels. As we wrapped each of the razor-sharp tips in oil-soaked strips of cloth, I hoped that somewhere in that group of arrows was one that would hit its mark.

"Find our best target," I told Lyum. "Something within range and easily spotted."

He used Teo's custom binoculars to locate a suitable target. Telios was just beginning to rise over the Sun Point Mountains, throwing a pink haze across the West Prairie.

"See that tent with the four banners on each corner, and the larger banner in the center peak?" he asked.

We all told him we could see it.

"Look to the west side of it and back about fifty paces to the first trebuchet you come to." When we didn't respond immediately, he took the binoculars away from his face. "Well? Are we all together here?"

"Yes, we're all together, Lyum," I said.

"How much time did you say you wanted to waste?" he said and gazed back through the binoculars. Peytynn shot him an angry look, but I couldn't help smiling.

"Again, look to the west of that trebuchet's base and you'll see a few barrels. They're stacked on top of each other. Those will be our best options from this height and angle. Should be well within our range."

I gave the final order. "Light the arrows. I'll fire first, then we'll go down the line so Lyum can more effectively guide each bowman. Listen to his guidance as each arrow is shot, and adjust your aim accordingly."

We dipped our oiled arrow-heads into the embers of the small fire, then raised our heavy-bows in the direction of the barrels. The arrow tips sparked and flared to a blue flame. I began the volley.

Lyum called out, "Good shot. Can use less angle on the ascension." I immediately loaded my next arrow, adjusted the angle and aim, and fired my second shot.

Peytynn aimed and fired his first shot. It flew from his bow with a twang.

Lyum said, "Good shot. Move ten degrees east, and put greater rise on the ascension."

Peytynn followed my lead and immediately lit, loaded, adjusted, and fired the next shot.

Destyr and Teo followed suit, with Lyum adjusting their first shots. Soon the sky above the West Prairie was lit by more than just the morning light. A small barrage of burning arrows hissed and flew toward a single target. They all landed close to their target, but none hit the barrel.

The soldiers who were standing guard around the trebuchet started yelling, and the entire encampment sprang into action.

Lyum began to call out adjustments more rapidly. "Give it a steeper ascension so it has less angle of descent," he called out. "Dammit, Destyr, a steeper ascension for you, too. You're all shooting way too far, and you're revealing our position with every damn shot you waste."

We each had a single remaining arrow and knew that after our last shots, whether they paid off or not, we would have to retreat. Once the enemy pinpointed our position, those trebuchets could have a barrel on top of us within minutes. But regardless of who triggered the explosion, it would signal the rest of the Austringer militia to move out en masse.

"Concentrate, dammit," Lyum hissed.

"Be calm, breathe deeply, and listen to Lyum's adjustments," I said.

We adjusted our angles and in a single moment sent four arrows into the air. They all flew in a thick smoking trail that soon separated as each arrow found its own path.

"That looks good," Lyum called. "Your best shots yet. Descent looks good. The first one missed. Looks like those suckers are ready with buckets of water. The second one missed. Too much angle, Teo. Dammit! The third one missed, too. Wait!" he screamed, forgetting he was almost within enemy lines. "The last one hit!"

He dropped to the ground in anticipation of an explosion. All the other Skirmishers followed suit, but nothing happened. Lyum slowly got back up and peered through the binoculars.

"They doused all our arrows, though it looks like one is sticking out of the barrel," he said. "It's funny, though. None of the soldiers are lingering near that particular trebuchet."

"How many soldiers are headed this way?" I asked.

"There doesn't seem to be anyone coming to get us," he said. "But I'm sure they had our location by the third volley of arrows. I saw men pointing this way. Uh-oh!"

"What is it?" Peytynn asked.

Lyum took one last look through the binoculars then grabbed his rucksack and swung it over his shoulders. "They're loading the trebuchets."

We slid down the gravelly slope to the footpath and bolted south, back toward the City Valley where our comrades were waiting. We had not gone a hundred feet when the first explosion occurred. It knocked us to the ground. The blast hit the ridge where we had just been hiding, and debris rained down around us.

I lifted my head up, coughing and wiping dust from my face, and my neck started to tingle. I clenched my teeth, determined to ignore the pain. With my hand pressed hard into my neck, I stood and ran to catch up with the rest of the Skirmishers, but I was having trouble breathing. Lyum dropped back a few paces to run next to me. He grabbed my arm and tried to move me along, but I could not go any faster. Instead, I began to slow down. Then I doubled over.

More explosions rocked the hills behind us, getting closer and louder. By now all the Skirmishers had surrounded me. Destyr and Teo paced and watched the perimeter as Peytynn and Lyum knelt beside me. Through the din and the never-ending rain of dirt and rocks, Lyum yelled into my ear, "You've got to keep moving."

Plumes of dark smoke tailed each blast, and clouds of stones and dirt were lifted into the air and then fell back out of the sky. Massive tree trunks and boulders were thrown in every direction. Then we all saw it at the same time, flying through one of the smoke clouds. A small dark barrel flipped end over end. At the top of its arch, it looked like it was suspended in the air for several seconds. Then as it began to descend, it seemed to defy all the laws of physics and tumbled forward, directly toward the hill to our right. A flame burned in a glass globe in the very center of the barrel.

"They're igniting them with an oil globe," Destyr said. "When the barrel hits something, it is smashed to pieces, along with the burning oil in the globe, which sets off the explosion."

Destyr and Teo looked at each other with the keen eyes of engineers who realized that someone else has come up with a great idea. Then the top of the hill above us separated and lifted up into the air with a deafening roar, and we were thrown backward on top of one another.

The larger debris settled, but smaller dust particles filled the air. Peytynn helped me up as the Skirmishers moaned and swiped dust off their shoulders and legs.

Destyr pulled and poked at his ears, and Teo also fidgeted with his. He rubbed them for a few seconds then took his hands away. He squinted his eyes and looked left and right as if searching for something. Then he tilted his head, listening.

"Wait a minute," he called out in a loud voice. "I think I've gone deaf."

We all tried our best to listen past the ringing in our own heads. A strange silence filled the valley, but it was not because any of us had gone deaf. It was because there were no more barrels flying through the air. The explosions had stopped.

Destyr was the first to answer. "Deaf, huh? Do you still hear the ringing in your head?"

Teo paused and rolled his eyes back and forth, then said, "Yes, I do hear the ringing in my head."

Destyr looked at Lyum and Peytynn. "And do you hear me talking to you?"

Teo stared at him, then his cheeks began to turn red. "Yes, I hear you."

Destyr grabbed Teo and brought his face close to his own. Slowly, with exaggerated pronunciation, he said, "Teo. You are an idiot!"

Teo shook himself loose, but his panic attack seemed to have passed. Meanwhile, Peytynn was trying to get me to straighten up. It was a difficult task because I was reluctant to remove my hand from my neck, and I fought to stay doubled over because the pain now extended deep into my abdomen.

"They've stopped the bombardment," I said, straining to speak, "which means they will be sending out soldiers to hunt for us." The dust made me cough, and my belly throbbed in agony. "You've got to get back to Cony. Leave me here. I'll follow you as soon as I can."

"Not a chance, King Tyrcel," Peytynn said. "We'll wait for your spell to pass. We don't leave any man behind. Especially our king."

The pain was tolerable enough that I was able to give Peytynn a quick smile. "Spell, Peytynn? That's a good one."

He took a deep breath, then helped me back to my feet. Though I didn't like my orders being dismissed so easily, I liked even less the notion of the Skirmishers being killed because of me. I was glad they were with me. Sweat turned the dust caked on my forehead into a runny mud that dripped into my eyes. Peytynn let go of my arm, and we all got back to running.

19

For days after the Skirmishers and I met up with Cony and his troops in the City Valley, Doldra's forces bombarded the West Spring Sister. Mountain-sized piles of debris fell from the sky onto the City Valley gate. I sent the Skirmishers to help with operations at the Great Pool, which was well out of range of the trebuchets.

One day, a terrible heart-wrenching sound started, like the high-pitched war call of thousands of falcons. It turned deep and thunderous like the snapping in half of an ancient ash tree, and large boulders fell out of the clouds. Debris rained down onto the City Valley gates, and for hours the gate wall was covered in a cloud of dust, which only added to the eerie nervousness that came on because we could no longer see what was happening.

Meanwhile, within that heavy black cloud the explosions of more barrels echoed across the City Valley, and the strange sound from above continued in random, long screeches.

Then came a long and grueling pause. The silence froze us more than the bombs had. The next sounds we heard were even more horrific. The entire valley was engulfed in a thunder clap as the war rig fell from the sky, followed by the screams of hundreds of men plummeting to their deaths.

The ten-foot-diameter stanchions that had been bored into the mountain centuries ago fell away, yanking the rig more quickly on its descent. Then the west-end cables gave way, and the rig swung downward for hundreds of feet until the cables reached their end and tightened, which snapped the rig free from its massive roller wheels and sent it slamming into the side of the East Spring Sister. It slid down the almost sheer mountainside, plowing trees and rocks before it into a huge pile of debris that halted its forward movement. But the sudden stop made it flip end-over-end until it caught in a deep trench on the hillside and flew into the air over the shops and homes that lined the lower mountainside.

It finally came to rest on top of the pile of dirt and stones that covered the City Valley gate.

The only positive outcome to the rig's destruction was that the citizens of the City Valley finally found their nerve and joined their warrior neighbors—the Austringers who were supposed to be their protectors—and began to form a supply line from the Austringer depot down to the forward command of warriors. The cable lines that carried the war rig had come down with the Spring Sister, but many of the secondary and tertiary lines were still working, and it was not long before the supply lines were running relatively smoothly.

It seemed that the current amount of destruction was, for the time being, enough for the northern forces, and they ceased their bombardment. Cony and I knew we had to secure the top of that new debris pile as quickly as possible. Luckily, reaching the top was hardly a bother for any Austringer. Some rappelled down from the East Spring Sister, while others climbed up from the section of the Main Road that sat—cratered and bloodied—at the base of the pile.

Within a day we removed all our fallen warriors from the wreckage of the war rig. Then Cony and I focused on the business at hand. The devastation was awful, but I quickly realized that my warriors were exactly where they needed to be. From the top of the pile we could see leagues north, up the line of the Main Road. And in the shadows below, where the light of Telios penetrated only half a day, sat the enemy base camp.

Cony stood on the back edge of the pile and raised a signal flag to notify the next wave of archers to ascend the hill. We were going to begin what would hopefully be the first of many barrages, and the upturned war rig was in a perfect position for our archers to be almost directly on top of our enemy's front lines.

We scrambled over the beams and fixtures that used to hang from the ceiling of the upside-down war rig. One side of the rig hung about ten feet over the edge of the pile, but most of it sat solidly on the mound. Archers and scouts were able to lie on the upturned ceiling and look down directly into the enemy camp. At first we were astounded by how close to our City Valley gates the northern army had dug in, but then we remembered that they weren't expecting any resistance.

From this vantage point, we collected intelligence and set up sighters for archers who stood on and within the wreckage.

"Your optics," Cony said to one of the sighters who was lying prone at the windy edge of the rig's ceiling. The warrior handed over his binoculars, and Cony lay down next to him. He watched the activity in the front lines of the enemy's camp and asked, "How much longer do you suppose until they attack?"

"Within the hour, I would imagine, sir."

I watched the tiny figures far down on the road. They had pulled their two trebuchets back to get out of range of our arrows. Every time they moved back, we used different bows and arrows to reach them. But that tactic could only last so long. The trebuchets could be well out of the farthest Austringer arrow range and still cause trouble well into the City Valley. We watched as the last few barrels were loaded onto the trebuchets.

"Tell the men on this pile to move back," Cony commanded.

"Aye, captain."

Cony rolled back into position and gazed down again at the enemy below. In the past two days, we had fired countless arrow barrages down on the northerners and still had a virtually endless supply of arrows at our disposal. But as I watched the barrels being pulled from the rear to their respective trebuchets, I thought, our advantage seemed to be over.

The pile was evacuated in less than a minute. Moments later, the first barrel arched its way up and landed on the north face of the pile, not far from the upturned war rig. The explosion sent dirt and stone flying in all directions.

After that, the bombardments continued at a staggered pace, and soon enough of the pile had been blown away that the war rig took its second tumble. It rolled like a massive log down the cratered northern slope of the hill and came to rest at the base of the pile.

The trebuchets on the Main Road were now focused on the City Valley. They blasted away for hours, and in between the explosions, when the dust settled, the pile was always a bit lower. In the intervals between bombardments, a platoon of Austringers would rush up the pile and loose as many arrows over the hill as possible before their sighter would order them to retreat just before the next barrel was about to be launched.

For the first two days, the pile was high enough that we had complete control of the valley entrance. But once the height was whittled down, things took a dramatic turn. On the afternoon of the second day, a platoon of warriors in tight formation were sending death into the skies above the northerners' front lines when suddenly the line of archers dissolved and scattered across the top of what remained of the pile. The Austringer warriors were no longer launching arrows but fighting hand to hand with the enemy. The northern horde had breached the pile.

I yelled to Cony, and he called the closest platoons to order. As warriors hurried to ready their weapons and shields, the fighting on the hill suddenly broke against us and a wave of darkly clad northerners rushed into my City Valley.

Adrenaline coursed through my body as I watched my fellow warriors fighting on top of the pile. As soon as I saw the dark swath of men rush down the hill, I no longer cared about the stabbing pain in my guts and the tightness in my neck. I saw my destiny rushing toward me and no longer believed I would die the sickened, slow, decaying death that Heike had set upon me. My heart grew strong with the thought that I would finally get to fight alongside my fellow warriors.

Cony shoved an overstuffed skirmish quiver into my arms and yelled, "Grab your bow. You're with my group."

In lowland hand-to-hand combat, Austringers fought in tight skirmish groups of three fast archers and three shieldsmen. The archers stood in the center of a wall of shields and fired over the shields' tops. Three Austringer archers could unload more than fifty arrows a minute, which was often enough to thin out the front lines of any enemy, man or giant.

Two platoons of Austringers formed battle groups, and we hurried to meet the enemy before they got too deep into the City Valley. The northern forces carried nothing but spears and swords, and before we were within their spear range, our skirmish groups broke their nerve with an onslaught of arrows. The northerners were trapped in the valley. To retreat meant going back up the hill, and any help from their comrades was slowed by a barrage of Austringer arrows flying down onto the debris mound from the heights of the East Spring Sister.

We kept up a dynamic front that moved closer and closer, until at last we were almost out of arrows and practically as close as the tips of our enemies' spears.

Cony gave the order, and I finally heard the surreal crash of true battle. My father used to tell me the only part that he hated about meeting an enemy was the deafening noise. He had no problem with the killing and had no fear of death. *That's why I had to be able to scream over all the dying and killing, he would say. A king who doesn't lead in battle will not be a king for long.*

Our archers dropped their bows and pulled out their long-daggers. The shieldsmen kept the front line but pulled out close-combat blades of all lengths. I joined my fellow warriors in one last war cry, and we lunged at our enemy.

The northerners' numbers might have been reduced but only down to a point where we were equally matched. The slashing and screaming of bloody battle continued for what seemed like hours. Cony and I fought at each other's side, protecting our backs and cutting our way to the pile that covered the gate wall.

Things moved quickly, and my thoughts felt like they were always far behind my actions. I moved from a conditioning that was not in my head but in every part of my body. With each passing minute, I felt something inside me changing. I became less and less concerned with my own defense or safety, and my fighting spirit soon turned into an all-consuming rage.

We had almost stopped the first wave of northerners when, as I pulled my long-dagger out of the belly of my latest kill, I turned to see two northerners rushing toward Cony. He was busy finishing off his own opponent and did not notice them. I yelled to him and rushed to meet his attackers.

I jumped on the closest northern soldier just as he was about to surprise Cony with a spear to his back. Cony spun around and dodged the other soldier's spear thrust. I had stopped Cony from being killed, but I lost my grip and my enemy and I tumbled loosely across the ground. My side and ribs crashed against the hardpacked gravel, and pain ripped through my body. My opponent got on his feet first and came at me. He reared up, his sword in both hands, ready to bring it down into my chest. I kicked his knee and snapped it into a backward bend. He fell, screaming, and I rolled toward him, using my momentum to give me enough force to bring my elbow down onto his throat.

I looked around for Cony. He was finishing off his opponent, and then the fight calmed down to the moans of the wounded. Only Austringers were left standing. We had defeated the first wave of northerners and hardly broken a sweat.

I wearily pushed myself off the corpse of my last kill, and Cony rushed to my aid. As he helped me to my feet, a round shadow flew over us. My heart leaped into my throat. This first barrel seemed to be a warning from the northern forces because it struck the base of the East Spring Sister but did more damage to the smaller hills that formed the eastern edge of the City Valley. The shockwave pushed Cony and me off our feet and sent us tumbling backward in a scorching blast of wind.

I was no longer able to help myself. Heike's curse and the battle I had just fought had sapped my strength. I put up no resistance as I fell into a ditch at the bottom of a low-hanging outcrop. I laid there for several minutes, listening to the stark ringing in my ears and feeling the tight throbbing in my throat.

Finally I came back to my senses and used what strength I had left to lift my head. Across the field above me, Cony stood unsteadily, like a man who had consumed too much barley wine. I called his name, and when he saw me trying to crawl from under the outcrop, he summoned a few other warriors to help me.

As he turned back to me, another barrel flew over the pile.

It landed in the middle of the City Valley—a perfect shot to deliver an explosion that would radiate out in all directions. The last thing I saw before I was knocked unconscious was a flash of light so bright that everything within a hundred yards—including Cony and hundreds of Austringer warriors—was vaporized into piles of ashes.

20

My best pest, is he? The clicking turned into a morbid hum.
No, d'ychus scum. He too is turning.

Then came the smell—the aroma of the most delicious goat and turnip stew. But it was mixed with the foul odor of death and decay. Every exhalation was difficult, and with them came that strange odor and taste in the back of my throat—something between the stench of rotting flesh, the taste of copper, and the sourness of vinegar.

A cacophonous bellowing in my head finally jarred me awake. It wasn't the first time I'd had a dream like that. Now I lay coughing, my mind stuck on the last words the terrible voice had said: *He too is turning.*

I could hear Austringer warriors and citizens of the City Valley moving all around me, but I was paralyzed with sickness and fatigue, unable to do much more than writhe in the dirt whenever the pain in my abdomen grew too strong.

At the thought of it, my belly erupted in a series of stabbing pains. My chest spasmed as I tried to take a deep, full breath, and I finally passed out into an unrestful blackness—not like sleep but more like my body's attempt to feign death in hopes that actual Death might be tricked into passing me by.

Eventually, the dark gave way to a bright white spot that pierced and blinded me. Even with my eyes closed tightly, I could not escape the white light. It demanded my attention, boring into my vision with a dull pressure that I could not will away. The frantic palpitations of my heart subsided, and I suddenly heard my mother's soft, loving voice. The sound filled me with warmth, and I no longer worried about the bright light, the pain, or the thirst.

Slowly, I realized the voice was not mother but Telios. Was the sun playing some prank on me? I grew confused and anxious. My heart sped up again. I tried to speak, but my vocal chords were no longer working. They felt as frozen as my arms and legs. I tried again and again but could form nothing more than mumbles from between my cracked lips.

"Ha...ha...how..." I stammered, but even a single syllable challenged me.

Always the impressive one, the voice said. *Such the hope of your parents, poor Tyrcel.*

The words reminded me of father and some long distant message he had given me. "Fa...fa...fath...wa...warn..."

My mind reeled. My father and many of the people I cared about were dead. I tried cursing Telios, blaming him for all my troubles, but only choked, broken syllables fell from my mouth.

Then a warm and loving sense washed over me. It soothed my frantic heart, and for the first time in days, I was able to relax. I blinked up at the bright sky, at the random puffs of clouds that sped past the dark shadows at the top of the mountains rising all around me. Finally, after a long time, the voice told me how much it wanted to wipe the blood from my cheek and dry the tears from my eyes.

I no longer cared that Telios was impersonating my mother. I just wanted to rest in the sound of her voice.

You must move from this place, she said. *Make your way to Olos.*

I knew, deep in my dream mind, that I could not. I tried to shake my head and blink my eyes to let mother know that I was sorry, but I couldn't move. I feared that Heike's curse had finally got the best of me.

The voice grew serious. *That's not the right answer.*

I blinked more frantically, and in the strobing in and out of the sun through my eyelids, I saw the shadow of a falcon pass over the rocky hillside across from me. I knew, beyond a doubt, that it was Stella's shadow. I stopped blinking and waited to see if the shadow would return.

But the voice said, *You must go to the giants' city. You must save our people.*

At the sound of a distant falcon screech, I opened my eyes and inhaled like a man who had just broken the surface of a pool to breathe in vital, dry air. I sucked in a huge dust-filled breath, which caused me to cough violently. Blood spattered my chin as my lungs struggled to clear themselves of all the dust.

When my coughing fit came to an end, I heard another falcon call. I squinted up into the bright sky. It was midday and Telios was at its peak, which caused the thermal updrafts in the City Valley to increase. There, floating in the warm glow, at all altitudes, were hundreds of falcons. I thought I was dreaming, and when I lifted myself up onto one elbow to get a better view, I realized that I was lying on a pallet at the bottom of an Austringer path.

The path led up to a cable-lift plateau at the base of Gavina. To my left and right, wounded Austringer warriors lay on countless other pallets and stretchers, frantically tended by a scant amount of medical personnel. We were all in line, waiting to be lifted up on the cables to the hospital quarters—and the Pyre Hall. I noticed that my pallet had been set off the main path some distance from the others.

After propping myself up for a few seconds, I was out of energy. I lay back down and cried dry tears until I passed out again.

"Well, for the love of all things feathery."

I opened my eyes just enough to see Peytynn leaning over me.

"Is he alive?" Destyr asked as he showed up pulling a barrow behind him. I was still on the pallet at the bottom of the cable-drop plateau.

"Of course he's alive," Peytynn said.

Lyum came into view. He knelt by my head and poured water over my face to clean away the dust.

"He's okay, right, little brother?" Peytynn asked nervously.

"He isn't dead," Lyum said.

"Thank the Sirens." Peytynn stood up and turned to Teo and Destyr. "Put him in the barrow. I don't think anyone's rushing to assist him." He looked around the area, pinching his nose. "And he smells like a the rotten wharves of Port Tallion."

"Give me a minute," Lyum said as he splashed water on my lips. "He's coming to."

Despite Lyum's attempt at washing, my eyes still had a considerable amount of dirt caked around them, but I began to move, and my lids made a few, desperate attempts to blink. As the sky came into view, I noticed that there were fewer falcons flying above me.

"Hold it, Peytynn. I think he's trying to speak." They brought their heads as close to my face as possible, but they did not lean in too long.

"For the love of the Sirens. Give him more water," Peytynn ordered. He sat back and took a deep breath.

Lyum seemed better able to endure the smell. He stayed next to me, lifting his head as far away as possible while still cradling the back of my own and trying his best to pour water over my face without drowning me.

Peytynn leaned a little closer. "Careful, brother."

After a few splashes of the water to my lips, my mouth moved like a freshly hatched eyas who knows nothing else but to search blindly up and keep its mouth open. Unable to use my limbs, I frantically tried to move my mouth toward the source of the water. Lyum poured more, but it was too much for my parched throat. I coughed up a spattering of water mixed with blood and dust.

"Dammit, brother," Peytynn said. "You're pouring too fast."

While trying to hold his breath, Lyum said, "Come over here and hold his head up. And give me a cloth—or your kerchief."

Peytynn pulled a rag out of his vest pocket and handed it to Lyum. He wiped my face until the entire cloth was brown.

"Gods, Lyum," said Peytynn as he stared down at me. "I've never smelled anything like that before."

Lyum continued wiping my face. "It will get easier. Come over here and help."

The water and Lyum's care revived me enough that my cracked and bloodied lips moved with a bit more vigor. I interrupted the brothers with attempts at a few syllables. "O...los..."

"What did he say?" Peytynn asked.

"Shut up and listen."

"O...los..."

They looked at each other, perplexed. "Sounds like he's saying Olos," Peytynn said.

Lyum nodded, and Peytynn wrinkled his brow, this time out of confusion and not just the smell of decay that hung over me. "Why of all these lowland Hells would he say that word? Give him another splash of water."

Lyum held my head up, careful not to strain my weakened neck. He splashed water onto my lips, and my head rolled in his hands as my lips desperately searched for more. He poured again. Soon my throat relaxed, and my frantic need to drink eased for a few moments. Lyum lowered my head gently back onto the ground.

My lips again tried to make the sound, "O...los."

Peytynn leaned in closer. "King Tyrcel?" He waited a few seconds and began again. "King Tyrcel, it's Peytynn. We've come to take you back to the Overhang."

"We can't get to the Overhang," Lyum said, but Peytynn shushed him.

"It doesn't matter where he thinks we're taking him. He's in no shape to protest anything."

My eyelids cracked opened, and my mind was fogged and confused, but I managed to hold onto the orders from that strange and luminous voice.

"N...no. Mus...get...to...O...los."

Peytynn leaned in close and asked, "Why Olos, King Tyrcel?"

I managed to mumble the single word, "Must."

Peytynn ordered Destyr and Teo to carry me to the barrow. They hesitated, but when Lyum impatiently began to lift my shoulders, the others forgot the foul odor and hurried to my side. They braced themselves for my full weight, but easily lifted my emaciated frame. Peytynn stood beside the barrow while the other three made sure my body was as secure as possible and that the few supplies were also tied down. Meanwhile, all around us the line of wounded men had hardly moved.

"Forget that smell," Peytynn said. He pointed to my neck. "Look at his skin. And the scars. They're purple."

The boys stared down at me. Telios was at his zenith so they had plenty of light to see just how sick I was. My skin was a pasty white and pulled tight over bones. My veins and arteries left deep gray trails all over my body. My lips were cracked and swollen from dehydration, and I imagine they distorted my face into a gruesome caricature of my once youthful visage. The wound that Heike had gouged into my neck pulsed with each weak heartbeat. But the worst part was how bad I smelled. The stench of infection and rot was a constant cloud around me.

"He kept repeating the word Olos," Peytynn said to Destyr and Teo.

Olos was one of three cities in the Midlyn Range and our only trading partner in the south. The giants who ran Olos were ruthless gangsters who only bothered with those who had something to trade or purchase from them. Centuries ago, after they had fled Heike, the smarter giants who came down from the hills realized that the Olos harbor was the best, most direct route to the equatorial lands, and they took full control of everything that came and went from that harbor.

Many years ago, after the Treaty for Peace was signed, Austringers frequented the city. But in recent times, the leaders of Olos had become more cruel and Austringers did less and less business in the city. Instead, they used go-betweens from the City Valley to get whatever they might need from Olos.

Despite the Austringers' hatred of giants, they knew that the rulers of Olos were more civilized than the average hill-giant. They were also accomplished miners and architects who were familiar with stone work, which meant that they had earned the grudging respect of the Austringer engineers.

"What can he want there?" Destyr wondered aloud.

"I have no clue," Peytynn said.

They stood in baffled silence for a moment until Peytynn said, "Well, it seems impossible to get up to the Overhang. And there's nothing but skirmish groups out in the valley and foothills."

"And it won't be long before the next bombardment and then the northerners' next attempt to rush the pile," Destyr added.

"They will need us to stay here, then. In the City Valley," Teo said.

Peytynn shook his head. "I don't see how four teenagers and one half-dead king are going to help an outnumbered army. We must follow a different path, and so far the only suggestion has been from the member of our group who looks like he's dead or dying. And that suggestion is Olos."

He looked at Lyum, but his younger brother was gazing off in the distance.

"A different path?" Destyr asked, sounding frustrated. "The path to Olos is certainly different."

"I know." Peytynn was looking down at me. The sun had dried the layer of dirt that stuck to my skin, and my breathing was so raspy that it led to coughing fits.

Lyum wiped the last of the blood and dirt from my face and kept fresh water on my lips.

I gazed up at the sky. Now only two shadows remained. They drifted across the Skirmishers' faces. My neck ached as I craned it to see the birds. I knew instantly that the bigger one was Stella, and Rymeo was up there as well. I could tell it was him by the odd spacing of the feathers on his right wing, the result of a long-healed wound he had sustained while dropping down on a massive pool-trout. He was the most rash of all the Buteo flock, and his hubris had almost cost him his wing, but instead the injury only caused him to fly a bit crooked.

I considered trying to crack a smile, but my desire was not stronger than the effort it would take. I dropped my head back down onto the pallet. I had no idea why the birds were up there, but it had to be a good sign. According to Austringer beliefs, Stella and Rymeo had been given to my brother as a gift from the Sirens. Aillil had scaled the cliffs of Hunter's Bluff and safely brought these two birds into his care. They seemed to know that their beloved master was gone, so they had found and followed the closest thing they had to him.

Peytynn looked up at the falcons moving in and out of Telios' light. Stella gave a piercing screech and with a flap of her wings climbed, breaking the circle and swooping in a southerly direction. Peytynn looked back at the long, never-moving line of wounded Austringers who were waiting for their turn to be pulled up to the medical quarters.

He turned back to us and said, "A different path does not necessarily mean the wrong path."

The Skirmishers had been walking through the foothills that surrounded the City Valley for half a day, cursing the Sirens for the never-ending stench. They took turns pulling me in the barrow, and whoever had that duty gagged and retched nearly the entire time.

While he and Teo pulled the barrow, a weary Destyr said, "This is why we need Morys."

No one spoke for a long time after that. I bounced along listening to the squeaking of the barrow's axle and the crunch of the Skirmishers' feet, seeing only whatever was in front of my face at whatever angle it happened to be rolling by.

We were nearly south of Gavina. Explosions sounded almost constantly in the distance. From what I understood of the Skirmishers' chatter, the enemy's scouts and outposts were focused at the base of Gavina and all the cable-drop plateaus that were outside the City Valley.

Peytynn looked up at the two falcons soaring above us. "Our guides are heading in a more southerly direction. I don't mind at all. I want to be as far from Gavina as possible when we hit the Main Road."

"South from here, he says," Teo whispered to Destyr as they struggled to maneuver the barrow over the loose, rocky ground.

Destyr whispered something that I could not discern.

Gavina loomed so large that it was hard to believe it was half a day's journey north. To any Austringer, perspectives were subtly different in the lowlands. We preferred looking down from the heights, not up from the ground. We felt that to look up from the ground meant one was a base creature—or sick or dying.

My head bounced to the side facing north. There was my Gavina. Telios' light covered this side of her throughout the day, so the mountain's various greens, grays, and browns were vivid. The forests that grew up from the foothills spread in great swaths of dark greens, blending with the white trunks of the dense aspen forests where the higher altitudes began, until the gravel, granite stones, and dirt took over. The very top of the mountain consisted of quartz-veined granite interspersed with black shrubs that disappeared into the clouds.

Destyr and Teo gazed over their shoulders at their beloved home, the largest mountain of all the known territories on Axis Solan. Teo slipped on the gravel. Regaining his footing, he said with a sigh, "Olos. As if the northerners weren't bad enough."

Stella and Rymeo led us into the largest southern valley of the Midlyn Range. Austringers referred to it as the Lesser Coverts Valley, but the giants of Olos called it Olon's Footprint. The myths of the old hill-giants claim that the first giant, Olon Mountain Builder, carved the valley during his many travels to access the River Shea. Austringers agreed that from their outposts on top of Gavina, the valley did resemble a massive footprint with a slow-rising westerly mound not unlike the arch of a massive sole.

Our path paralleled the River Shea, a branch of the River Ayah, which was once a clear stream that ran from the waters collected in the Great Pool and then south of Gavina to Tallies Harbor. But Shea was now nothing more than a muddy toe-deep trickle.

The Skirmishers stopped on what used to be her banks, their empty water skins in hand. Peytynn and his brother shared a worried glance with Destyr and Teo.

"There's still a little water in there," Teo said.

"Yeah, a trickle of mud," Destyr said. "Who's going to drink that?"

"If we follow this river...river bed," Peytynn broke in, "we will eventually hit the Main Road not a few hour's walk from the walls of Olos." He looked at Destyr and Teo and added, "Lyum and I will take the barrow for now."

Stella screeched impatiently as she and Rymeo circled in the high distance. Peytynn grabbed a handle-bar of the barrow, leaned back for one last relatively fresh breath, and said, "It won't be long now."

The Skirmishers came out of the Lesser Coverts Valley and sat in the shade and safety of the last few trees before the terrain fell off into the brown and green grassy stretches that lined the Main Road. From this vantage point, we could see a considerable expanse of the road toward the north and south. We could also make out the gray skyline of Olos in the distance.

And closer, where the road made its final bend toward the city, lay a cluster of dead men wearing the armor of the northern army.

"What do you suppose happened there?" Destyr asked.

"I have no idea," Peytynn said. "Teo, what do you see?"

Teo was studying the situation through his binoculars. "Looks like a bunch of different bits of I'd say five men, all strewn about on the road. And what looks to be parts of two horses."

"Anyone else around?"

"Not that I can see."

"Okay, but be sure," Peytynn said. "We need to take that road to get to Olos."

Teo looked over at Peytynn. "There remains, of course, the option of not going to Olos. We don't even know what to do once we get there."

Peytynn chose to ignore him. "Let's get moving. Destyr and Lyum, take the barrow. We'll get a little closer and figure out the best route."

Stella screeched, and both falcons dove out of their updraft and headed south. Rymeo made an ominous chatter, as though warning us of danger ahead.

"Keep your eyes open," Peytynn said. "I don't like the look of things."

There was a long swath of hip-high grass between us and the road. Running through the pasture would put us totally out in the open, and the Skirmishers would be pulling a barrow made unwieldy by my useless body.

"Teo, keep your optics on those falcons and the hills under them," Peytynn said. "And speak up if you see anything odd." He moved into the point position. "I'll stay out front. We'll head to that ditch next to the road on this side of those bodies. Let's move."

They took off with Peytynn way out in front. Teo walked as skillfully as possible while trying to keep track of the birds, and Destyr and Lyum gagged as they pulled the barrow. Peytynn reached the ditch and crouched in a kneeling position. He bobbed his head up and down trying to get a clear idea of the state of the road to the south of us.

Teo was looking at the distant rise in the terrain under the swooping falcons. From that low slope, two northern soldiers were sprinting through the grass, straight toward Peytynn's location.

Lyum and Destyr came to a sudden stop, jostling me out of my delirium. I heard their mumbled surprises and saw Teo waving his hands dramatically in a motion that urged Peytynn to take cover. But Peytynn looked baffled. All the Skirmishers were staring down the hill behind him in the direction of the falcons. He pulled his long-dagger from its scabbard and tried to peer over the top of the ditch.

Teo yelled, "Peytynn, get down!"

Two boots leaped over Peytynn's head. He dropped to the bottom of the ditch, and a northern soldier landed at the other end. The man picked himself up and turned toward Peytynn, who was holding his long-dagger out, ready for anything. The two studied each other for many seconds. The soldier looked down at the long-dagger then back up at Peytynn.

"That's not going to help you," he scoffed and pulled himself out of the ditch.

Peytynn stood up to watch as the man sprinted to the Main Road. Then he turned around just in time for the second northerner to land on top of him. The Skirmishers shouted his name as he and the soldier disappeared into the ditch. All they could see was the top of the soldier's head as it bobbed up and down.

Lyum dropped the barrow handle and raced toward the ditch. We could hear the sounds of a struggle, but before Lyum could reach his brother, the soldier yelled, "Let go of me, you southern cur."

The ground shook with what seemed like the beginning of a quake. I tried to lift my head for a better view. The soldier leaped out of the ditch and stumbled backward just as a huge shadow loomed up from the hills that lined the other side of the road. The shadow turned into a massive hand that grabbed the screaming northerner by his waist.

Peytynn scrambled back down the line of the ditch as fast as he could. Darkness covered his body as an enormous man stood over him. But the giant looked more like a massive granite sculpture than a man. His skin was like pocked and cracked stone, and his joints had ivy growing from them, which also dangled in sparse strands from his chin. This giant stood many feet over the height of the only other giants I had ever seen, Chod and Dosh.

The giant held the terrified soldier up by his collar as the man flailed and screamed. *Caught you, little sneaky pinky,* said the giant. It spoke in the common tongue but with a graveled pitch that no human voice could duplicate. He held the soldier directly in front of his own huge face. The soldier desperately slashed at the air between their two faces. The giant looked over his shoulder and shouted a thunderous cry. *Conj! Orkun! Dey'ehsy romyul!*

The ground shook under my barrow, and I saw two more massive men lumber up to the first giant.

As the first giant taunted the helpless soldier in his fist, he noticed the other soldier up the road running for his life. *Aaaarggh,* he shouted, with what seemed to be a happy-to-be-challenged tone.

He stepped with a single lumbering stride over the ditch. Then he took two more steps, pivoted 360 degrees, and used the momentum to launch the screaming soldier through the air. The other giants moved past Peytynn with a litheness that belied their seemingly cumbersome bodies. None of them had noticed the Skirmishers or me, lying helpless in the barrow.

In the common Midlyn tongue, the first giant called after the two soldiers, *There you go little pinkies. A reunion!*

The other two giants raced each other toward their prey, doubtless in the hope that the poor northerners might live long enough to give them a little more fun.

Conj! Orkun! Dey'ehsy farrah romyul! The first giant called to his cohorts and pointed toward the road, just as the man in the air, his screams now over, came down directly onto the other fleeing soldier. Both tumbled across the road.

The running soldier was only stunned and picked himself up just in time to be within reach of Conj and Orkun. He screamed one last terrified time before Conj wrapped his huge hand around his torso.

Ha ha! Now that's it for you, pinky.

Orkun was checking on the other guard.

Orkun, bellowed Conj. *O'achtull! Catch!*

The giant cocked his arm and tossed the soldier high up and over Orkun's head. Orkun saw the challenging pass and stomped on the other soldier's head just to make sure he was dead, then lunged off the road to catch the flying body. He dove almost fifty yards and landed terrifyingly close to us with a thunderous crash that sent a plume of dust and grass up into the air.

The first giant said, *Gruffah dey sulla.* He towered over Peytynn's ditch like a huge, surreal statue. He sniffed at the air and tilted and turned his head in all directions as if searching for an elusive smell. I had a good idea what the smell might be.

Finally, his yellow eyes looked down and saw Peytynn. The giant gazed at him for several long seconds in confusion. He and his friends had been chasing only two men, yet here was a third. He bent down to analyze Peytynn, who was frozen with fear. The giant wrinkled his brow and ran huge fingers through the ivy dangling from his chin.

Peytynn took advantage of the giant's confusion to spring from the ditch. But with just a small stretch of his arm, the giant had him fast around the waist. At the sight of his brother being captured, Lyum jumped up and yelled, "Get your hands off him!"

All three giants spun toward the high-pitched voice. They seemed shocked. Conj and Orkun let the now inanimate body of the soldier drop to the ground. They looked at each other for answers. Each shrugged his shoulders, then the first giant gave the order, *Dey'ehsy farrah gorthoth.*

Orkun met Lyum as he blindly raced to aid his brother and scooped him up like an ant in his palm. For such a large beast, he did very well at gently holding the boy. He yelled to the first giant, *Rotter, deysyss gorthoth, essyn Aus...Austringer.*

Rotter cupped Peytynn in his palm and yelled back to Orkun, *Essyn dey Austringer.*

Then he looked down at the helpless Peytynn and spoke in the common tongue. *You Austringer? Fight other pinky? Or you with other pinky?*

At the sound of his people's name, Peytynn sat up in Rotter's hands. "Yes! I am an Austringer. We do not come to make trouble like those other men."

Rotter laughed, *Other men!* His tone became more of a bragging conversation. *They strange, indeed. Never I met a pinky who talk to Rotter like those.* He eyed Peytynn more closely. *Mind you, pinky, Rotter love trouble from men. We of Olos not fear the trouble of men.*

Suddenly, a brave "Hurrah!" came from the pasture. Destyr and Teo were charging Orkun and Conj in a last-ditch attempt to save Lyum or protect me or perhaps just to die fighting. Before they made it halfway to Orkun, Conj swept around his giant friend with one massive step and scooped both Austringers up, one in each hand. Destyr and Teo slashed their long-daggers anywhere on Orkun's hands that they could reach, but the blades left hardly a scratch in his granite skin.

Rotter looked back at Peytynn. *We like Austringer pinkies,* he said with a huge, stony smile. *Rotter never see ones so small. You little pinkies fight hard. Not like stories we teach.*

"No," Peytynn said. "My friends are just scared and confused. They don't mean any harm."

Rotter laughed and turned to Conj. *Dorykkon deyssyn Austringer non-mallass.*

All three giants laughed like three storm clouds colliding together and shaking the ground with a thunderous clash. Rotter looked back at Peytynn. *My friend Conj says he is relieved that small Austringer pinkies don't mean harm. We really worried about that.*

DEYSYSS, ROTTER! The deafening call came from Orkun who stood in the pasture leaning over me, pinching his nose. *Farrahgh ortym mallass essyn Austringer.*

Rotter turned to Orkun. *Mallass Austringer?* He walked, with Peytynn in hand, across the pasture to join Orkun.

"Okay...uh...Rotter," Peytynn said. "That man lying in the barrow is the king of the Austringers. He is sick or under some sort of curse. When we found him, the only thing he said was the name of your city, Olos. We figured there had to be a reason, so we brought him here."

Orkun was still peering down at the barrow. He had temporarily forgotten about Lyum and relaxed his grip. Lyum grabbed onto the creases between the fingers of Orkun's hand to keep from plummeting to the ground.

Rotter! Orkun called. His tone had an edge to it that diverted Rotter's attention away from Peytynn's harried rambling.

Ignassu Orkun. Uhttentynn, Rotter replied.

Peytynn continued his desperate explanation. "He seems to be getting worse. His veins have become dark blue tracks all over his—"

Pinkling talk too much, Rotter said without turning his head to Peytynn.

Orkun called, *Rotter! Mallass essyn d'on dyssys Ahkkharu.*

Without breaking his long stride, Rotter stretched his arm down and dropped Peytynn to the ground. Peytynn was able to manage his fall and landed well, and Rotter was already yards away by the time Peytynn stood up. The giant took two more steps and was standing next to Orkun and me. By this time, Conj was also standing beside the barrow. He still held Teo and Destyr in his hands.

Peytynn walked up to the huddle of giants. "That is King Tyrcel Buteo."

Rotter knelt beside the barrow and leaned close to me. He sniffed the air around me and made a face that signified disgust. He mumbled something that only Conj and Orkun understood. In my bleary state, I could only make out the word *Ahkkharu* before a massive stabbing pain consumed me.

Rotter looked at Peytynn, his granite brow wrinkled in disbelief. *This your king?*

"Yes," Peytynn said.

Rotter looked like he was deep in thought. He pulled at the ivy vines growing from his chin and asked Peytynn, *What you know about Ahkkharu?*

"Ak... ka..." Peytynn tried to pronounce the word.

Ahkkharu! Rotter shouted again. *The sorcerer runt. The Blood Drinker.*

"You mean Heike?" Peytynn said. "Not much at all. Other than that he was rather a mad giant....whereas you three are...well...nice giants."

Rotter was looking down at me. *Austringer king still live?*

"Why...yes...I mean...last we checked he was still alive." He tried to move closer to me to check my condition, but Rotter effortlessly flicked him out of the way.

I tried to speak, but my throat was still so parched that all I managed was a weak, "Please..."

Rotter stood up, wrinkled his granite brow, and said, *Your pinky king make smell like Ahkkharu magic surrounds him, and you pinkies make no sense.* He turned and began striding across the field toward the Main Road. *Conj, evyck d'on dryssallun. Y Orkun, evyck d'on Austringer king.*

21

Peytynn, Destyr, and Teo had to keep up a brisk trot the entire way to Olos. Lyum had secured himself a perch on Conj's shoulder, where he seemed to be sitting comfortably. I, on the other hand, was held at arm's length by Orkun. He had picked me up, barrow and all, and tried his best to keep his cargo as far away from his nose as possible.

By the time the other Skirmishers reached the walls of Olos, the three giants were standing on the other end of the massive bridge that marked the northern entrance to the city on the Main Road. They were engaged in a discussion with two other giants, who sat upon massive boulders on each side of the wide arch over the road. Their skin looked as solid as granite, but it moved and rippled with the subtlety of flesh.

When the rest of the Skirmishers had caught up, we all entered the city. We found ourselves at the edge of a massive market square. I was surprised how familiar the streets of Olos looked. The buildings, as far as I could see, were not much bigger than what we were used to in the City Valley. Merchants and customers, who were human, walked in and about the stores dressed in the familiar clothes of the people of the north and south.

The architecture of the main street was also similar to the City Valley shops, except that everything here seemed to be made of gray granite. The buildings' walls were almost the same colors and textures as the giants' bodies. There was little variation among the stone walls except for the occasional storefront sign hanging from an awning. The streets were made of massive granite slabs, and each slab was at least twenty yards square, so that a single slab spanned the street. The streets of Olos had few seams, unlike the cobbled walks of the City Valley.

Beyond the roofs and shops of the market, other giants of all heights walked about. It seemed that the market was built to accommodate the human merchants and traders, and its small walkways and alleys kept the giants of Olos on the sidelines.

Our three giants strode along the outer edge of the market to the far end. The main street curved in a long, subtle turn toward the west. Above the rooftops and stone facades rose an ominous skyline. Flowing columns of black smoke rose above the massive buildings that sat stacked and clustered in the distance.

At the sight of those dark, distant buildings where the giants lived, I thought this must be how a stranger feels when first seeing Gavina. From every shore, no matter how far away, Gavina looked massive. When one finally nears her base, her size is overwhelming. Those buildings in the distance were piled so high on top of one another they created the illusion of a mountain.

I looked back over my shoulder and realized that the other Skirmishers had fallen behind. Then a shadow fell across the main road like an eclipse of Telios, and the three Skirmishers were plucked up by Rotter. He dropped them into a large net and swung it over his shoulder. They tumbled, grunted, and cursed as they righted themselves in the net.

All three giants turned down a short alley that ended in a ten-foot wall that they easily stepped over. Once we were out on the perimeter walkways, all I could see of the Olos Market was the back sides of the shops, which shrank as the giants moved into what looked like an endless expanse of gritty, reddish-brown sand and sparse shrubs. The air was humid and hot because the city was the last stop before the warm equatorial lands.

We soon reached another set of arches that resembled human architecture except for the size. The walls were massive and constructed of perfectly milled granite blocks, each the size of a small building in the City Valley. The blocks did not have any mortar between them but sat so tightly on top of one another that time and all of Axis Solan's quakes moved them very little.

Rotter led the way through the arches. Once in the giants' city, I saw that each building was actually a cluster of open rooms that sat on top of one another. The bases of the structures were solidly framed and seemed to have a complete set of stone walls, but as the levels grew higher, the buildings looked more like huge boxes set on top of one another, and no box had a complete set of walls. Many of them were open and faced huge verandas or rooftops, as though the giants enjoyed sitting out in the elements.

We walked down what seemed to be a main thoroughfare, so wide that at any time ten giants could walk shoulder to shoulder along it. Like the previous market, this huge city street was alive with activity, only here the activity consisted mostly of granite-skinned giants. I could not detect gender differences among the giants, who looked relatively alike. And they all wore massive chains and rings of gold, silver, and other bright metals and gems. The occasional human milling about looked worried because the giants paid little attention to where they placed their huge feet.

Finally, we stopped in front of a building that did not have any sort of steps leading up to its open doorway. Again, its entrance was a high-headed archway, coped and trimmed so that each stone edge was as smooth as glass.

Rotter yelled into the open archway, *Y'rog Missesh, solth Austringer dyss golonth pur d'ym.*

Solyth y'undreth sol, answered a voice from somewhere far inside. We entered a room whose ceiling was higher than any of the rooms in the Overhang. The stonework on the walls was organized in faux arches of granite surrounding sparkling quartz that was packed with green emeralds. The base coping was composed of two-foot-high rough-hewn granite blocks that twinkled with flecks of platinum. Symbols and strange shapes were carved on the walls. In the quartz, the carvings were faint reliefs that were difficult to see at first, but they were darker and more pronounced in the granite. All the surfaces were polished so smooth that the light of Telios shining through the open sections of the ceiling reflected in wild patterns along the length of the room. In my delirium, it seemed that these patterns shifted back and forth between simple geometric shapes and the symbols I had seen in Heike's torture den.

The hall's vivid brightness and fine artistry reminded me of the walls of the Overhang. In fact, certain sections and elements in the artwork were strikingly similar to the reliefs and carvings found throughout my home city. We walked toward another open doorway. The coping around the door was a delicate mix of carving and glass tile-work that I would not have expected from such brutish fingers. Behind the opening, dark shapes sat in various positions.

After Rotter set them on the floor, Peytynn, Destyr, and Teo squirmed out of the netting and stood up, gazing at the bright beautiful architecture around them.

Aussssstringersss, hissed Rotter, telling them to stop sightseeing and move.

We made our way across the wide threshold and into a huge, round room that rose more than a hundred feet to a massive domed ceiling. However, the dome was open-framed and composed of curved timbers, each inscribed with intricate symbols that were hard to make out because they seemed to rise right up into Telios' glare.

The silhouettes of Stella and Rymeo flew in and out of the bright white light and high above the beams of this chamber.

The timber frame rose out of the tops of the circular foundation walls, which were composed of large strips of chiseled granite and the same glowing quartzite as the foyer. The granite sections were finished with delicate, stone reliefs depicting giants in various seated positions, the details of which flowed from one granite slab to the other. The reliefs were so detailed that they almost leapt off the wall as if they were actual giants frozen in time.

Lining the circular base of the walls were twenty-one large stone slabs. The two slabs nearest the door sat directly on the ground, and the slabs along the walls rose in height until they ended at the tallest one, directly across from the entrance. Here the leader of Olos sat.

Each slab was of a different type of stone. Austringers were expert geologists and I recognized many of the boulders, even some of the rarer ones. One giant sat on a huge black, gleaming monolith of iron ore. The block was hewn smooth on five sides, and on the remaining natural edge sat a giant draped in gleaming metal necklaces and chains.

Another giant's seat looked like huge slabs of slate, melded together by ancient forces, all standing on end. The slabs were joined at their base, and as they rose up, they separated into thick individual plates. I was amazed at how comfortable the giant on this slate boulder appeared. He lounged in a groove on the front side of the boulder that had no doubt been formed by centuries of sitting.

The highest seat in the room, the one on which the leader of Olos sat, was a massive rose-quartz boulder that was riddled with pure veins of platinum and raw emeralds. None of its edges had been ground smooth. In fact, the boulder looked like it had simply been ripped from the core of a mountain cave and placed in the council room, stunningly beautiful and lustrous in its natural form.

Rotter, Conj, and Orkun stopped in the middle of the room in front of the highest slab, with Lyum still sitting on Conj's shoulder. Orkun leaned down and placed the barrow, with me in it, on the ground. After a few garbled words between them and the giant who was obviously in charge, they each moved to their own open slab and sat down. All the giants could see me lying in the barrow. A loud murmur swept through the room.

Rahyla Austringers, said a cacophony of huge voices.

Rahyla. That means hello, pinklings, said the bejeweled giant on the highest slab.

The entire room was well lit through the open ceiling, and the features of the giant's face were clear. There was an air of humor in the face of this huge creature.

In our language, he said, *that is how we say hello. Do you understand me?*

"Yes, we understand," Peytynn said.

At the sound of his voice, a murmur spread around the room.

Excellent, said the giant. *I am Missesh Olluns, the Governor of Olos. I am grown from the same lichens and ore from which the Ancient Ones grew. From the same pebbles as Olon Mountain Builder himself. That is why I can be the governor of this city. There is no giant who can claim to be better than me, Missesh Stone Crusher Olluns. From tossing boulders farther than any other giant alive to hewing the finest, most perfect cubes of quartz from the deepest caverns. You pinklings should know, I am not afraid of anything. In fact, I challenge you to challenge me to something!*

The giant sat forward and stared directly at the Skirmishers. They were speechless with fear and could offer Missesh no challenge of any sort.

Missesh began to speak again, *That's what I thought! You pinklings can call me Missesh. Or Governor Missesh. Or Governor Ollun. Or just Governor. I don't really care.*

Missesh continued to stare down at them. *So I have told you my name. It is customary that you do the same.*

"I'm sorry, Governor," Peytynn began.

Missesh, however, boomed out an interruption. *You call me just Missesh.*

Confused, Peytynn said, "Yes, Missesh. Well, my name is Peytynn. And these are my friends."

This time Destyr interrupted. "I am Destyr."

Their responses seemed to intrigue Missesh. He said to Destyr, *You, however, have to call me Governor Missesh.* His expression turned stolid, and he leaned a little closer to the three Skirmishers.

"Oh...yes...of course," Destyr stammered. "Please forgive me, Governor Missesh. I did not mean to insult—"

Missesh interrupted again, this time with a roaring laugh that shook the ground beneath us. The giants erupted into booming laughter. The Skirmishers looked at one another, back to Missesh, and then around the room at all the laughing giants. Peytynn and Teo moved a step away from Destyr. Up on Conj's shoulder, Lyum was laughing almost as loudly as the giants.

Don't look so serious Austringers, Missesh said. *You need to relax. So tell me the name of this last Austringer.* He turned to Teo, who trembled with fear.

"Uh...Governor Missesh, I am Teo Bromynn."

The laughter died out, and Missesh stared at them for an uncomfortably long time. Finally he looked down at me lying on the barrow. He sniffed the air and wrinkled his brow, then shifted slightly in his seat. Finally he looked back at Peytynn and the others.

Governor Missesh does not like what he sees. What brings you Austringers to my city?

The room was dead silent. The Skirmishers looked uneasily at one another. Peytynn began. "Well, Missesh, we were hoping...." he stammered. "We were hoping that you would help us figure that out."

The room was silent as the giants waited patiently for more.

Peytynn continued, "I believe we need you to help our king."

Missesh sat upright on his slab and looked around at the other giants in the room. *Did you hear that? He wants us to help his king.*

Another murmur filled the room.

Peytynn's tone grew stronger. "If you have no intention of helping, or simply cannot, then we will take our king and leave."

Missesh stared at Peytynn. *You, pinkling, are a bit too rash for Missesh. I thought Rotter here told you what we do to pinkies who try to make decisions for us giants?*

"Governor Missesh, with all due respect, we are of the opinion that our king does not have much time left. We found him in a state of great sickness, and the only word he could say was the name of this city. So we brought him here."

Missesh did not respond. In frustration, Peytynn blurted out, "What does Ahkkharu mean?"

The giants gasped, and Missesh leaned forward. *Do not be so careless. The Ahkkharu is no joke.*

"The other giants used that word when they saw my king. I just want to know what it means."

The giants whispered among themselves, and then a voice came from one of the slabs in the back.

It means death, Aussssstringer, said a giant. *The death brought on by the curse of being drained of your blood, with everything inside your body being turned to rot.*

Huggon! Missesh bellowed. *We must tread more lightly around these matters.*

Missesh turned back to Peytynn. *Forgive Huggon. On the one hand, he is right. This word is not something we use easily around here. On the other hand, Huggon needs to be more careful.*

Peytynn said, "Would you rather I use the word HEIKE?"

This elicited another gasp from the giants. Missesh leaned back and yelled, *Too quickly this has turned to a risky place. These words are not easily tolerated in Olos.* He switched to his own tongue, ranting at his subjects. *Dyahment rahshar fornigth, d'yss Ahkkharu, y Heike!*

The noise in the chamber settled, and Missesh turned to Peytynn, Destyr, and Teo. *You have brought your sick and cursed king to my city, Austringers. This is something that no giant likes.* He stared down for a long while then finally finished his thought. *Tell me, how long ago did pinkling king acquire such wounds?*

"Over a fortnight," Peytynn said.

Missesh sat with his back against the massive granite wall behind him. He looked to be lost in thought.

Another voice called out, *Why was he in Ahkkharu's forest? Why did he not travel up in the air, on your strings?*

"We don't know why he chose to take the Main Road instead of our cables," said Destyr. "Perhaps the cable lines were full of refugees. We found him after he had escaped Heike." Destyr caught himself. "Beg your pardon, but all we know is that he was out hunting on the northern bluffs when he found some evidence of treason."

What is it pinkling king say about Olos?

"When we found him," said Peytynn, "he would only say the name of your city." He pointed up at Stella and Rymeo, who were perched at the top of the timber-framed dome. "And those two falcons seemed to lead us here."

Missesh looked up at the falcons for a few long moments, as if recalling something in the back of his granite mind.

"Missesh," Lyum said in a more conciliatory tone. "All these events have occurred in the past fortnight. Our home is under attack, and while defending it, we found our king lying helplessly on the ground. We have never seen a sickness such as this. It seems to eat at him from the inside out, and his skin is turning gray. And, of course, there's the unbearable stench. We have no medicine that can deal with this. We need our king to lead us in victory against our enemies, so we brought him here in the hope that you might help. Since you are giants...and so was...well...Heike."

Missesh listened and stroked the vines growing from his chin. *Kings die every day. What do we care if another pinkling king dies?*

Peytynn took the opportunity to speak up. "Please, Governor Missesh. Whether or not you have the power to heal our king, I am certain that he would want us both to come to an agreement. Our home is being overrun by northerners. They can't live in their lands anymore, and so they are invading ours. And they are doing so at the expense of all that we hold dear."

Missesh looked bored. *What is your point?*

"I feel that King Tyrcel would agree that we humans and giants should stand together to drive the northerners out of our lands."

OUR LANDS, pinkling? It seems to Missesh that this concerns only your lands.

"Once they are through with us, their hordes will continue to move south, through Olos, to get to the equator."

We giants of Olos have no fear of these pinkling hordes. You saw, on your Main Road, what we do with pinklings who try to boss us around. He looked at his comrades, and they all gave knowing glances and nods. Rotter grunted the loudest.

"The next time you come across any northerner, it won't just be a few of them. They will come by the tens of thousands and plow right over Olos."

Missesh laughed at the thought. *The giants of Olos will never let any plowing be done over Olos. We will crush the pinkling hordes, and whatever organs we don't sell in Olos city, we will throw to the s'thull whales that hunt the Trench.*

"They will bring their trebuchets that can throw fire and make explosions big enough to destroy your city in less than a day."

Missesh sat up. *What about this treh...bu...shey?*

"It throws barrels full of fire. They have the power to turn mountains into piles of rubble. They have already done it to our mountains. That is what killed Heike."

A shocked murmur filled the air. Missesh looked to the giants sitting on both sides of him. They nodded as if confirming a rumor.

Missesh raised his hand to stop the other giants' chatter and asked, *So this is what burned the cursed forest?*

"Yes," answered Lyum.

"And what felled the West Spring Sister," Peytynn added.

The giants looked from one to another and repeated the phrase *Efflua d'syss mallass. Efflua mallas?*

They called the Spring Sisters Efflua. Both were as sacred to them as they were to the Austringers because the rivers of these two mountains supplied the entire Midlyn Range with fresh water. Even the giants of Olos could not live long without the water of the Spring Sisters. And their history claimed that the first giants of the Midlyn Range were born from the rivers fed by them.

Missesh quieted his council and demanded, *What has happened to Efflua?*

"Last we saw, at least one of them had been destroyed." Peytynn said, making a horizontal chopping gesture with his right hand.

The giants shouted curses in their language.

Destroyed? roared Missesh, filling the entire council room with a volume that carried up through the open roof. Stella and Rymeo leaped from the dome's arched beams. *How can this be?*

Destyr broke in. "That, my good governor, is the work of the trebuchets."

22

I don't remember much after that. I was carried out of the council room in a stupor, and my first clear awareness came in the form of an eyas. I felt a sense of elation and couldn't believe how easy it was to fly. I simply extended my wings and hardly had to do anything else. I rode on a warm draft that puffed up through my new, coarse belly feathers. The wind tugged on the feathers and felt good on my skin.

I could see the vast landscape spreading out in all directions below me. Behind me, the plains of southern Olos dropped precipitously into the long, deep trench that had been gouged out of the Midlyn Range by the floods from the Day of a Thousand Quakes. To my west were the treetops of the Feathered Forest. The pointed tops of the pines and the twisting branches of the cedars, with trunks so large that even a three-hundred-year-old giant was not able to reach his arms around them, swayed in the same breezes that kept me aloft.

I dove toward the treetops and at the last minute arched and let my momentum and a single flap of my wings carry me into a glide directly above the cedars. With one more strong swipe of my wings, I swept down, closer to the valley of rolling treetops. To my east I saw the fern fields that lay in the ever-present shadow of the foothills of Gavina. The ferns were interspersed with the yellow, white, and red curls of new fronds that had yet to stretch out and expand in the early morning light, then relax in the cool afternoon and evening glow of Axis Solan's five moons.

From this distance the young fronds looked like wildflowers. They waved in the breeze, but a yellow glow filtered through them so that their tops were the brightest, most brilliant green I had ever seen, yet those in shadow were devoid of color.

I angled east over the ocean of ferns to get a better view of the strangely lit foliage at the base of Gavina. I was no longer swooping over the fern field but rather diving headlong into an all-encompassing field of light. It blinded me so that I had to squint and dive away. The heat also startled me. As I dropped into a descent, the entire sky was filled with the strange light I had noticed on the ferns. It swirled between reds, ambers, and yellows that rolled like liquid fire caught in a glass orb. There was no longer any blue sky or white clouds, just the hot, yellow light.

I slowed my descent with a subtle angling of my wings and changed into a horizontal glide, heading north. With the change of direction, the details of Gavina came into view, the mountain that dominated the Midlyn Range and whose peaks were visible from the southern coast of the North territories, but only the bottom half of the great mountain was visible now. The top half disappeared up into the bright yellow light, as if hewn in half by a great ax, and all that existed above Gavina was nothing but the yellow-tinted sky.

With a twist of my wings, I felt the breeze lift up under my left side, so I angled toward the right to cut into the air a bit more and begin a barrel roll. When I felt that my belly was up and my back down, I opened my eyes. A sense of intense disorientation and confusion engulfed me. Below, or at least where I assumed the ground would be, was the bright yellow of the strange sky. Looking up past my chest, I saw the ground, and there was Gavina still looming in the distance. I felt a familiar tickle in my belly that I associated with flying upside down. Yet my belly felt like it should be facing the ground. I swooped into another roll, and when I again opened my eyes, I was not sure where I was. The view ahead of me was swallowed in the bright yellow light. Gavina was gone. The ferns and Feathered Forest were gone. The black scribble of the Main Road was gone. Light was all that existed.

I felt a strange warmth and comfort in it. It seemed to be what was suspending me because I no longer felt the breeze through my feathers. In fact, the feeling of movement had come to a halt. I had no idea if I was upside down or not. I flapped my wings and tried to turn around, but nothing happened. No matter how much I willed them to, my wings would not move.

This inability to move reminded me of another time when I was helplessly bound. I could not recall it in detail but knew it had happened recently. As I struggled to remember, a voice came through the light.

Nyrosh undu yrosh sha'ahghatttt...PEST!

I recognized the voice. It engulfed me in a shock of horror that surged through my body.

TYRSSSSSSSEL!

Fear engulfed me so completely that I thought of flying away, but nothing worked. Suddenly I had the sense that my wings were no longer wings but had turned to arms—arms that were just as useless as the wings had become. But they were attached to what I now perceived as my human torso, and my chest was no longer full of feathers. That realization confused me even more and made me want to run, but none of my limbs would move. Nor could I move my head from side to side.

Focusing my worried and scattered mind, I realized that I was lying flat on my back on a massive wooden table. I tried to flail and arch my back but could not. It seemed the only muscle in my body that wasn't paralyzed was my heart. It pounded heavily, causing my temples to throb with each pulse. I tried to speak, but nothing came out.

The voice was suddenly closer, right next to my ear. The sound *TYRSSSSSSEL* filled every inch of my mind, driving a spike of fear through my nerves. I tried to scream, and my body flushed with a warmth that felt like millions of needles piercing me. As the burning needles morphed into tingling warmth, I felt that my body had been released from an invisible vise, and I lay on the table like an inert pile of bones and tissue.

I lifted my head and opened my mouth wide, yelling as if begging the Sirens to end my suffering. After a few seconds of screaming, vomit spewed from my mouth. I gagged and dropped my head back on the table, shocking me with blunt pain across my skull. When I lifted one hand up to grab my throat, it flopped across my chest and slid off onto the table.

With my useless arms and a windpipe full of stomach acid, I was certain that my life was about to end.

A cold grip wrapped around both my shoulders, and I was rolled onto my belly. My head flopped back and forth and knocked against the table top as I was turned, coming to rest as I ground my chin into the table.

You have to hold his head, pinkling. That is one of your only two jobs. HOLD HIS HEAD! My'nyothg acrussar...

"Don't acrussar me, Noth. I forgot about that part," Peytynn said. "I'm a a bit distracted."

You have only two jobs.

Noth the giant turned me onto my right side.

"I'm not a doctor," Peytynn said. "I really shouldn't—"

Pinkling talk way too much. Like all pinklings. Believe me, Noth can do without you. Noth has caught heads much bigger than pinkling king. My fingers are too big to fit in your puny king's mouth. So hurry before he chokes!

Peytynn lifted my head up to keep my windpipe open then he stuck his index finger into my mouth and scooped back and down my throat. My chest convulsed, and I gagged as my throat filled with more vomit.

That's it, pinkling, said Noth, rolling me onto my belly. Peytynn's action had forced out the last of the black and bloody mess that was lodged in my throat.

If not for the sense of all-encompassing, surging pain, I would not have realized my heart was beating. My entire body pulsed with each heart beat, as if every inch of me was tight and swollen with infection.

I opened my eyes to a bright yellow light that felt like a massive blade shoved all the way through my head to the back of my skull. I waited for my eyes to acclimate and then saw, high above me, Stella and Rymeo circling at different heights. The clouds were crisp and white, but they sped by at speeds I had never before witnessed. This confused me, but then I remembered that I had seen the clouds that cause the white-blindness be whisked away in a random mountain wind, and my heart eased.

A strange sensation passed over me when I realized that my eyes were not actually open. I blinked again and suddenly saw my own body lying on a huge table. The table had rails along each side, which led me to believe it was a table used for the medical arts. The surface was made of granite, ground to a smooth shine. It seemed to be made for a man over ten feet tall. The table was sitting on a tall stone obelisk in the southern foothills of the Talliedes.

My heart raced again as I realized I was watching my body from some distant space higher than the clouds. The tower itself sat on a stony ridge overlooking a distant, dark ravine. Dark treetops rose out of the ravine and became brighter as they moved out in every direction across the landscape that surrounded the ridge. Despite my out-of-body perspective, I was aware of the soft breeze that drifted through the hills around me. This breeze cooled the heat that surged through my veins.

From this new perspective, I noticed Stella and Rymeo drifting and circling in the wide aperture of the ravine. I delighted in the sight of them, but before I could relax, a voice sounded from somewhere close. I couldn't see anything other than my own body lying on top of the cliff-like slab. The voice had a familiar timbre, not unlike that of my father. I tried to speak but found moving my mouth and lips difficult, as if all my organs of speech had frozen.

"Ffffff.... fffffah....ttthhher," I mumbled. The syllables seemed to come from a million leagues away.

The voice was soothing. It was my mother's, yet she was speaking in the tongue of the giants. *Connyn se dyyseus father'ne.*

I was confused and tried speaking again but was able to produce nothing more than mumbles.

Dy'yseus, said the voice again. *It isss time.*

From the center of my chest, a coldness grew that enveloped my core. Then my extremities succumbed to the chill, as digit by digit my hands, feet, fingers, and toes grew cold.

The falcons circled and screeched in tones they used after a victorious hunt. But they did not dive into the dark depths of the trees below. My heart pounded with fear, yet I could think of no reason to be afraid. The falcons screeched again. Their calls echoed in the distance and resonated for long seconds in my head. Then the screeches began to sound like human voices.

Please. Who are you?

Noth. Ey lessiud, de Noth, replied the voice.

I shivered, more cold than I had ever been. Something pressed into my right shoulder for several seconds, sending shockwaves throughout my body and creating ripples in the dream-hills that surrounded me.

My eyes sprang open as if commanded, their movement no longer giving me comfort. They were fixed on the white clouds that were speeding by, high above. I found that no matter where I looked, I saw these fleeting clouds. Then the two falcons came back into view, drifting in an updraft above my head. Once directly overhead, Stella rose up almost as high as the racing clouds to a height where she was nothing more than a black speck. Then she let her body fall.

She controlled her descent, angling herself directly down toward Rymeo. She flew straight at him, but before she got too close, Rymeo noticed her and made an attempt to dart out of the way. Stella let out a cry that pierced my ears, and landed on Rymeo's back in a burst of black and white feathers. They both shrieked as they plummeted, snapping and clawing viciously at each other. Soon, Stella had both her talons around Rymeo's shoulders, and as they fell, she slashed his chest with her razor-sharp beak.

I heard the familiar words again. *It is time.* The pressure on my shoulder eased. I began to feel warmer, as if I was breaking out of a cold sweat. I felt myself urinate. I tried to tell the voice that I needed help. *Nah... muh... muh...* My bowels evacuated. Excrement moved through me, dragging what felt like burning blades within my abdomen. I groaned and futilely tried to curl into a ball as the pain in my belly raged. But my muscles did not respond to my brain's request. Despite the searing pain, my eyes were locked on the two falcons falling into the darkness of the ravine in a burst of feathers and screeching.

The pain was so strong that it caused me to convulse, and my belly roiled. My bowels emptied again at the same moment that I vomited up into the air and all over my nose and eyes. I choked and struggled, unable to clear the black mix of clotted blood and bile from my face. More and more of the acidic vomit slid back down my throat.

I saw Stella fly up out of the dark ravine. Bulging through the tight grip of her talons was Rymeo's heart, still dripping with blood. It was a bad omen, and I was sure it meant I would die soon. No more breath moved through my airways, and the heavy pressure on my shoulders returned. I was lifted and rolled, and my head bounced against something hard.

Suddenly, the hillsides and mountains disappeared. The falcons disappeared. Strange voices began again.

Mynyothg acrussar, pinkling.

"I know, I know, Noth," said another, more familiar voice. "You don't have to keep telling me these things."

Well—yothg—why did you not do it?

"I've never done this before, oh great hill-giant witch doctor."

You watch words, pinkling. I can put a curse on you that will haunt you worse than anything the Ahkkharu could conjure.

"Shouldn't you be a bit more careful with that word around here?"

The voice bellowed and echoed in my head. *AAAAhhh! Noth not afraid of Ahkkharu. Noth's medicine just as strong! Plus, Noth is ten times bigger than puny Ahkkharu. That is why he move to that valley, where any stupid pinkling he meets will always be smaller than him. Now, pinkling, hold your puny king's head and clear his throat!*

I was on my belly. A hand held my head up over the edge of the table while another gently squeezed my cheeks to open my mouth, which was flushed with a burst of fresh water and swiped clean of any remaining blood and vomit. Deliciously cool air filled my lungs. Tears blurred my opened eyes, and something was pressing heavily against my back. My belly convulsed again. I gagged, and liquid oozed out of my mouth. A puddle formed in a bowl on the ground under my face.

"By all the Sirens that are holy," Peytynn exclaimed.

Nysoth mallass Aussssstringer. You and your Sirens. These things mean nothing in this world.

"At least we've got the bowl down there this time."

I spit up the remaining ooze that coated my throat. I was rolled back onto my side and finally got a glimpse of the giant who was standing by the table. I could only see his waist, which was right in front of my face and wrapped in a kilt. The skin on his belly looked like the hardest granite.

"Nuh...No...Noth," I mumbled, just before a long metal tube was inserted into my mouth.

I gagged and tried to push away the huge gray arm that held the instrument, but then fluid rushed down and filled my belly with a soothing coolness that calmed me. It had a flavor similar to the mint tea I remembered my mother giving me as a child. But the concoction quickly turned bitter, and my throat constricted. I was afraid that I would not be able to breathe again, but the bitter flavor left almost immediately, and the dry tightness also subsided. I began to choke and cough and was immediately rolled back on my belly, where I again vomited over the edge of the table.

You do better this time, pinkling.

Peytynn cradled my head in his hands. "Thanks, Noth."

Now we roll him over for the next flushing.

Peytynn tilted my head just a fraction to the side to get better access to my mouth for a final cleaning. "It looks like he's passed out again."

This happen sometimes.

23

The sound of rushing water was all around, seeming to engulf my body, so that I felt the flow of the current moving across my arms and legs. And yet, I felt no anxiety. I scanned my body. There was no longer any aching pain, just a strong sense of fatigue and a dry, empty feeling in my chest, despite my submersion.

My neck still seemed to be weak, so I was only able to see what was directly in my vision. I was lying in a stream bed. To the right and left I could see the slope of the stream's edges, and towering above me were tall cedar pines that swayed in the breeze and rose up into the hills.

Suddenly the water slowed, pushing a last few seconds against my head. I now found myself lying in the soft sediment of a dry stream bed, and my body did not seem to be at all wet. I blinked as if to clear water from my eyes and noticed that my vision had cleared. Above the pointed tops of the cedars was a vivid blue sky, which brought me peace, and I relaxed. I tried again to take a deeper breath. My chest and throat were tight, though with each attempt to breathe, more air filled my lungs and helped calm me.

I closed my eyes, exhaled, and rested my head. Relief washed over me. My body felt refreshed and whole. Then the smells and sounds of my surroundings slowly became apparent. I was confused by the dank odor of old blood and the acrid stink of potions and other homemade distillations. I heard voices and the faint clanking of metal on metal.

I opened my eyes and was no longer in the river bed. Instead, I was lying on a familiar granite table in what looked like a huge circular laboratory, half of which was lined with perfectly coped shelves that held large leather-bound books and stacks of rolled-up parchments. Many of the bound edges of the books contained the same images and symbols I'd seen in Heike's hovel. The thought sent a chill down my spine.

The other half of the room was lined with shelves that had many different shapes and sizes of bowls and jars sitting on them. Any other available surface area in the room was covered with mounds of candles, as in Heike's lair.

A shadow moved across my face. The huge bodies of Noth and Missesh stood at the head of the table. I heard Peytynn's voice down toward my feet. I tilted my head and focused my eyes on my friend. Peytynn leaned over me and said, "King Tyrcel, you look like a mountain billy's hind quarters."

I smiled and tried to laugh but could only cough. Peytynn quickly brought his hands behind my head so I wouldn't bump it against the table during the coughing fit. "You've got to relax. You're in a very weak state," he said.

Then a booming voice startled me. *Yes, pinkling king, you are in a very weak state. This is, of course, because you are a pinkling.* Missesh was looking down at my prostrate form from fifteen feet up. *You have been lying here for so long. I was about to tell Noth to throw you to the s'thull whales in the Great Trench before your foul stench infected the entire city. But your little pinkling friends begged us not to.*

"Th... thanks for that," I said with a feeble smile.

Peytynn gently lifted my head and tilted a cup to my mouth. The instant the water hit my lips, I was revived. I grabbed Peytynn's arm with more strength than he expected and forced him to keep pouring the water, which soothed my aching throat and chest. When it was gone, I begged for more. Peytynn filled the cup again, but when he came back to the table, Noth stopped him.

No, pinkling. Too much at once will not help him.

Peytynn looked frustrated, but he deferred to Noth.

My body felt weak, but at least there was no more searing pain. And the water I just drank was the best thing I had ever put to my lips.

In a few minutes, pinkling, you give him more.

I waved my hand to get Peytynn's attention.

"Where are the others?"

"Teo and Destyr are at the Olos Market trying to scrape up some food you might be able to eat."

I nodded, although the effort was taxing.

"It seems that the kind giants of Olos don't really eat the way we do," Peytynn said with a smile at Missesh and Noth.

Missesh broke in. *Your small pinklings will be back soon enough, pinkling king. They are with my son, Sithesh. He does not like to waste time among the stinking pinkling market, so he will only be gone as long as your little friends require.*

Just the small amount of effort I had expended to talk wore me out. But I remembered the last member of the Skirmishers.

"And Lyum?"

"He's busy showing off to our giant friends," Peytynn said. "Apparently they have never seen magnets used the way he has arranged them in his various designs. In fact, the giants have agreed to help us with Doldra's horde, in exchange for a few of Lyum's gadgets."

I was a bit confused. "Won't they be too small for them to use?"

Missesh broke in. *Don't worry, pinkling king. We will make them bigger.*

I smiled at the thought of how smart Lyum was, then remembered the rest of what Peytynn had said. "The giants have agreed to help us?"

"Yes," Peytynn said. "First off, it seems Noth here has cured you of Heike's curse."

Missesh and Noth exchanged a quick glance, and then Noth started cleaning up the area around the medical table. *Only time will tell us how fixed your puny king is.*

Peytynn shrugged off the comment. "You are looking much better," he said to me. "We've got plenty of things to talk about, but let's not stress you right now." He tilted the cup of water to my lips, which I drank as if it were to be my last. "Get some rest, and soon I will bring you something to eat. Noth believes you should be on your feet in a few days."

Yes, pinkling king, boomed Missesh's voice, with a huge smile. *The task at hand is big. But we giants are just as big.* The smile disappeared as he continued. *We giants know that it is in our best interest to rid the Midlyn Range of northerners. But it is you Aussssstringers who are being run out of your homes in the mountains. We giants of Olos know how that feels.*

He straightened up to leave as Noth collected the filthy bowls from the floor and put them in a large wash basin.

Missesh paused in the doorway and said, *In return for our help, puny pinkling king, we giants of Olos will need much from you Austringers, beyond some of the stones that you turn into magnets. We can discuss these things once we push the northern pinklings back into the Straits.*

24

"Well, I guess it's about time you started acting like a king, King Tyrcel," joked Peytynn. "We Skirmishers can't carry your weight forever."

I tried to look stern and commanding, but despite the impending battle, I could not prevent a slight smile. It had been almost a week since Noth had removed Heike's curse. In that time my strength had come back, but while I healed, the City Valley was overrun by the northern horde. I no longer suffered the debilitating pain from Heike's bites, yet the Great Pool in the center of my home's valley was now polluted with the run-off of war and the disgusting filth of the invading army.

With a small contingent of giants, we Skirmishers returned to the City Valley. Through the southern foothills I was able to test my fighting ability as we cleared out any enemy encampments that were dug in across our path. Work was so easy and quick with the help of Missesh and his kind that I was not completely sure of the state of my fighting strength. Luckily, along the way, we gathered any remaining skirmish group of Austringer warriors, and they were happy to see their king return in good health and with such effective reinforcements. By the time we were on the outskirts of the City Valley, we had several thousand warriors behind us.

I felt much better, but my mental energies still seemed to be scattered. Often I found myself having trouble keeping my thoughts in any cohesive order. I would grow confused, and I often ended up having conversations with myself in an attempt to sort out the confusion. Soon these conversations grew into a cacophony in my head, and I had to force myself to focus on whatever I was doing at the time. When I returned from these mental conversations, as often as not, I found the dialogue was not just in my head but clearly audible to anyone around me. I couldn't help but think of my father.

Now as we stood behind one of the small foothills that formed the perimeter of the City Valley, I told myself to ignore the voices for the time being and focus on what waited on the other side. Our plan was to get to the top of this hill, where we would have the height advantage, and rush the enemy's western flank. The northern front was primarily focused on Gavina. Trebuchets and mercenaries were well dug in around her base. Their focus elsewhere allowed the giants of Olos to lift the thousands of warriors up to a ridge that lined all sides of the foothill in front of us.

With the rest of our warriors, Peytynn and I hurried around the top of the hill to the other side, then climbed down onto a ledge that overlooked the entire City Valley. My first glimpse of the scene below was heart wrenching. As far as I could see, across the entire expanse of my once beautiful home, was a dug-in militia of mercenaries, soldiers, tents, and trebuchets. At first, I thought my clouded mind was trying to trick me, but I could not blink away the reality of the scene.

It was not long before our presence was detected. And once Missesh and his son stood up behind us, two of the trebuchets that had been aimed at Gavina were slowly turned in our direction.

At the base of the foothill on which we were assembling was an empty swath of valley wide enough that we didn't want to risk our few remaining arrows trying to hit any targets from this distance. As my warriors assembled, the northern forces came to life and quickly had a new front line facing our direction. A single man rode his horse up to the edge of the front lines, dismounted, and walked out to stand in the shadow of the ridge on which we were gathered. He did not seem concerned by the fact that any one of us could put an arrow in him.

This was the first battle that I would lead. My emotional state was a mix of fear and anger, both of which were being distilled into a firm resolve that helped me focus and accept that my own death might be near. I did not mind dying for my homeland, and I wondered if this was how father had felt before he stepped into all the battles he had won.

Shadows passed over me. I looked up expecting to see a flock of falcons but instead saw dark boulders flying over us and into the mass of northerners assembled below. Missesh and his giants were softening up our enemies with a barrage of boulders that crashed into clusters of enemy soldiers, while others landed and rolled over anything in their path. The boulders sent the front-line soldiers scattering in fear. The shouts of my enemies raised my spirits, and the sight of the destruction made my fellow warriors—who stood waiting for my word—restless.

The barrage was effective, and one of the trebuchets facing us was badly damaged. I was grateful once again to have these giants on my side.

Peytynn and I looked at each other. Our spirits were high. I yelled across the vast landscape below, "Northerners! I am King Tyrcel Buteo. King of the Austringers. I demand that you turn around and find another way to the equator. You have done enough damage to my homeland. Turn and leave the Midlyn Range immediately."

The mass of enemy fighters below me stood frozen at the sight of Missesh and his son. Only one of them replied—the single northerner standing at the base of our foothill.

"Austringer king," she yelled, "I am Queen Laurdin Doldra."

Peytynn and I looked at each other, stunned to discover that the bold soldier was a woman. I had heard about Abbo Doldra's daughter. It was rumored that she could fight better than any man. She wore no armor like the rest of her horde, but just skins and two long swords on her hips. And unlike the soldiers behind her, she held no shield. As I got a better look, I realized that she had only one arm. Protecting the stump of her right arm was an ornate bronze shoulder guard studded with a row of spikes.

She stood brazenly within my bow's range, but I wanted to hear what she had to say before running her through.

"She looks like one of the scouts in the Hollow Valley," Peytynn said, "where we ignited the trebuchet barrels. I think she had both her arms then. Looks like she got caught in one of our barrages."

"Aye. Hopefully that will slow her down a bit."

Laurdin shouted, "King of the Austringers! Have you not heard what happened to your precious Sentinels? And do you not see across your valley the desolation that we wrought when we crushed your precious Spring Sister and smashed your city's gates open? What else do I need to do to make it clear that we have no intention of leaving?"

I assumed that because Laurdin was doing the talking, the rumors of Abbo Doldra's death were true. "Excuse me, my lady," I said, "but I do not negotiate with common soldiers. Let me discuss your timely retreat with the leader of your troops."

Laurdin's reply was curt. "You are speaking with the Queen of the North." She pulled a sword from its scabbard and slapped it across the bronze shoulder guard. "Do you see my shoulder? This is where I let one of your arrows catch me. A poison arrow, no doubt. The poison was too weak to kill me but would not let my arm heal, so I cut it off. Does that sound like something a common soldier would do?"

She waited for a reply, but Peytynn and I were both at a loss for words.

"Believe me, Austringers, I am the one and only leader of this standing army that now commands your homeland, and one arm is all I need to do the job. I welcome any of you to come down here and see for yourself."

A murmur went through the warriors behind me.

"We have thousands more fighters than you do," the queen continued. "Even with a few giants on your side, you are helpless when you are not in the safety of your mountains. And we have proven that we can destroy those mountains. We can outlast you for as long as we need to."

"How effective were your greater numbers in the Hollow Valley?" I yelled, but a huge hand pushed its way between Peytynn and me, forcing us to jump aside.

Missesh growled at me. *You pinklings talk too much.*

Then he yelled down the slope, his voice booming so loudly that Laurdin finally took a few steps back. *Northerners, I am Missesh Olluns, and this is my son, Sithesh Olluns. Before he was a hundred years old, he had hewn the tops of mountains and mined with his own hands the depths of the same mountains for their stores of granite and quartz. For one thousand nights and days, I wrestled the Shirk, who haunts the mountains of the Midlyn Range, and caused panic in the hearts of the oldest giants. Never once did I grow tired. It was the cursed Shirk who feigned death so I would release it and let it scurry away to lick its wounds. I stand before you at the age of five hundred years.*

Peytynn gave me a questioning look. I said across Missesh's giant shins, "You have to let them get this stuff out. He'll finish soon enough."

Missesh continued yelling. *I am the Governor of Olos, the greatest and strongest city in all of Axis Solan. Descendant of the hills and stones of the great Olon himself, who rose centuries ago to be the ruler of all the Midlyn Range. Olon, known to destroy with just his hands mountains bigger than the ones you have destroyed. Know, northerners, that today you will all be crushed. We giants of Olos do not leave Olos for no reason. We are only here to crush you.*

For a few moments, Laurdin stood her ground. Then she turned and said something to one of the guards who stood behind her. The guard backed up and hurried to the closest trebuchet. On his way, he passed the corpses of men who had been flattened, and right before the trebuchet, sunk halfway into the ground, sat the boulder that had done the killing. Soldiers were already arming the trebuchet.

"Governor Missesh," Laurdin called. "We have no issue with you giants. We only desire to move through this island."

Missesh laughed a deafening *Ha. It is the opinion of the giants of Olos that those who just want to move through the Midlyn Range do not destroy mountains along the way.*

Laurdin said nothing.

And you, queen of the dead northern pinklings, have destroyed three of our most sacred mountains. Mountains that were built by the hammers and furnaces of the first giants. Mountains that were made to keep pinklings out because all you pinklings do is mumble and steal and argue about gold. These were mountains that have fed hill-giants and sated our thirst. For these mountains, the giants of Olos will not let you pass.

As Missesh threatened, a barrel flew up and over our heads. It disappeared behind me, and soon a massive explosion emanated over the ridge of our foothill. The force of it made Missesh and Sithesh bend almost to a kneeling stance, protecting the Austringers who stood in front of them. We were engulfed in a dark cloud of smoke, and when the debris cleared, Missesh and Sithesh were already standing again.

In the ensuing quiet, Laurdin shouted one last warning. "Austringers and giants of Olos, do you see that we can throw things back at you? Stronger things than just big rocks. Let that be another reminder of the power that we hold over you. With just one more word, I can unleash as many more barrels as I want."

The barrel had landed at the base of our hill and gouged out a massive ditch, but the explosion had not killed any Austringer warriors because we were assembled on the ridge high above it. However, a few of the giants who stood waiting to attack were helping each other up after the shockwave had thrown them back. I was saddened to see the remains of several other giants lying around the crater. Huge boulders that looked like feet and limbs were strewn about.

Peytynn was also looking down at the destruction. "If these giants needed any motivation to help us—" Out of respect for Missesh, I gave Peytynn a quick look that shut him up. We both turned back to face the northerners.

Missesh yelled with a rage that shook the ground, *You queen of the soon-dead pinklings, you have committed your last crime against the giants of Olos. No matter how many pinklings you have behind you, the giants of Olos will never be outnumbered.*

Then Missesh said something that I did not understand at first. *And those are not just big rocks. AAAAAARRRRGH!!!!* The sonic boom of Missesh's voice forced Laurdin and many of the northern soldiers to take a few steps back. When the noise ended, I felt a distant tremor underfoot.

Then the massive boulder that was lodged into the ground in front of the closest trebuchet began to move. First the granite started to wave and flow as what looked like huge stone muscles collected to move a frame that weighed tons. The section of the boulder that was above ground lifted up, and two arms stretched out and a huge head appeared on top of two rounded shoulders the size of hills. The giant uncurled itself and stood, and the pit in which he had lain barely rose past his ankles.

The giant roared at the terrified men who were arming the trebuchet. They scattered in panic as the giant brought the first devastating swing of his fists down on the trebuchet's timbered frame. It buckled and collapsed into the dirt. The giant continued crushing as much of it as possible.

At the same time, all the other boulders that had been sitting motionless in the northern encampment opened and transformed into huge granite men. Once they were standing, the giants went into a frenzy, smashing anything within reach.

Austringers sprinted past me. Some warriors hailed me as they jumped down the slope while others shouted their war cries as they launched their spears down the hill.

As the men and giants surged past me, I thought back to what Peytynn had said earlier.

"I believe you are right," I said.

Peytynn was about to bring his face mask up over his chin, but he paused and asked, "How do you mean, King Tyrcel?"

I smiled, glad to have the chance to lead my people into battle. I wore the scar on my neck like a trophy. It had lost its sickly gray hue and was the color of a well-healed human scar.

I pulled my two long-daggers from their sheaths, brought them down behind my forearms—in the typical Austringer attack position—and before I leaped down to join the melee, I said, "I think it is time I started acting like a king."

Acknowledgments

The following are just a few of the people to whom I am eternally indebted for their time and effort in helping to get this novel published.

If it wasn't for Loretta Lawrence, Claire & Bruce Lawrence, and Sarah Linde, I may have had to resort to picking through my neighbors trash for scraps of food to stay alive. You have been there for the roller-coaster ride that is JB Lawrence, and still, for some reason, want to talk to me. Please know that the publication of this story has as much to do with you as it does with me.

The gals at Possibilities Publishing Co., Meredith Maslich and Terri Huck for their patience and guidance in making this story so much better.

Frank and Carol Masci for your initial editing of what was once an over 500 page book. It was a noble effort at a time when the novel was not sure what it wanted to be.

Jon Bass for your undying and unconditional friendship, photography skills, and help with the finer details. You are my brother.

The1Nav, for his true-brother-love, and for being–literally–the one person who first inspired me to keep going with this work. Sorry for my phone phobia, but know that I love you.

Tina and Steve Lee, Stephanie Goyne, and Nakina Webster; your help with the campaign was such an essential part to getting this book published. You are my family and I love you all so much.

John Masci for your insightful marketing advice and of course being my friend since we used to walk to kindergarten and first grade together. I'm not sure why, but you've always stuck by me, and I love you for that.

Jeff Arsenault for your fine artwork and patience with me as both you and I have been at this for the past two years.

A huge thank you to David Saidman, Lisa Sachs, Dan Stebbins, Carol & Woody Luber, Brooke Fiske, Amy Saidman, Amy Goyne, John Larkin, Nhananh Nguyenkhoa, Carol Reitz, Carol & Ron Andre, Birgit Müller, Beth Thomas, Eric Anderson, Willy Bowles, and of course, you Aunty Sandy.

Being absent-minded and scatterbrained, I am sure some names have been forgotten. If any names have been missed, I apologize, and will make it up to you in the second printing.

Made in the USA
Charleston, SC
23 April 2015